Roy Gould spent five years as assistant stage manager on three West End musicals before joining the BBC and working for TV comedy legend David Croft OBE (creator of "Dad's Army"; "Hi de Hi"; "Allo Allo", etc.) as a lowly second assistant director before David Croft promoted him to become the director for his shows. On leaving the BBC, he formed his own production company and, as producer, won two Royal Television Society Awards. Having always wanted to write, he decided to stop making excuses and to sit down and get on with it. As well as "The Secrets of a Small English Village", he has now written two stage plays and full-length film screenplays, as well as being halfway into his next novel. Married for a very long time to Sarah, he splits his time between London and Norwich.

Dedicated to David Croft, my comedy hero and mentor; and Mum and Dad, for being there and letting me follow my dreams.

Roy Gould

THE SECRETS OF A SMALL ENGLISH VILLAGE

AUSTIN MACAULEY PUBLISHERS™

LONDON ∗ CAMBRIDGE ∗ NEW YORK ∗ SHARJAH

A CIP catalogue record for this title is available from the British Library.

ISBN 9781528994750 (Paperback)
ISBN 9781398406551 (ePub e-book)

www.austinmacauley.com

First Published 2021
Austin Macauley Publishers Ltd
Level 37, Office 37.15, 1 Canada Square
Canary Wharf
London
E14 5AA

Where does a wise man kick a pebble – on a beach? Where does a wise man hide a leaf – in the forest...and if a man had to hide a dead body, he would make a field of dead bodies to hide it in.

From *The Sign of the Broken Sword*
by G. K. Chesterton

Chapter 1

Having never seen a dead body before, Alice wasn't actually sure that she was looking at one then. She hoped she wasn't, but feared she was, and in the driveway of the Old Rectory. Heavens above.

Up until that moment, nothing really untoward had happened to Alice, apart from being informed by her doctor that she might be a little overweight. In reality, she was rather short and dumpy, but her doctor hadn't wanted to upset her so just said,

'A little overweight, perhaps; nothing to worry about; do you take much exercise?'

She didn't, she had to admit. This was the spur for her to get her old bicycle out of the shed. It was a little rusted up, so she asked Neil Hardy, the local builder and handyman, whether he would bring it back to life; he did. When she tried to press some money on him, he, of course, refused as he always tried to do for the locals where he could. Alice had taken a calculated risk that he wouldn't take her money this time as she had very little of it. From that moment, early every morning she would mount her trusty steed and pootle off around the village; down Church Lane, past the ancient church and Old Rectory, continuing down the narrow lane towards the stench that came from Broome Farm.

Screwing up her face, Alice would try and quicken her pace past the field which had become a graveyard of rusting vehicles of all shapes and sizes, amongst which mud-splattered pigs snuffled around looking for food. Even at that time in the morning, Borley's rather dim-witted son, Toby, could be on a huge JCB machine digging deep holes in the field for no apparent reason.

She would pass Borley's beautiful Elizabethan manor, which was now in a very sorry state and half-hidden behind a rotting London double-decker bus, in which Borley and Toby actually lived, then up the little hill. Here, Alice would fiddle with the three-speed gear lever, the mechanics of which she never understood, as the hill refused to get the slightest bit easier to peddle up whatever gear it said she was in.

That morning she had ridden by the Old Rectory, even though she had seen, what she had thought, was a dead body. The reason she had ridden by was because she didn't want to believe she had seen a dead body. By riding on around the village, as if there was no dead body, would, she hoped, make it not exist at all; just her imagination silly playing tricks. Yes, just silly tricks.

Having arrived outside Chantry Bowman-Leggett's cottage, Alice would normally dismount and lean her bicycle against the wall. There would be no need to put a lock or a chain on it, as she knew people did in the town to stop their bicycles from being stolen, as nobody was going to steal her bicycle in this village of that she could be sure. This morning however she did not stop but cycled on back to the Old Rectory gates. She smiled, telling herself what a silly she was to think that she had seen a dead body on the gravel driveway. A trick of the light, she told herself; the sun casting strange shadows through the trees. Yes, what a silly – oh dear! There it was, where she thought it was, and it was what she thought it was, surely. This was no shadow. It was a very solid figure. Yes, there could be no mistake; a naked body; well nearly naked. It had on, what looked like, black stockings and one dangerously high stiletto. A naked woman? Oh, dear.

'Chantry, Miss Bowman-Leggett, Chantry.' Alice was running down the path.

Chantry Bowman-Leggett swallowed a pill and put the box back into her cardigan pocket.

'Oh, Chantry,' said Alice as she opened the kitchen door.

'Whatever is the matter, Alice?' Chantry poured some hot water from the kettle on the Aga, into the teapot to warm it.

'It's the Old Rectory. Those people; those,' she paused a moment as if to think what to call them, 'people.'

Chantry pulled herself up to her full height and then turned to take two cups and saucers off the dresser and place them on a tray. 'I have no wish to hear about those deviants on a Sunday morning.'

'But they're dead.'

The kettle screamed, Chantry Bowman-Leggett, however, did not; she started pouring the boiling water into the teapot.

'What are you talking about, Alice?' She crossed over to the fridge and took out the milk.

'They're all over the lawn and the drive and…' she said, conjuring up more bodies in her imagination, 'shall we call the police?' Alice was jumping from one foot to another like a child in a playground wanting a wee.

Chantry put down the milk jug and pulled off her apron.

'What we must do, first of all, is to stay calm. You will have to show me.'

'Oh, I couldn't go back there,' said Alice.

'Stiff upper lip,' said Chantry Bowman-Leggett, 'stiff upper lip. Let us get to the bottom of this.'

And with that, she walked confidently out of the cottage door and off towards the Old Rectory. She did not think, for one moment, that she would find a dead body but had decided to clear the matter up, once and for all, otherwise she knew that Alice would go wittering on about it whilst drinking her tea and the one thing that annoyed Chantry more than anything was her friend's wittering.

The first body they encountered was the one that Alice had seen. Not a woman at all but a naked man dressed only in torn black stockings, a suspender belt and one ridiculously high stiletto-heeled shoe; the other shoe lay upturned in the gravel some six feet further back. Alice wretched. Chantry, although taken aback having not really expected to see such a sight, kept her head and decided that attack was the best form of defence.

'Do not be sick, Alice,' she barked. 'Now is not the time.'

Alice was somewhat at a loss as to know when the right time might be. Chantry took in the spectacle. Another body lay in the doorway, half in and half out of the house.

'We must investigate,' announced Chantry, taking control despite herself and making off toward the house.

'Oh, I couldn't go in there, I really couldn't,' cried Alice.

'You must get a hold of yourself, Alice, it is imperative that we get the full picture immediately before deciding what to do for the best.'

'But we must call the police, surely?'

'We must do nothing of the sort at this juncture. We must not be precipitant.'

She continued towards the threshold and edged around the second body in the doorway and looked up the stairs, where another was spread-eagled, head first, half up and half down the stairwell. She closed her eyes and took a deep breath and called out,

'Mister Bennett? Misses Bennett? Hello, are you there?' She stopped to listen. No answer. The only sound was that of the hall clock ticking.

Meanwhile, Alice had taken a wide birth, via the lawn, to the front door. She was now frozen to the spot staring at the corpse in front of her. Chantry turned.

'Really Alice, where's your mettle?'

'I'm sorry, Chantry, but, but,' she faltered and her stomach started to heave before being sick into the Bay tree nearby. Chantry closed her eyes in exasperation.

'If you insist on behaving like this, then you must make yourself useful in other ways.'

'Thank you, Chantry.' Alice had no idea what she was thanking Chantry for, it just came out, along with a residue of vomit.

Chantry walked back over to her; they were now either side of the doorway corpse.

'Clean yourself down and then summon up the members of the village council and get them to meet me in the village hall in fifteen minutes,' barked Chantry.

'But won't they all be in bed? What shall I tell them?'

'Nothing; just say that Miss Bowman-Leggett has called an extraordinary meeting; that will have to do.'

'Right,' said Alice, turning and kicking the corpse below her. She screamed.

'Shh, Alice.' scolded Chantry, 'Now, not a word. Just leave the explaining to me.' Alice nodded and tottered off down the drive. Chantry Bowman-Leggett watched her go and then, taking a deep breath, sighed. 'Oh, Chantry, whatever are you doing, you silly girl.'

*

Perhaps now would be as good a time as any to leave Chantry while she is making her through the carnage to attempt to explain her background and the Bowman-Leggett families' place within the history of the village. The reason?

Well, although one may not approve, this knowledge may make it easier for the reader to understand her actions.

A great house had stood on this site for about a thousand years. The original Hall was said to have been built by a soldier or nobleman who fought with William, Duke of Normandy, at Hastings. Popular myth had it that his name was Legat or Legayot and that he was the archer that fired the arrow which landed in King Harold's eye as depicted in the Bayeux Tapestry making him a Bowman called Legat, and so the family became known as Bowman-Leggett. Of course, as it is heavily disputed that Harold was hit in the eye by an arrow in the first place, Chantry's family took this story with a pinch of salt.

The Bowman, they thought, was more likely a simplification of Beaumont. It is known that Robert De Beaumont was a close confidant of William and was made the 1st Earl of Leicester after the Normans conquered Harold's army. This Beaumont may have been related. Who Legat or Legayot or Leggett was is also not known and the entry in Burke's Landed Gentry fails to explain anything. What is known is that a Great Hall was built on the site just after William became king and that the church was built alongside it, both paid for, most likely, by heavily taxing the local people. The church was built in order that the family could thank God for their great good fortune and a settlement gradually grew up around these grand buildings, which, in turn, became the village itself.

Throughout the centuries, the old Hall was replaced by a more modern house, which, in turn, was knocked down or altered until the Georgian period, when the building in which Chantry was now rooting about in was built with the Bowman-Leggett name having been passed from father to son, unbroken, from time immemorial.

Amazingly, every male heir fathered another male heir. Some were worthy of the Bowman-Leggett name, others not so. For many hundreds of years, the Bowman-Leggett family owned all the land in the area and all the properties built on it including the Leggett Arms and Home Farm, where they grew and bred all the produce needed for the grand household. Sadly though, over the years, parts of the land or buildings had to be sold to pay off the women who bore children conceived on the "wrong side of the blanket" or the debts incurred through gambling. The most infamous, and the one that could be said to have precipitated the downfall of the family, occurred in the early nineteenth century when Henry Bowman-Leggett, having inherited everything on his father's death took a carriage straight from the family solicitors in the Temple to Brooks Club in Pall Mall and celebrated his great good fortune by playing the more than aptly named game of chance called *"Hazard"*.

As was his custom, he partook of far too much port wine, and, as a consequence, bet his newly acquired house on the roll of the dice. Rumour had it that the reason for this foolishness, apart from being blind drunk, was because the Prince of Wales stood at his shoulder and having the opportunity to suck up to the heir to the throne, Henry insisted on His Royal Highness blowing on the said dice to bring him luck. Unfortunately, Henry had, seemingly, overlooked the fact that the royal personage had no more luck at games of chance than any mere mortal and was up to his neck in gambling debts himself. So it is probably needless to impart that Henry's dice, even though covered in Prinny's spittle, still came up a three, which, according to the rather complicated rules of the game, meant he lost. The Prince, it is said, laughed so much at Henry's misadventure that he took to his bed for a week with exhaustion. Edward Hinckley, who had won the game, donated the Bowman-Leggett house to the church as he was already the owner of several large properties around the country so in no need of another to live in and felt that it might be a good idea to show the Almighty his Christian side to help him through the gates of paradise when the time came. The church, as throughout English history, was not backward in coming forward when it came to accepting gifts and grabbed it with both ecclesiastical hands. Caring nothing for appearances, Henry turfed out the occupant of the next largest house on his estate and moved his own family into it.

And so the Bowman-Leggett fortune diminished greatly over the years and the family was forced to move into smaller and smaller properties. Finally, Chantry Bowman-Leggett, the very last in the line, moved into a tiny cottage within the village. It says a lot for the community that, with one exception, even though the Bowman-Leggett fortune had dwindled into nothing, their name was still said with reverence and Chantry was always treated with the utmost respect as the matriarch.

One thing the family did not lose, over the years, however, was the right to use the Bowman-Leggett family vault in the crypt of the church. This right had been handed down over the centuries and nobody thought to question it. Even when Chantry stated, publicly, that after her death she would be the final person to be laid to rest in the vault and it would be sealed up for eternity, nobody in the village objected. However, taking no chances, she obtained a court order, the basis of which was, as there were a lot of spurious claims to being true heirs to the Bowman-Leggett family name, mostly from Americans in places like Utah or Texas, these should be discounted from any legal rights in this regard and they were not to benefit in any way from any legacy which may be left. The judge, who had known Chantry's father for many years, rubber stamped the order without a second thought.

Chantry's Christian name was, it must be said, unusual and, perhaps, should be explained. When Chantry and her twin brother were born, their father, Augustus, being somewhat eccentric, wanted to name them after his favourite characters in Chaucer's *Canterbury Tales*: Chanticleer, a cock and Pertelote, a hen. Their mother being a devoted and Christian wife, who would not have dreamed of going against her husband's wishes, agreed. However, when it came to the day of the christening, Augustus's mother insisted on clothing the babies for the ceremony; pink for a girl and blue for a boy. Unfortunately, the old dowager, who was partial to a little sherry at breakfast was a trifle worse for wear by mid-morning and got herself into a bit of a muddle. Over the font, the babies were handed to the vicar, one by one, and given the sign of the cross and it was only after this had been done was it noticed that the baby in pink possessed a little penis. On checking, the baby in blue, it was discovered, did not. Tears were shed but the vicar endeavoured to calm the proceedings by stating that he would just christen them again, but this time in the correct order. Their mother, however, would not be pacified in this way and insisted that if it was God's will to have them christened so, then they must stay that way. So the boy, Pertelote and the girl, Chanticleer, grew up.

Pertelote or Perty as he became known went off to Public School where, the new boys, thinking that they had misheard his name called him Bertie. Perty, although embarrassed by the name, nonetheless had his pride and when he caught the innocent young perpetrators, he thrashed them to within an inch of their lives.

Chanticleer, being a girl, did not go to school as, in keeping with the family tradition, she was expected to be on hand to help her mother. Her education, however, was not altogether overlooked and she was taught her letters and numbers by a kindly part-time teacher who came to the house every morning and it was she who first shortened Chanticleer to Chantry (pronounced,

Sharntry) as a pet name. It did not take long for the whole of the village to address her in the same way.

Perty, even though he was given a good education, had inherited a great many of the bad Bowman-Leggett genes and, in the period which became known as the Swinging Sixties, could be found in all the trendy London nightspots, trying to be part of the "In Crowd", mingling with such luminaries as the cockney photographer, David Bailey. In truth, Perty was not that interested in Bailey, who he thought was too common, but he did fancy the mini skirt off Bailey's model girlfriend, Jean Shrimpton, who he endeavoured to sidle up to and whisper, what would be termed in these enlightened times, as extremely lewd and un-PC, suggestions. "The Shrimp", as she was known by the press at the time, to her eternal credit, ignored Perty's advances, although it was rumoured that Bailey did accidentally swing his Nikon around a little forcefully once and made contact with Perty's nether regions.

Sadly, it was Perty's penchant for living in the fast lane that ultimately brought him to a sticky end. Driving back in his E-Type Jaguar after an alcohol-fuelled school reunion at his old alma mater, he took the corner too fast coming out of the pleasant Surrey village of Hindhead and careened off into the treacherous Devils Punchbowl, plummeting to his death. This left the Bowman-Leggett family with no male heir for the first time in their, exceedingly, long history. The only true Bowman-Leggett surviving was the impoverished Chantry, who had never married. Having interned what was left of her brother in the family vault, Chantry now saw it as her destiny to defend the good name of the village that her ancestors had started and to make sure it would be remembered as the best and most decent place in England's green and pleasant land.

It was with the thought of this destiny swirling about her aching head that she surveyed the scene in front of her in the Old Rectory on this Sunday morning.

*

In the drawing room, wine glasses were strewn everywhere. On a table a large punch bowl contained the dregs of some sort of fruit punch and outside the open French windows she noticed the remains of a roasted suckling pig on a spit; great chunks of which had been unceremoniously hacked off it and plates with half-eaten pork rolls littered the patio. In an armchair, the body of Philip Bennett, the Old Rectory's owner, sat slumped, fully clothed. A large wine glass lay on the floor under his drooping hand as if he had dropped it as he fell asleep, which, in a way, he had, only permanently.

Making her way upstairs, Chantry looked down on the naked woman who had one leg fortuitously caught in the spindles of the bannisters, which had stopped her from plunging to the bottom and breaking her neck. Unfortunately, she was dead anyway, splayed out head first half up and half down the stairwell.

In the first bedroom, Chantry was confronted with three bodies. One, a naked man except for a leather jockstrap, was shackled cruciform above a double bed which was covered in black satin sheets. His head was hanging down and his features oddly contorted but Chantry could not help thinking that he looked familiar. A stark-naked woman was slumped at the man's feet like a discarded rag doll. Hanging over the edge of the bed was another female, dressed as far as Chantry could see, as a dominatrix, in a tight black rubber catsuit and cat mask; a floppy-looking cat o'nine tails lay on the floor near her limp black-gloved hand. Chantry closed the bedroom door and leant against the landing wall and took some deep breaths. She reached into her cardigan pocket and popped a pill expertly. She attempted to take stock: Seven dead bodies, so far. How many more, she wondered as she grabbed the door handle of the next bedroom.

By the time she had explored every room in the house she had counted thirteen bodies in all; everyone apart from Philip Bennett downstairs was either naked or partially clothed in what she thought could be termed as hideously kinky gear. *What was to be done?* She thought. *Was Alice right and the only sensible thing to do was to call the police? Or was this the time to throw caution to the wind and formulate a more drastic plan of action?*

Closing all the doors behind her she knew that if she didn't think quickly, the future of the village would be at stake. There was nothing to be done for those in the Old Rectory; they were dead and would stay that way no matter what she decided. They could not be saved, but the village could. The village was still a living, breathing thing. She closed her eyes and took in deep breaths. *Yes, above all else,* she reasoned, *she was the last surviving Bowman Leggett and it was her duty to see to it that the village was saved, no matter what.*

Chantry's head was spinning as she came down the stairs and she found it difficult to focus as she made her way to the front door, nearly tripping over the body on the threshold. She held onto the door jamb to steady herself. As her head stopped swimming, she could make out two small figures on the driveway.

'Whatever do you think it is, Molly?' She heard one of them saying.

'I'd say it was a dead body, Jane.' She heard the other answer.

The ladies were Miss Molly Cox and Miss Jane Fox and they had lived together in a small cottage, in the village, for nearly fifty years. They seemed totally oblivious to Chantry who was standing staring at them. The two old girls circled the corpse.

'It wasn't meant to kill them, Molly,' said Jane.

'No, it was only meant to make them a little ill,' said Molly.

'Oh dear, oh dear, oh dear,' they said in unison.

'What wasn't meant to kill them,' asked Chantry striding over to them?

'Oh, Miss Bowman-Leggett,' said Molly, 'I'm afraid that Jane and I have done something dreadful.'

'Something awful,' said Jane.

Chantry stared at them. 'What?'

'We spiked their fruit punch. I have used the correct expression, haven't I Jane?' asked Molly.

'Yes, I believe so,' said Jane.

'We spiked their fruit punch,' repeated her friend.

'Just to make them feel a bit poorly so they wouldn't come back. We've been doing it for the last three months, upping the dose a bit, every time they've had one of their get-togethers,' said Molly.

'Unfortunate phrase, Molly,' said Jane.

Molly stopped to think for a moment.

'Oh yes,' she said, 'so it is. But they are get-togethers, aren't they?'

'A bit too much getting together. That's what we were trying to stop.'

'What did you put in the fruit punch, ladies?' asked Chantry.

'Deadly Nightshade,' said Molly Cox.

'*Atropa Belladonna*,' said Jane Fox.

Chantry tried to stay calm.

'Go on, ladies,' urged Chantry.

'We crushed the berries and put them in with some gin and lemonade...and some other things.'

'They put it in their fruit punch.'

'A loving cup Mister Bennett called it.'

Chantry was beginning to understand. She now recalled the half-drained punch bowl in the drawing room.

'You said other things. What other things?' she asked.

'What? Oh, nothing important,' replied Molly, throwing a glance over to her friend.

'No, no, nothing important,' agreed Jane.

'You see, they have a glass or two before they start doing what they do,' continued Molly.

'Get together?' asked Chantry.

'Yes, get together,' the two ladies said together.

'Now ladies,' said Chantry, who had decided that she had heard more than enough and nothing further would be gained from talking, 'I'm afraid that there are more like this inside the house. I need you to get some sheets, which, no doubt, you will find in the airing cupboard, and wrap them up like Egyptian mummies.'

'Won't the police wonder why they are all wrapped up, Miss Bowman-Leggett,' asked Molly?

'We aren't calling the police, dear,' said Chantry.

'Aren't we?' said Jane. 'Does that mean we won't be getting into trouble?'

'Yes, Jane,' said Chantry. 'Now get started as we don't have much time.'

'Right,' said the two old women together and they waddled off towards the house.

'Oh, I do hope we won't have to go on the run again, Jane,' said Molly.

'Oh, I do hope not. In any case, I don't think I'm capable,' said Jane.

'No, me neither. It will have to be more of a totter this time,' replied Molly.

———————

Chapter 2

George Alexander was sitting up in bed, waiting. His wife, Elizabeth, entered the room carrying a large tray, which contained a plate of full English breakfast and a set of condiments including tomato ketchup and Worcester sauce. Under her arm was a large pile of Sunday newspapers along with the magazines. George received the tray gracefully.

'Thank you, dear,' he said.

'I'll bring up your tea directly, George,' said Elizabeth.

George grunted whilst sprinkling on some Worcester sauce, a dollop of ketchup and a little salt and pepper over the egg, bacon and sausage.

As Elizabeth was making her way downstairs, the doorbell rang. This rather flustered her as, it being a Sunday morning, nobody ever called. She was rather at a loss as what to do for the best. Did she get held up at the door or did she make her lord and master's tea first? But what if it was important? *Best to answer the door*, she thought.

Upstairs, sitting in the bed, George was tucking into his eggs and bacon when he heard Elizabeth calling.

'George. George, dear.' She came into the room. 'George, dear.'

George looked up from his paper, a piece of sausage halfway to his mouth.

'I'm sorry dear,' said his wife, 'but Alice Elms is downstairs. She says that Miss Bowman-Leggett has called an extraordinary meeting of the village council.'

'When?' said George, masticating his sausage.

'Now, dear.'

'Well, tell Alice Elms that I am having my breakfast.' He dipped a piece of bacon into his egg yolk. 'It is Sunday morning and Miss Bowman-Leggett can go hang.'

At that very moment, Alice poked her head around the door. 'But George,' she said, 'it's a matter of life and death; well, death mostly.'

George Alexander was not happy.

The front door opened, and Sue went into a full rant. Her face was like thunder.

'Lost your bloody key at some tarts house have you, Colin?' Through the blue mist of anger, she suddenly realised that it wasn't her husband standing on the doorstep but Alice Elms.

'Good morning, Susan,' said Alice, trying to hide her embarrassment, 'It's probably not a good time.'

A tear formed on Sue's cheek.

'He's stayed out all night this time. He usually crawls in at about four in the morning smelling of cheap scent, with some pathetic excuse.'

Alice looked suitably sympathetic. It was public knowledge around the village that Sue's husband was a serial philanderer and that was why he stayed in London all week and only came down for weekends. It was public knowledge because Sue told everybody about it. That's how she coped. Colin always denied anything was going on and would tell anybody, who'd listen, that his wife was a bit delusional and to ignore her. The village tended to ignore both of them as best they could.

'Now, Alice what can I do for you?'

Alice informed her of the meeting and asked if she could possibly spare the time; she realised it was difficult under the circumstances, but Sue waved it away.

'I'll be along in a minute,' she said.

Alice pottered off to her next port of call.

Penny Bright and Neil Hardy were going at it like newlyweds. They weren't newlyweds. Penny was married to someone else, but he was away. Neil was footloose and liked it when Penny's husband was away. Penny was on top, riding him in ecstasy.

'I love it when you use your screwdriver my little handy man,' she growled.

'Little?' he said. Neil never felt the need for "dirty talk" but Penny seemed to enjoy it, so he let it go.

'My big, big handyman. Hammer in that nail.'

The doorbell rang.

They ignored it.

It rang again.

'Don't stop now,' said Neil. They kept at it. Then:

'Cooee, Neil?'

Outside, Alice was crouched and had pushed the letterbox open and was calling through it.

'Neil, Cooee, Neil?'

At this, the loving couple got out of sync and when Penny should have been going up, she came down. Neil let out a yell.

'Christ,' he shouted.

'Cooee, Neil?'

Penny fell onto the bed and they both started giggling as Neil, naked, climbed off the bed, and hobbled over to the bedroom door and, from the landing, shouted down the stairs.

'What is it, Alice? Sorry, it's my day off.'

'Yes, yes, I appreciate that; I don't need any work done, it's just that Miss Bowman-Leggett,' and she explained about the meeting for the third time.

As Neil did not answer, she crouched down a little more to take a look through the letterbox to see whether he was still there. What she actually saw made her slam the box shut very quickly. She slowly pushed it back open and putting her mouth to it continued:

'Oh, and if you should happen to see Penny, on the off chance, will you tell her about the meeting for me?'

In the village hall, Chantry Bowman-Leggett was finishing putting chairs around a table in the centre of the room.

'What the bloody hell is going on Chantry? Bloody eight o'clock on a Sunday morning. Is nothing sacred?' stormed George as he crashed through the double doors?

'I'm afraid not, George,' she said. 'I'm sorry to pull you away from your egg and bacon but I have things to say that can't wait.'

'Really,' said Neil as he came through the door closely followed by Penny. 'I didn't want to get up this morning,' he continued.

'You could have fooled me,' whispered Penny, nibbling his ear.

'I'm sorry, Chantry,' said Sue as she came in all of a fluster, 'bloody Colin didn't come back last night.' All, except Chantry, rolled their eyes. Suddenly the cruciform figure flashed before her.

'I know,' mumbled Chantry to herself.

'Pardon?' said Sue.

'I said, oh no,' Chantry corrected herself. 'Now, I think we'd all better sit down as I have something to tell you that will come as a bit of a shock.'

Chairs were pulled up to the trestle table. 'As a village, we are facing a crisis.'

'Pub a bit too noisy at closing time?' interjected Neil.

Chantry was not going to rise to Neil's flippancy.

'This is a real crisis, Neil. The future of the whole village could be at stake and as a Bowman-Leggett, I will do everything in my power to avert it.'

'All very dramatic,' said George, 'even for you, Chantry.'

'Not nearly dramatic enough, I'm afraid, George,' she said.

'Spit it out Chantry,' said Penny, 'I've still got some more exercises to do.' She winked at Neil.

Chantry stood and peered down at the assembled council.

'Last night, as I'm sure you are all aware, the residents of the Old Rectory held one of their nauseating parties.'

'And you were upset because you weren't invited.' Neil smirked.

'You'll be laughing on the other side of your face in a moment, Neil, I assure.'

Penny snorted, suppressing a laugh.

'And you, Penelope.'

Penny made a "oh I'm scared face" at Neil. Chantry always called her Penelope when she felt she had over stepped the mark.

'I have called this extraordinary meeting of the village council as a matter of urgency. We are in the middle of an emergency. What are you doing, Alice?'

Alice was scrabbling about in her bag.

'I haven't got my note pad to take the minutes.'

'I think under the circumstances, Alice, the less evidence lying around the better,' replied Chantry, stopping her.

'Come on old girl,' said George.

Chantry, her head aching again, gathered herself to deliver her news to the group.

'I have to inform you that the residents of the Old Rectory, Philip and Sarah Bennett, are dead.'

George sat up, 'What?'

Chantry held her hand up.

'There's more, I'm afraid. All their…' she paused a moment, thinking what best to call them, '…guests, from last night's party, are also dead.'

'Oh, come on,' said Neil with a laugh.

'I'm afraid it's true, Neil. I've seen for myself. The bodies are strewn all over the house.'

'Has anyone called the police?' George looked shocked.

'No,' said Chantry.

'Why not for heaven's sake?' he growled.

'I haven't got my phone,' said Neil. 'Has anyone got a phone?'

There was general consternation in the room. Chantry banged the table.

'Everybody, I must have order. We will not be needing any mobile telephones. In my considered opinion, the last thing we should be doing is calling the police.'

'Not call the police? Why ever not, for God's sake?' said George rising from his seat.

'George,' said Chantry looking him in the face, 'George, dear. All I ask is that you think about it for a moment. Just think about it. Ask yourself what the consequences will be if we have the police swarming about the village, poking their noses into everyone's lives, looking for motives. And what about all those media people, trying to dig up any dirt they can find? Do you really want the police and all those hideous newshounds coming into the village and raking over everyone's past? Is that really what you want, George? Do you really want your past probed into? Do you understand what I'm saying, George?' Chantry looked him straight in the eye.

George stared back at her, his mouth half-open, a glazed look in his eyes, as if looking way, way back into his past.

'Yes, yes, I see what you mean.' He slumped down, defeated, in his chair. He had gone deathly white and started to shake.

Penny looked over at him and took his hand. 'Are you all right, George?' she asked.

He was unable to speak. He looked up at Chantry as if to ask something then thought better of it.

'I'm calling the police,' said Neil after a moment.

'No,' barked George, stopping the handyman in his tracks.

'What?'

Chantry looked over at Neil and then at Penny.

'Tell me,' she said, 'what do you think the newsboys will make of the story that the wife of the *Senior News Readers* from the BBC is having a fling with the local painter and decorator?'

'But there's a murderer on the loose, surely we must do something,' said Neil.

'In my opinion, these deaths are an inside job. I believe the killer to be still in the house, and as dead as his victims.'

'How the hell do you know that?'

'Instinct, my dear Neil.'

'You didn't kill them, did you?'

'Don't be so ridiculous.'

'I wouldn't put it past the witch,' whispered Penny in Neil's ear.

'My dear Penelope, I am so pleased that we no longer live in the Middle Ages, otherwise I'm sure you would have me strapped to a ducking stool before luncheon,' said Chantry.

'Have you stopped to think about this, Chantry?' said Neil.

'My dear boy, I have been around the house and have seen the carnage first hand. Believe me, what I am about to suggest has come after a great deal of thought.'

'Surely if it's an inside job then there won't be too much fuss,' said Penny.

'Oh, there will be fuss; sex always causes a fuss. Let me tell you, what happened in that house will only be the start of it. Once those hawks have got their teeth into this…'

'Beaks,' said Neil, 'Hawks don't have teeth, they have beaks.'

'Oh, do shut up,' barked George, still shaking. 'Once those newshounds have got their teeth into the place, who knows who'll be bitten next.'

'You've changed your tune,' remarked Neil.

Chantry threw a glance at George, who sank even lower into his chair.

'My family founded this village; they built this village; the Bowman-Leggetts have helped guide this village for over a thousand years. I, being the last in the Bowman-Leggett dynasty, have a duty to protect the name of this village. I will not sit idly by whilst a pack of wolves tear the place apart with gossip and innuendo. Those deviants at the Old Rectory have come into this place from elsewhere and I will not let their, degrading, deviant, behaviour contaminate my ancestors' memories. It is my duty not to allow that to happen.' She took a breath. 'I am asking you all to come together and fight for the good name of this village; I am asking you to put all other considerations to one side and help me in my job as leader of this community to, to…' Chantry stopped, not really sure what the analogy should be.

'To push this all under the carpet,' said Neil, helpfully.

'In a manner of speaking, Neil.'

George sat up a bit. 'How do we do that, Chantry? How many bodies are there?'

'I counted thirteen.'

'Thirteen,' exclaimed Neil, 'Sweet Jesus.'

'How the hell do we get rid of thirteen dead bodies without anybody noticing?' asked George.

'We hide them,' said Chantry matter of factly.

'Hide them?' exclaimed Neil.

'I know just the place.'

Neil looked at her.

'So you've got it all worked out.'

'I've an idea that I think may work, yes.'

'Well, come on then, spit it out.'

'We will put them in the Bowman-Leggett family vault in the church.'

'Bloody hell, Chantry, you have got it all worked out,' said Neil. 'You're a proper Miss Marple in reverse, aren't you?'

Sue, who had been very quiet, suddenly piped up.

'But how are we going to get the bodies into the vault? I, for one, couldn't touch a dead body. Could any of us?'

'Count me out,' said Penny, giving a shudder.

'They will be wrapped in sheets and blankets.'

'But that doesn't answer the question on how we get them from the Old Rectory to the vault,' said George.

Penny shifted uneasily in her chair.

'I really don't believe that anybody is honestly thinking of actually doing this,' she huffed.

'Penny, it is none of my business whether you are cheating on your husband with this young man.' Chantry nodded towards Neil. 'The fact that everyone in the village knows about it is neither here nor there.'

'Do they?' said Neil, sitting up a little shocked.

'The thing is, we, as a community, are not here to spread the word further afield; meaning to your husband.'

'Are you threatening me?' Penny was up on her hind legs.

'Get off your high horse, Penelope. No one in this room is threatening anything; no one in this village would say a word to your husband. But let in a hoard of gossip mongers such as the national press,' she paused for effect, 'Let in the television reporters from a rival television station. Then let in a lot of policemen. You only need one policeman to tell one rival newsman who your husband is. You only need that newsman to do a bit of digging and dig they will, about all of us; wouldn't you agree George?'

She turned to him as he sank once more into his chair and covered his face with his hands.

'You only need that to happen and it doesn't take a genius to work out that it wouldn't take long for him to buy one of the regulars in the pub a drink or two, and we all know who that would be.'

'Ronnie,' said Neil.

'No names, no pack drill,' said Chantry, pursing her lips.

Penny's head fell forward.

'All right, all right, Chantry, you win. But I'm not touching them.'

'I think we should just get on with it. The quicker we do it the quicker it gets done,' said Sue. Chantry looked at her.

'It's all right, Chantry. I understand,' said Sue.

What did she understand? Chantry wondered. *Did she understand everything? Did she understand that Colin was at the party and was now hanging above a bed, stark naked, with two women at his feet? Did she know that her husband's life had ended as part of a sadistic threesome?*

'So,' she continued, pulling herself together, 'are we all agreed on the plan?' People nodded their heads or mumbled a sort of assent. 'Good. Now, we are going to have to go about this speedily and stealthily; the less others know about it, at this stage, the better. George, bring that First Aid stretcher; Alice you and Penny can bring the large tea trolley from the kitchen; we need some sort a large barrow and some rope, Neil. Don't let anybody see what you're doing and meet me at the front door of the Rectory and be careful not to fall over the body on the driveway.'

'What about me, Chantry?' said Sue.

'Yes, well, I think you should come with me, my dear,' Chantry replied.

And with that, they all went off in their different directions.

For a moment Sue and Chantry walked together in silence. Chantry took Sue's arm as they made their way out of the village hall. For once Chantry didn't know what to say. Sue eventually broke the impasse.

'It's all right, I had a feeling he'd gone there. He tried to get me to go. He said it would liven up our marriage.'

'Oh, Susan. I didn't know how to tell you,' Chantry stopped.

'As soon as you started telling us about the place, I knew you'd found him in there somewhere,' said Sue, 'It was written all over your face.'

'We'll get him out of there and put him in your bed. You could say he died in the night, a heart attack or something,' reasoned Chantry.

'They'd have a post-mortem, wouldn't they? A post-mortem. They always do with an unexpected death. And if he's been poisoned with the rest of them, then they'll find traces in his blood, won't they? They'll find poison in his blood and think I poisoned him.'

'Did I say they'd been poisoned?' Chantry was watching her.

'I assumed it was poison, wasn't it?'

'Yes, yes, I would have thought so now you mention it,' said Chantry.

'Well then, I'd get arrested, wouldn't I? And to save myself, I'd have to tell them about the others; then you'd all get arrested and I wouldn't want that. No; why should you all suffer because my husband couldn't keep his dick in his trousers?' She spat the last bit out between gritted teeth and then smiled again.

Chantry winced. *Poor woman,* she thought, *she has had to put up with so much.*

'The selfish bastard. The stupid, selfish bastard deserved it. If he'd acted like an adult as opposed to…' She stopped.

'What will you do?' asked Chantry.

'What do you mean?'

'How will you explain Colin's disappearance?'

'I won't. He's retired, so his work colleagues won't miss him. His parents are both dead; only child. Let's face it, he was in London during the week, hardly ever here and when he was, he'd find an excuse to leave again as soon as he could. And I don't need his money although I do have access to his bank accounts. I have his PIN numbers and everything; the bloody idiot had them all typed up and stuck up on the inside of the bureau. His work pension goes straight into his account. I'll just use his card and pull the money out of the hole in the wall if I should need to. I won't because I don't need it. You see?'

'My, you have worked it all out quickly,' mused Chantry.

'Oh, I'd worked it all out ages ago. I've often fantasised about killing him. I've lain in bed more times than I care to think, staring at the ceiling, wondering what would happen if I did. In fact, I had it all apart from what I'd do with the body. This has just saved me the trouble of doing it myself.' Sue gave a weak smile and they walked on.

The village was still deserted as Chantry Bowman-Leggett, accompanied by the newly widowed Susan, strode back to the Old Rectory. The village was always this quiet; sometimes it was hard to believe that anybody lived there at all; sometimes you could sit on the bench outside the churchyard wall and not see a soul all day.

Chantry's head was aching badly and, when Susan was not looking, she popped a pill from her cardigan pocket, into her mouth and threw it back. She felt a trifle dizzy but she was determined that nothing would get in her way to save the village, her village, from shame and ridicule.

The high heeled body was still on the driveway but was now wrapped, expertly, in a bedsheet. Sue shuddered as they stopped by the gate.

'Is that?' She stopped, looking down at the mummy.

'No, dear, he's upstairs,' replied Chantry, patting Sue's hand.

From behind her Chantry heard a loud whistle and turned around to see George's head poking out from behind a hedge.

'Chantry,' he called, in a loud whisper, 'is the coast clear?'

'Yes, hurry up,' hissed Chantry back.

Out from behind the hedge which surrounded the Village Hall, the members of the village council emerged; Penny and Alice pushing a large catering trolley on top of which was an old canvas First Aid Stretcher, which had been standing upright and fixed to the wall of the hall next to one of the fire buckets for as long as anyone could remember. The trolley's wheels rattled on the roadway making a sound that could wake the dead...

'Lift it up, lift it up,' hissed Chantry.

'What's the bloody point of having a trolley on wheels if we're going to carry the bloody thing?' said Penny.

'Just get it in the house, quickly for goodness' sake and stop complaining,' scolded Chantry.

With much muttering, they picked up the trolley and tottered through the gate and along the drive.

'I can't do this,' said Penny as they were about to pass the mummified body.

'We have no choice, my dear,' said George, as they continued towards the house.

'What's she got on you?' said Penny.

'You wouldn't believe it if I told you,' replied George, 'so let's just keep focused on the matter in hand, for the moment, shall we?'

'Take the trolley up the staircase and onto the landing, we shall use it to ferry the bodies from the bedrooms to the stairs,' Chantry called, discreetly, after them.

Neil came into the drive pushing a sack barrow and carrying various coils of rope, string and duct tape. As soon as he saw the body, he stopped in his tracks.

'Come in quickly, Neil,' Chantry beckoned. 'Haven't you got a wheelbarrow,' she said eying up the sack barrow.

'I thought it would be easier to stand them up in this,' Neil replied.

'How would we keep the body upright?' asked Chantry.

'We'll tape them in with this,' answered Neil, picking up the Duct tape.

'Oh yes, yes I see,' said Chantry, a little sceptically, 'I think I need to get George to help us.'

Chantry Bowman-Leggett stood in the middle of the road, looking like an aged lollypop lady who'd forgotten her lollypop. She looked both ways, craned her neck a little and then beckoned. Neil came out of the Old Rectory gate pushing the sack barrow, with George holding onto the body to keep it steady. The head of the deceased hung over one side. As fast as they could, they made it over the narrow road and through the gate and into the churchyard. Chantry, giving one more look to make sure they hadn't been seen, followed them.

But they had been seen. A spy was lurking, albeit a very bleary-eyed spy in the shape of Ronnie Randell, who had been sitting on the bench in the lych-gate, waiting for Sam, the landlord to open the Leggett Arms. His eyes were a little out of focus, but he recognised the Bowman-Leggett woman, at least he thought he did, but couldn't make out who the others were, although one of them appeared to be floating.

Arriving at the church door, Chantry pushed at it and it opened with an echoing creak. Making sure the coast was clear, she beckoned them to follow.

Everything in the church seemed to be as it should be at this time on a Sunday morning; cold and empty. But something had changed; something that couldn't be seen. Behind a screen, a "state of the art" sound system had been set up the previous day in a tiny side chapel by Ryan Roberts, a young geeky looking lad of around sixteen, along with his girlfriend, Kylie Gordon.

Chapter 3

The Reverend Jonathan Martin, the parish priest, had officiated at the church for many years; for more years than most people could remember. Chantry Bowman-Leggett could remember, but she'd been in the village almost longer than God himself.

The years preaching to his flock had taken their toll on the Rev. Martin's voice; years of listening to the Rev. Martin preaching had taken their toll on his flock's hearing. So as his voice got quieter and quieter the congregation heard less and less. It got so bad that when asked if they enjoyed his sermon the members of his flock who were hard of hearing had to admit that they hadn't realised he'd given one. So, after much thought and to-ing and fro-ing, it was decided that some funds, which had been put aside for minor repairs, should be utilised to see if they could purchase, second hand, of course, some sort of sound system including a microphone that the Reverend Martin could use during the service. Chantry was, as could be expected, privy to all this but the meetings to decide what should be done had been so long ago that she had quite forgotten them.

Hearing of the problem, Ryan put himself forward to help find the right equipment. He had to admit that he had no problem hearing the Reverend but then again, he was only sixteen and his hearing was as keen as mustard.

He informed the Vicar that he had trawled all the popular online sites and had found a nearly new sound system that not only had the type of microphone one put in a stand, which looked to him quite old fashioned, but it also came with one of those small microphones that somehow was attached to your head and seemed to grow out of your cheek. A thin cable ran down the wearer's back and was attached to a tiny box with an aerial that beamed the voice back to a transmitter and then through speakers that could be strategically placed throughout the church.

Ryan assured the Vicar that he would be able to wander about the church unfettered. The Vicar tried to point out that he had never "wandered about the church" and that he liked to stand still as much as possible as he had a gammy knee, from his time on National Service when he had smashed it falling off one of those climbing ropes on an assault course and fell on top of the instructor so hard that both of them had to be invalided out of the Army. Needless to say that Ryan did not listen and nagged the Vicar until he gave in.

Ryan, therefore, was duly despatched to purchase this wonder of audio engineering for as little as he possibly could.

When presented with the head microphone, the Reverend Martin expressed his doubts as to whether he could carry such a contraption off convincingly. His main fear, being, that it would fall off or he'd forget he got it on and think the end nearest his cheek was some sort of insect crawling up his face and that he would be tempted to hit it with his hand, which would, more than likely, break it. It would create such a noise as he bashed it and it would be amplified all around the church and deafen the, albeit small, congregation that attended the Morning Service.

As luck, or should that be fate, would have it, this very Sunday; this Sunday when Chantry Bowman-Leggett and her two accomplices were wheeling a dead body down the aisle, had been picked to launch the new sound system onto the unsuspecting congregation. Ryan and his sidekick, Kylie, had been working on concealing the speakers behind pillars all through Saturday; Ryan had even contrived to conceal one up on a beam near the image of Christ in the stained-glass windows above the altar. In truth, Kylie thought that Ryan was pushing God's patience a bit when he leant the step ladder just above the window and climbed up, turning, when he had got level with the crucified Christ, and throwing his arms out so in the light it looked like he had been crucified. Kylie had always worshipped Ryan, but she worshipped Christ more and felt rather uncomfortable at what she thought to be a tasteless, and rather blasphemous, joke.

They had been having a problem with the transmitter pack on the head radio mic, as it either faded when the wearer walked up the aisle or created a tremendous feedback screeching which sounded like the most blood-curdling scream being let loose in the church. The noise could be terrifying as they had discovered only the day before, when they seemed to have frightened the living daylights out of Mister Bennett, the owner of the Old Rectory, when he had wandered in around Saturday lunchtime. Ryan and Kylie may have been young, but they were more than aware of what went on once a month in the house opposite. They had heard the gossip around the village; they had heard that the goings-on every first Saturday in the month were a disgrace to the village and in the Old Rectory too. How could God allow such a disgusting bacchanalia so near to His house they thought?

They had been playing around with various knobs and switches on the amplifier, such as echoes and distort along with tone from a high treble to a big booming bass sound; the last of which they had just finished experimenting with when Philip Bennett wandered in. Ryan and Kylie were behind the screen and were quietly adjusting the settings. They watched him wander down past the pews, his hands plunged in his pockets. He had a huge smile on his face, and he kept laughing to himself. He walked up the steps into the pulpit and started turning the pages of the large Bible that lay on the Golden Eagle stand.

As they watched him, they felt uneasy. He flicked the Bible's pages without, in their mind, any reverence; to them he was defacing the Holy Book. They both felt the gorge rise in them. They both wanted to scream at him for his lack of respect.

'And God sayeth unto them,' Philip Bennett bellowed, suddenly from the pulpit, as if he was reading from the Holy Text, 'That thou shall not fornicate with thy neighbour's wife.' He paused and leant forward over the pulpit as if he was bearing down on the invisible congregation. 'Unless,' he continued, 'you come to Philip and Sarah's house on Saturday night, when you can roger her senseless whilst her old man is looking on and more than likely joining in.' He laughed loudly at his own outrageous joke; his laugh was so loud that he did not hear Ryan and Kylie audibly gasp in shock and horror at his blasphemous remarks. Ryan wanted to go and punch Bennett on the nose, but in reality he knew that he didn't have the courage. Kylie was on the verge of tears; she was going through a very religious phase in her life and felt extremely hurt and confused that God could allow such behaviour in His House.

'God isn't going to allow it,' whispered Ryan.

'How can you know that?' asked Kylie, wiping the tears with her hand.

'Don't be alarmed,' he said quietly, 'but God is compelling me to act on His behalf.'

Now, whether Ryan really felt he was being guided by the Almighty or was just acting on an impulse, it is not for us to say but for now, let us give the lad the benefit of the doubt and say it was God's hand that made Ryan reach for the controls and put the small radio microphone on. He turned the Graphic Equaliser to its base setting and then turned up the echo and began to speak.

'Philip Bennett,' he said not sounding at all like a sixteen-year-old boy. Bennett jumped and looked around.

'So, Philip Bennett, you see fit to come into My House. Do you come to defile My House?'

Was this Ryan's voice or God's? Kylie stood in awe.

'What the fu…?' Bennett stopped himself. He'd just been trying a glass of Miss Cox and Miss Fox's gin and lemonade concoction and was feeling a little trippy. He started to giggle.

'You find it funny,' said the voice rising in anger. 'You are in the House of God; My House!'

Philip Bennett paused a moment and tried to pull his thoughts together, but instead they seemed to be going further away from him.

'Who the hell is that?' he slurred slightly; his voice, seemingly, not coming from his own mouth.

'You use the name of the Devil's pit in My House?' Ryan was warming to his task.

'Who are you?' Philip heard himself shouting. The voice seemed to be coming from around the stain glass window. He looked up at it, but the sun's glare was coming straight through, and he found it difficult to focus.

'I am the Lord thy God.' It came out before Ryan realised it. 'I am the resurrection and the life.'

Kylie was aghast; *was he was pretending to be God in God's House, or was this actually God?* She thought. *Surely, they'd both be struck down by a bolt of lightning if it was just Ryan playing about.*

The owner of the Old Rectory was staring up at the stained-glass window. The figure on it seemed to be moving. It was speaking to him. He swayed slightly.

'Philip Bennett, you have sinned against me; you have sinned against your fellow man with your lewd and lascivious behaviour.' Ryan was on a roll and ignored Kylie's attempts to silence him. 'All those who cavort with the Devil shall be damned forever after. He who lies with his neighbour's wife shall burn in the fires of hell,' Ryan roared.

Had he not partaken of the brew that Miss Cox and Miss Cox had laced with their own, lethal, concoction, his brain would have been clear and he'd have, quickly, cottoned on to the fact that someone, somewhere in the building was pulling his leg. But he had taken a draft or two and it was rapidly taking an effect without his knowing.

'What do you want?' he asked the disembodied voice.

'You must rid the world of this evil,' said the booming voice of Ryan's God. 'Those that sin with you must be consigned to damnation. You, Philip Bennett, must be consigned with them.'

'How?'

'It is for you to decide how this is to be done, but it must be done tonight,' said Ryan the God.

It was then that a deafening screech came from the speakers and the feedback bounced off the stone walls all around him. Bennett covered his ears and fell to the floor in agony.

'Oh, Christ,' he muttered, suddenly completely paranoid, 'What have I done?'

Was this a ploy? thought Ryan; *is he about to get up and start laughing? Were they about to be caught?* Bennett did get up, unsteadily and falling up the aisle staggered towards the doors. As he reached them, Ryan could not resist turning the knife just a little more and with full voice he bellowed,

'Philip Bennett, your time and the time for all your followers is nigh!'

Bennett crashed out into the graveyard, the ancient gravestones swimming in front of his eyes.

Both Ryan and Kylie stayed silent, half expecting him to come back; he didn't.

'You'll be damned in hell, Ryan Roberts,' whispered Kylie.

'I was just doing God's bidding,' said Ryan.

'How do you know that for sure?' She looked at him.

'I just do, Kylie. He spoke to me, I'm sure of it.' Ryan had turned bright red and was hyperventilating slightly.

'Are you about to have one of your asthma attacks?' she asked looking him straight in the eye.

Ryan got out his puffer and gave himself a blast.

'I'm sure it was God talking through me. What else could it be?'

Kylie wanted to believe Ryan. She was in love with Ryan, although she hadn't told him so. They hadn't kissed or anything up until that point. She kissed him now. Ryan went redder, pulled away and gave himself another quick blast of his puffer, just in case. Ryan felt stirrings that he only usually had when alone in his bedroom.

Was this feeling brought on by a nearness to God or someone a little closer?

Chapter 4

Chantry stopped by the door to the crypt.

'You are about to enter a very private place,' she said, as she unlocked the large oak door and switched on the two 60-watt light bulbs.

'Bloody hell, it's huge,' said Neil.

'Good God, there are coffins,' said George.

'Well, of course there are coffins, what did you expect, bottles of wine?' snapped Chantry.

Slowly the two men struggled to lower the body, still on the sack trolley, down the stone steps whilst Chantry unlocked the iron gates to the Bowman-Leggett family vault.

Arriving at the bottom, the full extent of the vault could be taken in. There were a few stone tombs but mostly the place was full of old and dusty coffins piled on top of one another in corners, and along the middle of the space. Three or four arches were full of them.

George and Neil stepped forward a little to get a closer look. 'Is this legal?' asked George.

'Is what legal?' said Chantry.

'Having all these coffins on show like this,' George continued.

'They're not on show,' said Chantry, 'this is the Bowman-Leggett family vault. Apart from the first few who are buried under the nave, this is where all the Bowman-Leggetts are buried; well, the ones that got back to England, that is, the others are strewn over Agincourt and the Somme.'

'But they're not buried, are they?' said Neil, 'They're out in the open.'

'This is not out in the open,' Chantry replied curtly, 'this is a sanctified burial place and has been for nearly a thousand years.'

'But I thought they were all entombed,' said George.

'Yes, well some of them are; the early ones, but when the family fell into financial difficulties, they decided just to put them down here and leave it at that,' said Chantry. 'I put my brother Perty in the centre there, and I shall go next to him when my time comes. I shall be the last to rest here.'

'Really?' asked Neil.

'I am the last of the true Bowman-Leggett line.' Chantry looked at them. 'After I am laid to rest down here, the doorway we've just come through will be walled up.'

'But why?' asked George.

'Well,' started Chantry, 'after I'm gone, there will be no others to be buried here so that will be that. No one will have any need to come down here again.'

The three of them stood for a moment in realisation. It took Neil to break the silence.

'So what are we going to do with our friend, here? Plonk him into one of the coffins with your ancestors?'

'Certainly not,' returned Chantry, shocked, 'Whoever heard such a thing? We will put them in the Monks' Cell, which is over here,' she said, making her way through the maze of coffins and over to another oak door.

'So what's in there? More coffins?' asked Neil.

'No, not more coffins, but...' Chantry stopped and looked over at the others.

'But what?' asked George.

'It's probably best that I open up and let you all see for yourselves.'

'Why is it called The Monks' Cell?' asked Neil.

'You'll find out in a moment,' answered Chantry, turning the large iron key. 'What you are about to witness has never been seen by anybody, to my knowledge, besides members of the Bowman-Leggett family. And,' she continued, 'not many of those have been in this room. It will come as a bit of a shock, so prepare yourselves.'

'As if the last hour has been a bundle of laughs,' Neil added.

'I must say, this is all a bit dramatic, Chantry,' said George.

'Oh, it most certainly is,' said Chantry, pushing open the door. Neil and George stepped back in horror as a shaft of light from the two sixty-watt bulbs in the main vault threw shadows over three walls of the room and the six aged truckle beds on which lay the bones of six humans. Hollowed out eyes from the skulls looked towards them or up into the vaulted ceiling.

'Jesus Christ!' exclaimed Neil.

George looked away. Chantry continued.

'Don't worry. These have been dead for well over eight hundred years.'

'Who are they? How did they get in here?' asked George.

'They lived in here for a while. They were monks, that's why it's called The Monks' Cell, by the family. Sadly, they also died in here.'

George looked at Chantry. 'What happened?'

'The story goes that one of my ancestors locked the door, from the outside, one night and left them to die.' Chantry stared at what was left of the poor souls.

'Why?' asked Neil.

'The plague.'

'The plague?'

'You must remember that in the fourteenth century nearly half of the population died as a result of the Bubonic plague; the Black Death,' said Chantry, 'Nobody had seen these strange men before and it's said that soon after the monks arrived in the village, one of them fell mysteriously ill. Rumour of the plague had been going around the district for a while although none had yet been affected in the area. People said that the monks had recently come from France, where the plague was thought to have started and they feared that the monk was infected, and the village had to do something to stop it from spreading.'

'So what happened?' George looked at her.

'Nobody is certain, but the incident is alluded to in a journal kept by an ancestor at around the time. A meeting took place of the village elders.'

'The medieval version of us,' said Neil.

'Precisely, Neil,' said Chantry, 'The meeting was convened and it was decided that the plague, as this was thought to be the reason behind the man's illness, should be contained. They came in the dead of night when the monks were sleeping. The guilty party made their way down those stairs, opened that iron gate into the vault, crept up to this door and turned the key in the lock and left them.'

'So they couldn't get out and starved to death?' asked Neil.

Chantry nodded, 'I'm afraid so.'

They all looked over to the skeletons in calm repose.

'So what did they do, just lie down and die?' asked George.

'I wouldn't have thought so,' said Chantry 'I expect they prayed and when that didn't work, they probably tried to break the door down. When I found them, their bones were all over the place.'

They both turned to look at her.

'It's a long story,' she sighed, 'but after my parents died, my brother and I decided to investigate. Up until then this key had been locked away in a safe deposit box at the family's bank. We had no access to it until my brother took over as head of the family. We had both, of course, read the story of the monks in the vault, but neither of us really believed it, thinking it was just one of those tales handed down throughout the generations that, in the end, turned out to be an old wives' tale. In fact, our father spoke about it in a way that he thought it to be a myth. That said, he refused, when pushed by Perty and myself, to find the key in order to get to the truth of the matter. Having, eventually, got our hands on the key, I'm afraid that youthful curiosity took the better of us and we came down here and opened the door. The place was dusty and smelt of decay, as can be imagined. The bodies by now, of course, were just a mass of bones. One was just behind the door as if he had been trying to get out at the time of his death – you can still see the scratches he made with his finger nails. One lay on his bed; the others strewn about the room. There must have been such panic, poor things. Of course, we have no way of knowing.' Chantry stopped for breath, 'They may have tried to eat each other.'

'Good God,' said George.

'A pretty hideous God if you ask me,' said Chantry.

'Perty was resolved to just lock the door and walk away and not think about it again, much in the same way, I would think, that our ancestors did. Nobody wanted to do anything about it. They wouldn't even talk about it. Perty put the key back into the safe deposit box and thought no more of it. I, on the other hand, had nightmares about these poor souls and tried to come to terms with how the village could do such a thing. After Perty was killed in the car crash, I became the only living heir of the Bowman-Leggett dynasty.'

She turned and looked over towards the newest looking coffin. 'The day after I put Perty's body down here. I realised that I needed to face the horrors of the place and try, on behalf of all my ancestors, to make my peace with these gentlemen. So I came down here with dustpan and brush and a cloth and attempted to put what was left of the poor souls together again. I cleaned them up and placed them on the beds; I have no way of knowing whether I put the correct arm or leg with its corresponding torso, but I did my best for them. During all this I apologised for the dreadful wrong that had been done, but, at the same time, endeavoured to explain that although I thought what the village had done to them was wicked and murderous, they had to see the other side of this. Above all else, the village elders' job was to make sure that the inhabitants of the village were safe. What would seem horrific to those who discovered their crumbling bones was, in fact, the only sensible option, under the circumstances. Lock them in and protect others from the plague.'

Neil looked around him, 'After you'd put them all together, didn't you think to call the police?'

'Whatever for? The perpetrators of this particular crime had been dead for well over eight hundred years themselves. Their punishment, should there be any judgement higher than us, would have been metered out long ago without the help of the local constabulary. Which brings us back to the matter in hand.'

'And that's what you think we are doing now?' asked George.

'I do, George, yes.' Chantry looked at them. 'I know you think I'm mad and, perhaps, bad for talking you into doing all of this, and to be honest I never thought you'd go along with it, but I truly believe that my ancestors got it right. It was important to save the village above all else. But that does not mean that we will not treat the dead with less respect. Having put these gentlemen together, I went around to see the Vicar; not the Reverend Martin, it was before his time; and got him to say a little prayer over them before locking the door again.' Chantry stopped and looked around her. 'I think,' she continued, 'we need to finish putting in the new intake before Morning Service.'

That said, they unloaded the body and, carefully, laid it on the stone floor of the cell. Then they made their way up the stone steps, along the nave of the church, down the gravel path and across the still deserted road and back to the Old Rectory.

Chapter 5

By the time they returned, Molly Cox and Jane Fox, Sue and Alice, had fully mummified the others in various sheets and duvet covers. They each had been tidily knotted at their head and feet. Penny stood, with her arms folded, in the hallway having completely refused to touch any of them.

The next task, Chantry told the assembled group, was to get the bodies from the bedrooms and onto the landing and from there down the stairs to ground level. After some hesitation, they worked out that they could be lowered down by ropes, but the worry was whether the head would bang down the stairs.

'We need a board or something to tie them too,' observed Neil.

All of them stood about scratching their heads and looking aimlessly around them. It was Alice who came up with the solution whilst standing by the front door. Next to her was a large walk-in cloakroom. She went inside and took a look around as the others went off in various directions to see if they could find an answer. Without any real enthusiasm, she parted the coats that hung on the rail. Above the rail was a shelf full of hats of various types, amongst them a couple of very colourful woollen bobble hats. Next to these were two pairs of goggles which, on first inspection, Alice took to be more props for the household's sex games. In the corner, she noticed, was a large, long black canvas bag with handles and a zip fastener running from top to bottom. Not having a clue as to what it could be she started to unzip it.

'Neil,' called Alice quite loudly and in a somewhat excitable voice.

The others came out of their various rooms to see what the noise was about. Eventually, Alice appeared from the cloakroom with a pair of very long and colourful skis, which dwarfed her by some two or three feet.

'Will these do?'

'Brilliant,' said Neil, excitedly. Despite himself, he was beginning to enjoy the practicalities of what they were doing. 'What we need to do is set up a sort of pulley device; a block and tackle.'

'What's that?' asked Sue.

'Dead bodies are heavy and when we're lowering them down the stairs, we don't want gravity to run away with them so they go crashing to the floor.'

'Oh God, no,' said Penny, feeling sick.

'So we control them. We lower them down in a controlled way.' And having said that he ran up the stairs with a coil of rope.

Throwing an end of the rope through the banister rail, twice along the landing. He then called down to Alice to bring the skis up the stairs, which she did with great difficulty.

Using the strong duct-tape, he bound the two skis together and then attached the rope onto them with a knot most Boy Scouts would be able to recognise but may not, in adulthood, be able to name any more. He then beckoned to George to help him lift the first body onto the skis with the feet near the end which curled up, rather aptly. Neil then bound the body to the skis with some more rope.

'Right, Sue and Alice, get down the bottom and grab the end of the rope and slowly lower the body down the stairs. Penny, you guide the bottom of the skis, so they go straight and don't hit the bannisters on the way down,' ordered Neil.

'Do I have to?' asked Penny in her best little girl voice which usually made Neil feel sorry for her.

'Yes,' he said firmly. 'You won't be taking any weight. I've used the banister rails as a sort of double purchase system. It helps take the weight off the load. The ladies will be able to lower the body down slowly.'

With that, he pushed the skis over the edge of the top of the stairs. Alice and Sue took the weight and realising that it wasn't as bad as they thought it would be, let the body slip down the stairs in as a controlled manner as they could with Penny walking backwards down the stairs making sure it was going straight.

'Just a little faster, ladies,' said Neil.

The body's descent duly increased in speed until eventually stopping at the bottom.

Neil then untied it and he and George lifted it off the skis and tied it to the sack barrow.

Getting the deceased into an upright position, they pushed it through the front door and down the drive with George hurrying ahead as fast as he could to make sure the coast was clear, crossing the narrow road and through the church gate, up the path and down the aisle. The two of them bumped the trolley with its dead cargo down the steps of the crypt and into the Bowman-Leggett vault. Looking at each other, they both gave a shudder and without uttering a word wheeled the body to its final resting place with the medieval monks.

Meanwhile, back at the Old Rectory, the others were busy at their tasks. Chantry had organised her crew like a production line. Molly Cox and Jane Fox were tasked with cleaning up the rooms after the corpses had been taken out. Sue, Alice and Chantry herself lifted the bodies, one by one, onto the old First Aid stretcher which was taped to the large tea trolley, whilst Penny stopped it from rolling away. Then they wheeled that out of whichever room they were in and onto the landing. From there, the four of them lifted the body off the stretcher and onto the skis in preparation for its descent into the hall. Sue and Alice then took their positions downstairs, rope in hand, to lower the body to the ground floor with Penny keeping it on the straight and narrow.

Having lowered it, the crew lifted it off the skis and lay it on the hall rug to await Neil and George with the sack trolley to ferry it to the church. The ladies then repeated their actions with another corpse.

Four bodies had been transported to the vaults and another was on its way down the stairs when it suddenly went off-piste. A cry went up from Alice.

'Whatever is it, Alice,' asked Chantry, dashing out of one of the bedrooms?

'Constable Dealey. I'd quite forgotten, Constable Dealey in the excitement,' Alice replied, shaking.

'What about Constable Dealey?' said Sue.

'It's nearly time for his breakfast,' said Alice.

'So?' Penny shook her head. She was not happy that she was hunched halfway down the stairs with a dead body above her.

'I always make his Sunday breakfast,' replied Alice, 'before he does his round of the village.'

Chantry came down the stairs and past the body.

'Oh, Alice, of course,' she said. 'The only time we see him is on a Sunday morning.'

'I've never seen him,' said Penny.

'That's because you stay in bed until Sunday lunchtime,' said Chantry.

'How do you know that?' asked Penny.

'It's obvious, dear,' replied Chantry throwing her a knowing look. 'Alice, you must get back to your cottage immediately and find a way of keeping him there.'

'But, how will I do that?' asked Alice.

'Use your feminine wiles,' said Chantry.

'But I don't think I have any feminine wiles.'

'Of course you have dear. Every woman worth the name has them when it comes to getting men to do what you want,' continued Chantry, 'Perhaps today is the day you offer up the ultimate sacrifice.'

'You mean? Oh, I'm not sure I could do that,' replied Alice.

'Of course you can dear,' said Chantry, 'Remember the reputation of the village is at stake.'

'Oh,' repeated Alice as she wandered off down the drive wondering how she could summon up the courage.

———————

Chapter 6

Police Constable Michael Dealey, was one of the policemen who were stationed in the nearest town, part of whose beat was the village. There were, in fact, three police constables whose job it was, during their shift, to make sure all was well and law abiding in the village. Two of the said PCs had, in fact, never set foot in the place after their first day in the area, as they could see no point in wasting the time or effort. Nothing happened in the village as far as they could see and nothing was likely to happen.

PC. Dealey, on the other hand, did visit the village regularly every Sunday morning when he was on the morning shift which started at 6 a.m.

He liked the place. He found it peaceful and enjoyed walking around it, taking in the church and the Old Rectory. He would smile and shake his head every time he walked past Borley's farm. How could a man have such a beautiful period home and let it run to rack and ruin and live in a double-decker bus?

There was, it must be said, another reason he liked the village and that reason was Miss Alice Elms.

He first came across Alice one morning when she was, a little later than usual, partaking in her morning perambulation of the village owing to the fact that it had been raining and she saw no point in going out to get wet just for the sake of it. She cycled aimlessly around the corner in the middle of the road on her way to visit Chantry at her cottage, when the police car, which Constable Dealey was driving, appeared in the other direction. The Constable, having passed his advanced police driving test, was quick to take evasive action and swerved to avoid the collision. Alice, however, had not passed any form of test to become a cyclist and being quite new to balancing on two wheels, panicked and turned the handlebars a little too forcefully. Unfortunately, instead of turning them to point the bicycle's wheels away from the path of the oncoming police car, she turned them instead in the opposite direction and proceeded to hit the side of the car and knock herself to the damp ground. The Constable, fearing the worst, leapt out of the car, knocking his door into the flattened bike and its rider.

Now, it should be noted that some people, including most members of the police force, would have looked upon Alice's actions as rather stupid and after making sure that she wasn't badly injured might have cautioned her to 'take more care, in the future' and 'learn to ride a bicycle properly on the correct side of the road'. This was not Police Constable Dealey's way. In his mind, when something bad happened, he reasoned that it must have been his fault. The reason for this Martyr Syndrome? That was easy; it was what his wife, Sheila, told him on a daily basis. It was so ingrained into his psyche that, even though common sense told him loudly and clearly that he could in no way be blamed for whatever it was that befell him, he could not and would not believe it to be so.

Constable Dealey leant down and, gently, turned Alice's head towards him.

'Don't move for a moment,' he said, 'let's make sure you haven't done any real damage.' He was thinking about all his training; how one must always be careful not to move someone until you are absolutely sure that their back wasn't broken or something equally serious.

Alice sat up a bit and in doing so the Constable decided that she was, probably, just shaken up a bit. Getting his hands under her armpits, he gently lifted her to her feet. Alice, although flustered at being knocked over, was not so devoid of her feelings that she experienced an acute thrill having this knight in policeman's uniform coming to her rescue.

'Oh, please don't worry, Constable,' she said, with a slight quivering in her voice, 'I'm quite all right. Oh yes, quite all right.' She felt a blush come to her cheeks as she stood, his arms still around her. She looked up at him and smiled. For a brief moment they stayed in this position. He smiled back at her but then, coming to himself, he relaxed his grip and stood back from her.

'As long as you're all right,' he said, in the most formal and policemen-like way he could muster.

'Yes, yes,' said Alice, 'Nothing's broken. Just a bit damp.'

'Damp?' inquired Constable Dealey, a little confused.

'On my legs, from the rain,' continued Alice.

P.C. Dealey found himself looking down at Alice's legs. He thought that he would not be allowed to look at his wife's legs like that.

'What are you looking at?' she'd ask.

'Just looking at your legs,' he'd said once in an unguarded moment.

'Well don't,' she bit back. 'It isn't a gentlemanly thing to do to look at a lady's legs. That's the way that common men behave.'

Alice's legs, although a little short, were not unattractive; he could see quite a lot of them as her skirt had ridden up revealing more thigh that she would usually expose. Not that she thought of that sort of thing, normally, having never thought that a man would want to look at her legs in the first place.

'Do you live far?' The Constable asked. She had caught a glimpse of him catching a glimpse of her legs and she blushed some more. She rather liked the fact that the Constable had been looking at her legs. She felt a thrill.

'Oh, not far,' her little girlie voice came as a bit of a surprise even to her. 'Just up the road,' she continued trying, unsuccessfully, to return it to her normal tone.

'Then allow me to push your bicycle back for you. It may have got damaged in the accident. I don't think you should ride it until I've had a jolly good look at it.'

Alice thought his turn of phrase made him sound like a true gallant.

PC Dealey picked up the bike and gestured that she lead the way. Alice limped slightly.

'Are you all right, really?' he asked noticing.

'Oh yes,' said Alice, for she was. She had no idea why she was limping; nothing seemed to be hurting.

Perhaps it's because something should be hurting, she thought, *the reason why I'm limping.* But nothing was hurting, so she knew that she had no reason to limp, but she couldn't just stop limping, as it would look like she had been doing it just for effect, which, of course, was exactly what she was doing.

'I'm just a little stiff, I think,' she said, almost to herself, perhaps to convince herself and she limped off down the street with the Constable alongside her, pushing the bicycle.

Once inside the cottage, Alice insisted on making PC Dealey a cup of tea and offering him a plate of biscuits.

'Oh no, I'd better not,' he said at first.

'Why ever not? You've been working since early this morning you need to keep your sugar levels up,' said Alice, having read in some magazine or other that snacking in the day was good for your metabolism.

Again Constable Dealey found himself hearing the words of his wife, ringing in his ears.

'You eat too much, Michael. You have a dreadful middle-aged paunch on you. That's from sitting in that car all day.' PC Dealey's wife did not allow him to have biscuits in the house, even though she bought them for herself, as she insisted that she had an overactive metabolic condition, which could only be controlled by having sugar. Michael Dealey often wished that he had an overactive metabolic condition, but he knew that if he did, then his wife would insist that it could only be stabilised by not having sugar, or indeed anything else which was pleasant to eat. So, throwing caution to the wind after Alice had put the plate within easy reach, he took a biscuit and by the time he left, he had eaten five or six and had two cups of tea. Luxury.

In the following weeks, whenever he was on duty on a Sunday, he would make a point of dropping in to see Alice, and it was on around the third such visit that the subject of fried breakfast was brought up. Alice, just making polite conversation, commented that, as a child, Sunday's always meant a good fry-up. She imparted that her father would get up and make a full English breakfast and insist that "his girls" as he called his wife and two daughters, stay in bed whilst he did the honours. It was, he said, his way of making up for the fact that they were good enough to cook for him throughout the week. It was during the telling of this heart-warming story that Police Constable Dealey let slip that he had not had a fry up breakfast since he'd been married.

'Why ever not?' asked Alice incredulously.

'My wife doesn't like the smell of fried food. She says it makes her feel ill,' he replied.

'Oh, but a man must have a hearty breakfast once a week surely,' said Alice.

'Oh, I don't know about that,' said the PC without any real conviction.

'Well,' said Alice, 'The smell of fried food doesn't make me feel ill, so allow me to cook you eggs and bacon.' Constable Dealey held up his hand in protest.

'No, no. I'm fine. A couple of biscuits will do me,' he continued rather unconvincingly.

Alice was not to be put off and within minutes, rashers of bacon were sizzling in the frying pan and two eggs were on the side with a couple of slices of bread cut and ready to be put into the fat to make fried bread.

'I'm afraid I don't have any sausages but I'll get some in for the next time,' said Alice, excitedly. She had never cooked a meal for a man apart from her father before and she realised that she was really rather enjoying it.

And so, from then on, every Sunday when PC Dealey came to the village, he would, first of all, park his police car slightly up the road from Alice's cottage, so it didn't look too obvious who he was visiting and then he'd walk the fifty yards to the back door of the cottage and knock politely. Every time he parked the car, he thought that perhaps today Alice would not be pleased to see him and every time he would be pleasantly surprised that she was completely the opposite. She would greet him with a sunny smile and the smell of frying sausages wafting through the kitchen. He was so used to his wife totally ignoring him when he walked in, her eyes glued to the television, her only gesture to his existence would be to call out that she hoped that he'd taken his dirty shoes off and put his slippers on as it wasn't her intention of going around clearing up after him all day.

It was with all this history in mind on this dreadful Sunday morning that Alice let herself in through the back door and stood frozen to the spot. The knock on the door, when it came, made her jump out of her skin.

PC Dealey saw her jump through the glass of the door, and as was usual for him, he felt his heart sink. Alice walked over to the door and opened it as she usually did, but Constable Dealey could see that all was not well.

'Are you all right, Alice?' he asked.

'Yes, yes,' she said, forcing a smile.

He did not need to be a detective to know that she was not telling the truth. Something was missing. There was no smell of sausages cooking. No bacon or eggs on the side ready for their turn in the pan. No thick slices of bread ready to be made golden brown in the bacon fat. The whole atmosphere, in fact, was the complete opposite to what he now thought to be normal for a Sunday morning visit to Alice Elms little cottage. And it was all his fault. It had to be his fault.

'What have I done, Alice?'

'You haven't done anything, Constable,' she said.

Now he knew he had done something. She never called him Constable these days, not since the start of the cooked breakfasts. She had been Alice and he had been Michael. Now this morning; no cooked breakfast and no Michael.

'I'll put the kettle on. I'm sorry, I'm just popping upstairs for a moment,' she said, realising that she needed to pull herself together somehow. Part of her wanted to confide in him, but she knew that if she did, the game would be up and, as Chantry had said, the village would never be the same again. Alice liked the village as it was, and she liked Constable Dealey more than she knew she should. Trying to give a reassuring smile, Alice left the kitchen and trundled up the stairs to her bedroom.

PC Michael Dealey sat at the kitchen table. He was having a very strange sensation; it was, he knew, his heart sinking. He had experienced it many times before. Just about every time he walked into his own house, to be exact. He had entertained the hope that he would never feel it entering Alice's house, but, sadly, today he did. And he was annoyed and saddened to discover the sinking feeling was going further down and deep into his soul and deeper into his policemen's boots.

Upstairs, Alice found herself staring blankly into space at the bottom of her bed. She looked down upon it, staring at it for the first time. It was, what the salesman called "a small double". It measured about four foot across. It was plenty big enough for Alice on her own. She had gone to the shop to buy a single bed but had been talked her into buying this small double instead. It was, said the salesman, cheaper than a single. She found it strange that something bigger could be sold for less, but, then again, she never did understand the logic of commerce and so agreed to buy it. So now she stood staring down at it; a small double bed that had only she had ever slept in; a double bed that she thought would only ever be slept in by herself. Then a thought caught her off balance.

'Oh no,' she said to herself, remembering Chantry's final words to her before she left the Old Rectory. 'He wouldn't want to, would he? I couldn't, could I?'

Taking a deep breath, she opened her bedside cabinet and bought out a box of pills that the doctor had prescribed her. She had told him that at times she felt a bit lonely and depressed; not deeply depressed but just a bit low, sometimes. So he gave her a prescription for these pills, which, he said, were a sort of "pick me up".

'What sort of pick me up?' she had asked, a little warily, not usually being a pill-popping person.

'Well, when you're a bit low or when you feel a bit lonely, take one and it will make the world a slightly brighter place,' he answered.

When Alice had picked up the pills from the chemists, she read the little leaflet folded neatly inside the box. It informed her that they were a form of Valium and she was to take one, two-milligram pill, whenever the need took her, but not to take more than three a day. She looked at the pills now, and taking a deep breath, she popped out a pill from its foil covering, put it on her tongue and chased it down with a sip of water from the glass she always kept by the bed. Stopping for a moment, she glanced towards the door, her eyes boring through the thin walls of the cottage. In her mind's eye, she could see PC. Dealey sitting in the kitchen. Without a moment's hesitation, she popped out another pill from the strip and almost threw it into her mouth and gulped down the water, washing the Valium down her throat before she had time to change her mind. Putting the box of pills back into her bedside cabinet she started towards the door. Then before even she realised what she was doing, she rushed back to the cabinet, pulled out the box and popped another pill, this time without the aid of the water. Gulp.

'Well, it says I can take three a day. I'm just taking them all at once,' she said to herself, probably a little too loudly. She strode back towards the door then stopped. She felt distinctly odd. She turned slightly and leant against the door jamb. After a moment she realised that she was looking at herself in the full-length mirror hanging on the wall opposite. Then, something else slowly dawned on her, she was smiling. Realising she was smiling, made her smile some more. Then she giggled. She brought her hand up to her mouth to try and stifle it but to no avail. She giggled some more. Her whole body felt light and as she turned toward the stairs, it seemed to her that she was bouncing. She virtually bounded down the stairs, letting out a joyous laugh as she went.

'Are you all right, Alice?' called PC Dealey.

'Oh, yes, I feel absolutely marvellous,' she replied, hanging onto the doorframe at the bottom of the stairs, draped like a femme fatale. 'And now it's time to get my dear Constable Dealey his fry up. We need to keep his strength up, after all,' she said with a giggle, crossing over to the fridge and opening the door. She had no idea if she was doing it deliberately, but she bent over more than was absolutely necessary to bring out the sausages, eggs and bacon.

Constable Dealey, who was sitting opposite the fridge could not avoid witnessing the spectacle in front of him. His heart, which had been sinking fast was now shooting up into his throat and beating very fast indeed. Down below, things were stirring. A part of him, he thought long dead, was springing back into life. He wanted to get up and rush across and take this wonderful woman in his arms, only the pain in his loins made it almost impossible for him to move without doing himself a nasty injury.

Alice rose with the ingredients in her hand and turned around to face him.

'I've bought different sausages this week,' she said, her cheeks burning, 'They're spicy ones. I don't usually like sausages, but I must say the thought of a spicy one does sound enticing.'

PC Michael Dealey could hardly hold himself back. 'Lovely.' His voice came out as a high-pitched squeak.

Alice turned back to the kitchen worktop and went about the business of making a cooked breakfast. Constable Dealey could not take his eyes off her. An aura filled the room which, mixed with the aroma of spicy sausages, bacon, eggs and fried bread, made a heady brew.

'Some tea?' said Alice, who along with preparing the fry up, had also put the kettle on and made a pot of tea.

'Lovely,' squealed PC Dealey.

Alice poured the tea into the cup and brought it over to him. The smell of the tea, mixed with the smell of the fry up and the aura which was over the room was all getting too much for him. He wanted to grab her as she put down his teacup. He wanted to pull her towards him and kiss her, passionately.

'Sauce?' said Alice, holding up a bottle of Worcester sauce. 'I got a bottle when I bought the sausages.'

'Lovely.' The squeak was, if possible, even higher than before. Dogs would soon be at the door if this continued. Alice plated up and brought his breakfast over to him and put it on the table. As she went and fetched her own plate, he could smell her.

'Love....' His voice cracked and he took a gulp of tea to try and calm himself.

They both started to eat. Constable Dealey's appetite was enormous. He couldn't stop wolfing it down. Alice, who usually pecked at her food like a blue tit also found that she could not eat quickly enough to satisfy her cravings. The spicy sausages went down especially well with both of them and they could each feel the heat rising within them. Before long they were looking at each other whilst shovelling the food into their mouths. The fuel from the food made their bodies hotter and hotter. The spice from the sausages made them sweat profusely. PC. Dealey splashed a dollop of Worcester sauce over his breakfast, which made the whole thing even hotter. Inside both a furnace was burning. The steam was rising. Something had to be done soon or they would both spontaneously combust.

They put down their knives and forks, at the same time. Both still masticating and looking at each other, their eyes bulging. In a moment they stood and looked longingly at each other. They, momentarily, pressed their mouths together in the start of a kiss. They came apart, realising that they still had food in their mouths. They both took a swig of tea and pushed their mouths together again. Neither of them breathed. Neither of them spoke. Before even she realised what she was doing, Alice; little shy, dithering Alice; had taken her uniformed hunk by the hand and was leading him upstairs to her bedroom. Before long they were on the small double bed, running their hands up and down each other's clothed bodies. Soon after, Constable Michael Dealey was attempting to unbutton Miss Alice Elm's cardigan and at the same time she was negotiating the buttons on his uniform tunic. It was exhausting work, but neither of them was willing to give up. Cardigan; tunic; trousers; skirt. All eventually removed and strewn on the floor, where I think we will leave it and them, on the small double bed. Two heated bodies in carnal embrace.

Chapter 7

Ryan Roberts and Kylie Gordon walked down the path in preparation for their big day. Morning Service was less than an hour away and the launch of the new sound system was imminent.

They were surprised to see the church doors wide open and could only think that the church elders were there already getting ready for the service. Inside, though, all was quiet.

'Miss Bowman-Leggett?' called Ryan.

'Miss Elms?' said Kylie.

As there was no answer, they continued down the aisle and went behind the screen. Ryan started to turn on all the equipment while Kylie looked on lovingly. *He was so clever*, she thought, *and when he takes off his glasses, he is really quite handsome,* a thought she turned to *"quite fit"* to sound up to the minute, even inside her own head she castigated herself when she was sounding un-hip, or whatever the hip phrase was at that moment.

Back at the Rectory, the final body had been loaded onto the sack trolley and Chantry looked at her watch. It was just on five past ten, which meant that they had fifty-five minutes before the Morning Service but only about twenty before the Reverend Jonathan Martin arrived to get himself ready and into, what he jokingly called his "frock to greet his flock". So few came to the church as a congregation that he sometimes wondered why he bothered to turn up at all himself, but, as he had told Chantry, talking to ten people was better than talking to no one at all. She thought he was overstating the numbers a little, ten people in the pews was a very good day, indeed, except on high days and holidays.

'Chop, chop,' she said, clapping her hands, 'nearly there but time marches on.'

'And waits for no man,' added George, somewhat exhausted.

'Exactly,' said Chantry, 'it's nearly time for Morning Service and we don't want the dear departed to bump into the Vicar, do we?' She looked over towards the body which Neil and George had just put into an upright position on the sack trolley. 'I'll go over with you gentlemen. Ladies?' She looked around at Penny, Sue, Molly and Jane, 'I suggest you get back to your houses and freshen up before we all meet up again at the service.'

'I don't go to church, Chantry,' said Penny, rather disdainfully.

'That's as may be, Penny, but today may I suggest, that you make an exception. Needs must when the devil drives, and he's most certainly has his foot on the accelerator today.' Chantry was looking straight at her. 'I feel most strongly ladies that we should all stick together today. We have lots more to do before we are finished.'

'Like what?' Penny was in danger of stamping her foot.

'Like getting this place tidied up, for a start. You don't think we can leave it like this do you? Oh no. The Old Rectory needs a jolly good spring clean.'

'Count me out,' said Penny.

'Nobody is to be counted out, Penelope. We are all in. Yes, we are all very much in it together.' On this, she turned and ushered Neil and George toward the front door with their load and they set off down the path towards the church.

'All for one,' said Molly Cox.

'And one for all,' finished Jane Fox.

'Oh, for Christ's,' Penny shouted petulantly.

'Chantry's right, Pen,' said Sue, 'there's no turning back now. We have to see this through to the end.'

'I thought this was the end,' said Penny.

'Sadly, I think we've hardly started, actually,' mused Sue.

Ryan and Kylie were both were very quiet as they went about the business of finishing off setting up the equipment ready for the Morning Service. They were both trying to ignore the events of the day before. By the time that Chantry, Neil and George came through the main church doors, they were confident that the microphone was working well so to give it a quick test Ryan decided to throw out some biblical quotes.

'I am the Lord thy God, which bought them out of the land of Egypt, from the house of bondage,' boomed Ryan in his God voice.

Chantry, for probably the first time in her long life, completely lost control and jumped back, bumping into the sack barrow, which Neil dropped to the floor.

'Holy…' Neil looked about him.

Ryan popped his head from behind the screen, the microphone still attached to him. 'Are you all right, Miss Bowman-Leggett?' his voice boomed again, but this time as a sixteen-year-old.

'Ryan Roberts, what in God's name do you think you're doing?' exclaimed Chantry.

'I didn't mean to frighten you, I was just testing the microphone,' replied Ryan, looking past the old woman and straight at the mummified shape in the barrow.

'What's that?' he asked, pointing.

'It's nothing,' said Chantry waving her arms about as if that would make it disappear.

Kylie appeared from behind the screen.

'It looks like one of those mummies I saw in the British Museum.' Her school had visited the Tutankhamen exhibition a year or so earlier.

'It's a pretend mummy,' said Chantry airily. The two youngsters were walking towards them.

'Is it a dead body?' asked Ryan, without a hint of horror.

'Haven't you two children got anything better to do than stand there gawping?' asked George, irritated.

Kylie did not like being called a child. She didn't feel like a child, especially after what he had experienced with Ryan the day before.

'Is it Mister Bennett from the Old Rectory?' asked Ryan.

Chantry paused for a moment.

Kylie put her hand to her mouth. 'You don't really think it is, do you, Ryan?'

'Why do you ask if it's Mister Bennett, my dear,' asked Chantry., astounded.

'Well,' said Ryan. He turned to Kylie, 'Shall I tell Miss Bowman-Leggett about yesterday?'

'What about yesterday?' Chantry looked at the two of them.

'I only did it because he was mocking God and the Bible and stuff in the pulpit.

'Did what for heaven's sake?' growled George.

'I'm afraid that I have a confession to make,' said Ryan.

'What sort of confession?'

Ryan looked at Kylie and she nodded bravely to him.

'It's both our faults. Mine as much as Ryan's, although he did all the talking,' blurted out Kylie.

'Whatever do you mean?' Chantry peered down at them, 'What talking?'

'I pretended to be God,' said Ryan, shamefaced.

'God?' all three adults said in unison.

'On the sound system. We were trying it out yesterday when Mister Bennett came in. I think he was drunk or something,' Ryan continued.

'Drugs,' interjected Kylie, 'I've seen programmes on the television about them. He was all giggly at first. They said that Snack can make you giggly.'

'Smack,' said Ryan, 'Smack makes you giggly, then you become paranoid and never pass your exams. A policeman from the drugs unit in the town came to our school.'

'Mister Bennett was giggling and then got paranoid. He was very upset.'

'But what do you mean when you say you talked like God?'

And Ryan explained everything that happened in the church the previous afternoon. After hearing the story, Chantry exchanged glances with the two men.

'What I don't understand is why he didn't cotton on,' huffed George.

'Atropa Belladonna,' mumbled Chantry under her breath.

'What was that?' asked George.

'Nothing. We must get on. I'll explain everything later,' answered Chantry. She then turned to the two teenagers, somewhat in a quandary.

'Now, Ryan, Kylie, you are both junior members of the village council and as such, perhaps you should be told the truth.'

'No, Chantry,' said George abruptly, 'they're only children.'

'I'm not a child,' said Kylie.

'Nor me,' said Ryan.

'No, quite right. They're right, George.' Chantry nodded. 'They're quite grown up now and it's time for them to learn the realities of life.'

'I really don't think that's a good idea, Chantry,' said Neil, 'Who knows who'll they'll blurt it out to?'

'Will you blurt it out?' asked Chantry, turning to the youngsters.

'Blurt what out?' asked Kylie.

'Are you really grown up enough to keep a secret? A very big secret?' asked Chantry.

'Dear God, Chantry, we'll all end up in prison,' said George, with a knowing shudder.

'In prison?' said Ryan and Kylie in unison.

Chantry looked at them, 'Yes, that's how big a secret this is.'

'About 20 years with good behaviour-sized secret,' said Neil through gritted teeth.

'I'm grown up enough,' said Kylie.

'And so am I,' said Ryan, wishing, inside, that he really was.

'Then follow us down into the crypt. I have something to show you,' said Chantry, beckoning them.

'Come on you men, we haven't got all day.' Chantry gave a slight nudge on Neil's arm to get him and George to continue down the nave to bump the last corpse down the steps. They stopped at the edge of the vault and Ryan and Kylie gasped at the coffins.

'My dead relatives,' said Chantry.

'Is this one of your dead relatives?' asked Ryan, nodding towards the body.

'No, not mine, but somebody's.' As she said this, she felt a sudden sadness. It was the first time that she'd allowed herself to humanise this horrible nonsense. 'Oh, what have you done?' she muttered to herself under her breath.

'Right,' she continued, a little too forcefully, as if to rouse herself to the task and led the two young people past the coffins and towards the oak door pushing it open to reveal the ancient bones of the medieval monks and twelve shapes shrouded in cotton bed sheets and duvet covers. Both Ryan and Kylie gasped.

'I don't have the time to explain anything at the moment.'

'Are they all from the Old Rectory?' asked Ryan.

'Yes,' said Chantry, beckoning George and Neil to bring in the final body.

'Were they bad people?' asked Kylie.

'Well, I don't know whether one would say they were bad people, but their behaviour had a lot to be desired, especially in a village like this.'

'Is that why you killed them?' asked Kylie.

George and Neil nearly dropped the body on the floor.

'Oh, no, we didn't kill them,' answered Chantry quickly.

'We didn't kill them,' yelled Neil, panicking.

'None of us killed them,' said George in his sternest voice.

'You mean they just died because their behaviour had a lot to be desired?' asked Ryan earnestly.

'In truth, we're not sure how they died, only that nobody in this village killed them,' answered Chantry, trying to put out of her mind what Molly Cox and Jane Fox had confessed to her. *No*, thought Chantry, *punch infused with a little Deadly Nightshade was not the murder weapon.*

'First of all, you must put it out of your mind that you were in any way to blame for all these,' she hesitated, 'deaths. They were silly and naughty people, who did silly and naughty things and have now suffered for it.'

The two teenagers nodded.

'And although I don't think that putting the wind-up Mister Bennett was very a Christian thing to do and risking the Almighty's wrath by taking his name in vain like that, I'm a fine one to talk, under the circumstances. I will say, though,' she continued, 'it would be in your best interests not to say anything to anybody, to your friends at school or, indeed, to your parents. All of us here may be fully aware that you are innocent of any wrongdoing, but others may not see it that way if you understand me.'

George and Neil exchanged glances and shook their heads.

'If, for any reason, in the future, your parents ask if you saw or heard anything about the people from the Old Rectory, you are to say nothing. If they ask if you saw them leaving the village, don't pretend you did, just say you saw nothing. Under these circumstances, nothing is good, do you understand?'

'We were both in here sorting out the Vicar's sound system. We couldn't possibly see anything else,' said Ryan with complete conviction.'

'And you won't have seen any of us today except in the church at our devotions.'

'At your prayers,' said Kylie.

'Good girl,' said Chantry, rather relieved, 'That's all settled then. So now we must lock up down here and get on our Sunday best to give thanks to the glory of God.'

Both George and Neil shuddered at the rank hypocrisy of it all.

'The Reverend Martin will be arriving at any moment,' Chantry continued looking at her watch and hurrying the others out of the door of the monk's cell and locking it. 'Now, Neil, this door will need to be bricked up,' she said out of the blue.

'You what?'

'I've been thinking. You can use the stones that have fallen out of the churchyard wall in the far corner, by the field. That part of the wall has been in a state of total collapse for the last ten years. It's all overgrown there and nobody will notice a few stones missing.'

'You're pushing it, aren't you?'

'This room needs to disappear, Neil. Perty and I were discussing that very thing only the day before he died. What with one thing and another, I never got around to it. If we wall the doorway up, it will look just like the other arches in the vault. No one, apart from us, need know it ever existed. But don't do it yet, there is something I must do in there first,' she said, almost to herself as if working it out in her mind. 'Now, hurry along and get out of here before the vicar arrives,' she said shooing them up the steps and through the door behind the choir stalls.

It was at this moment that they heard the unmistakable voice of the Reverend Jonathan Martin, talking to himself in the porch of the church, as he straightened up various church notices on the corkboard.

'Quick, hide,' said Chantry.

George and Neil ducked down into the choir stalls with the sack trolley clattering onto the stone floor. Then, without prompting, Ryan started to speak very loudly.

'And up there, Miss Bowman-Leggett, Kylie and I have fixed speakers and hid them behind the pillars.'

'Well Ryan did most of the hanging,' continued Kylie, even louder, as the Vicar started his journey down the aisle.

'Hello, hello, what have we here?' The Reverend Martin said in his usual jocular manner.

'We're just showing the new sound system to Miss Bowman-Leggett, Reverend,' said Ryan proudly, 'I hope you don't mind?'

'Of course, I don't mind, Ryan,' he said, kindly, 'So you have it all working then?' In his voice, if you listened carefully, you could hear a distinct hope that they hadn't got it working.

'Yes,' said Ryan, starting off towards the screen, 'come and have a look.'

Chantry marvelled at Ryan's ingenuity and calm.

'I really think I should get on, Ryan,' said the Reverend, taking a step toward the vestry.

'It won't take a moment,' said Kylie, taking Reverend Martin by the arm and steering him over to the screen before pulling him, gently, behind it and out of sight.

'It's really been great fun to set up,' continued Ryan, clamping the headphones over the Vicar's ears, as Chantry beckoned the two men from their hiding place.

Scrabbling to their feet they grabbed either end of the sack trolley and ran up the aisle. Tripping on a raised floor tile, George lost control of his end and it clattered to the floor.

As quickly as he could, Ryan started banging the head of the microphone to cover the noise.

Both men leapt in between a row of pews as the Vicar popped his head out from behind the screen.

'Whatever was that noise?'

'I was just making sure the microphone was on,' said Ryan, as Kylie pulled the Vicar back behind the screen, 'See?' said Ryan, tapping the mic head again and turning up the reverb a bit so it echoed around the old church walls so that George and Neil could make their escape.

'It's very loud,' shouted the Rev. Martin.

'Sorry, wait a minute and I'll turn it down,' he said peering through a gap in the screen to make sure the coast was clear. He removed the headphones from the Vicar.

'Well,' said the Reverend, good-naturedly, 'I do hope we don't deafen the congregation, any more than they are already.'

Ryan said that he would make sure that he would set the sound levels at around four or five, just enough to 'Lift your voice.'

He handed the Rev. Martin the head microphone along with the battery pack.

'When you put on your vestments, put this battery pack in this pouch under them.' Ryan handed over the pack which was in a little cotton pouch with two lengths of pink ribbon attached.

'I made it,' said Kylie, proudly. 'You tie it around your waist.'

'How clever of you, Kylie,' said the Reverend, not sure that he really wanted to walk around with a pouch around his waist held on by a pink ribbon.

'And you put the microphone on your head and hook it over your ears, like this,' said Ryan, placing the mic on the Reverend's head as he described, 'and you drop this wire down the back and plug it into the battery pack.'

The Reverend Jonathan Martin smiled a kindly smile but inside wished to God that he had never agreed to all of this. He knew it would be unchristian to back out now, knowing how hard the two young people must have worked to get this all set up, but it did not stop him lifting his eyes to heaven in the hope that some divine intervention might make the gadget explode or at least fail to work.

'Oh, well, I must remember all that,' was all he said a little resignedly.

'I'll come into the vestry and make sure you have put it all on right, after you've got dressed, shall I?' asked Ryan.

'Yes, yes, give me ten minutes and then do just that,' he said as graciously as he could.

'Chantry, Chantry.' It was Sue. She was running up the path towards the porch.

'Whatever is it, Susan?' she asked.

'The cars,' said Sue.

'Cars?'

'Yes, I went around the back of the house and I suddenly saw the cars. The cars are around the back of the Rectory. What are we going to do with the cars?'

For a moment Chantry was completely stumped. She hadn't thought about the cars.

'Colin's car is there as well,' said Sue matter of factly.

Chantry was stumped for a moment, then had an idea, 'I think we may need a little help with that,' said Chantry.

'From God, you mean?' said Sue.

'Oh heavens, no. I was thinking more of Borley Broome.' And with that, she gave a little laugh, 'I believe we may have blown it rather with the Almighty, don't you think? I'll sort the car problem out after the service.'

The service, that Sunday, was very much like every other service that the Reverend Martin had taken over the years, only a great deal louder and accompanied by deafening bursts of high-pitched feedback. The members of the congregation who were deaf thought that their hearing had, miraculously, returned, and those who were not feared that they soon would be and were grateful when the whole thing was over.

After the service, Chantry, along with the others stood around outside the church waiting for the rest of the congregation, such as it was, to drive off back to their own villages.

'It was good to see you both in the church this morning,' said the Reverend Martin shaking hands with Neil and Penny.

'I thought I'd pop in and pay my respects,' said Neil.

'Me too,' agreed Penny, unconvincingly.

'I'm sure that God will have appreciated that. We rarely see anybody from this village in the church, apart, of course from Miss Bowman-Leggett and Miss Elms, who, now I come to think of it, I don't remember seeing this morning.'

'No, Alice has been taken to her bed, this morning,' replied Chantry mischievously.

'Oh, dear. Is she poorly? Perhaps I should pop in and see her.'

'Oh, I don't think that will be necessary, Vicar. She has everything she needs, I'm sure,' said Chantry.

'Right, well, I hope to see you all next Sunday,' he said as he walked over to his car and got in, 'God bless.' And with that he started the engine and drove off.

'Thank heavens for that. Well, that's Stage One out of the way,' said Chantry, watching the car disappear into the distance and turning to Neil, 'Now, what I suggest is that you get cracking by bringing in the stones from around the back. Penny, George, you can help.'

'I've done more than enough, thank you,' said Penny haughtily.

'Not one of us has done nearly enough as yet, Penelope. I'd be exceedingly grateful if you, Susan, would give a hand spring cleaning the place with Miss Cox and Miss Fox. Penny, after helping with the stones, you can join the others in the Rectory.'

'And what will you be doing, during all this?' Penny was feeling belligerent.

'I will be popping down to see Borley Broome as I need to ask him a rather large favour.'

'It's all right for some,' Penny grunted.

'The thought of spending any time in that smelly bus of his doesn't fill me with delight I can assure you but one must make sacrifices for the good of the village.'

Chantry stood hovering over Penny, who, by the look on her face, wanted to murder Chantry Bowman-Leggett and dump her in the vault with all the other stiffs.

Going to talk to Borley did not please Chantry but, she had no choice, all things considered. She little thought when she woke that Sunday morning that she would spend the first few hours directing operations, like some demented army commander, to rid the village of thirteen dead bodies. But she was pleased that she had succeeded in carrying out phase one of the operation. So far, so good.

Chapter 8

As Chantry made her way down the narrow road towards Broome Farm, she was acutely aware that before she won this war, she would need to succeed in more phases than she cared to think about. Phase two had now to be put into operation, which was to rid the village of all of the cars. She knew that they wouldn't be able to leave the village, but she also knew that it must also be made to look as if they had. In other words, she needed to make seven cars vanish forever. Nothing must be left of them. Without understanding the whys and wherefores she was aware that all cars had various numbers that could identify them. Apart from the obvious number-plates, she knew that there were numbers on the chassis and the engines of all cars, not that she knew where to find them herself.

They had to go.

Her head was hurting and she felt quite dizzy so she stopped to pop another pill. She was taking far too many today, she knew, but it was the only way of keeping herself going. This was not a usual Sunday and the strain of the morning had taken its toll and as she reached the bend in the road she wondered if she would make it.

'Stiff upper lip; can't do anything about it; carry on, carry on; no point in getting upset about it; what's done is done,' she mumbled to herself like a mantra. She pulled herself upright and continued steadfastly on her journey.

If the wind was in the wrong direction the stench could hit you from a mile away. This morning the wind was most definitely blowing towards the village. Along with a pulsating headache and the dizziness this brought on, Chantry was feeling decidedly nauseous.

'It's just like *Eau de Cologne*,' Borley would say, gruffly, then laugh. 'The smell of shit won't kill you.'

What lay ahead of Chantry was not an idealist's idea of an English country farm. It was, in fact, no one's idea of an English country farm. It was a smelly and dishevelled carbuncle on the side of the village; a boil that needed lancing and then have gallons of antiseptic applied and given a thoroughly good clean.

It could be said that Chantry Bowman-Leggett was the smartest, most upright member of the village and the very opposite said of Borley Broome. Borley was a large red-faced, farmer who, it seemed, had only one set of clothes and they were the ones that he stood up in and, likely, slept in.

Whereas Chantry Bowman-Leggett's family had built the village from scratch, the original Manor House and its successors and Chantry was the matriarch and pillar of the village society, Borley Broome farmed his land without consideration for the rest of the village and apart from hogging the battered armchairs by the fire in the Leggett Arms, with his oversized son, Toby, cared little or indeed nothing for the village itself. Whereas despite a lineage, which came down from William the Conqueror, Chantry Bowman-Leggett had little or nothing in regard to money, Borley Broome was, by far, the wealthiest man in the place and thought to be one of the wealthiest men in the county. He was, and there could be no doubt about this, the tightest man with his money and ever since he acquired the leasehold of the Leggett Arms, he had never paid for any drink he ordered in it.

Throughout many decades now, the Broomes had added property after property to their village portfolio. No one save Borley himself and no doubt his accountant knew what proportion he owned but most of the villagers were more than aware that Borley Broome owned more of the village than all of the other owners of properties put together and he did so by some margin.

He was, to sum up, a multi-millionaire; he lived, however, like a tramp.

His house was Elizabethan with timber-framed wattle and daubed walls and original mullioned windows. Inside the place were priceless pieces of furniture: original Chippendale chairs and Sheraton tables.

On the walls were hung, or so it was said, portraits by Holbein and landscapes by Constable. Every single object in the house was worth a great deal of money and covered in an inch or two of dust and mouse droppings. On the driveway outside the front door stood a red double-decker bus, just like the ones that used to run throughout London. On the side of the bus was printed the faded legend "Clapperboard Catering" and in smaller letters underneath, "TV and Film Location Caterers".

The name, Borley Broome, was not the one he was born with. Although he had been called it since his school days. The name Borley was his mother's maiden name. Edith Borley was not a woman who had been born into money, although she certainly married into it when she became involved with Jack Broome, who, at the time, was in line to inherit the farm from his father, William. On William's death, Edith Borley decided that the name Broome was not good enough for land-owning folk which she was now part of. With her father-in-law not even cold in his grave, Edith announced that the family, henceforth, would be known as Borley-Broome and letterheads and cards were printed as proof of the family's newfound status. Chantry's father quipped at the time that 'a new Broome was sweeping clean'. Edith, it seemed, felt the Bowman-Leggetts had had too much of it their own way with regard to status and all because it had a double-barrelled name. As far as she could see, the Bowman-Leggetts were a spent force and it made no sense to her that the family, which had imposed its status for many years by reckless moral behaviour, should be given preferential treatment in the village.

Looking through her late father-in-law's accounts it was clear to Edith that the newly named Borley-Broomes were far richer than the Bowman-Leggetts and so it was, in her book, they who should be given the most respect within the community. To rub the Bowman-Leggetts noses in the mud further she bullied her husband, Jack, into buying up the cottage that Chantry's parents, were attempting to sell in order to be able to survive, for the smallest amount that he could get it for. The Bowman-Leggetts, being desperate for cash, realised that, loath though they were to exceed to the Borley-Broome offer, the market for run-down cottages in a small village in the middle of nowhere, at that time, just before Hitler jackbooted himself into Poland, was poor to say the least.

Jack Broome, who never thought of himself as Borley-Broome, attempted to put his wife off investing all his money in the property market, but Edith was not to be dissuaded. She insisted that property was the area to be in. Jack maintained that farming was the business he grew up in and was the job he understood but Edith closed her ears to her husband's thoughts and like Lysistrata kept other things tightly closed, as well, until she got her way. Jack had no choice but to go along with his wife's wishes if he was to have any chance with his wife's body.

Needless to say, the cottage that had belonged to the Bowman-Leggetts, became the property of the Borley-Broomes and nine months from the day the contract was signed, a new Borley-Broome was introduced to the world. From what Chantry could recall, the baby was called either William after Jack's father or Clifford after Edith's. The reason for the confusion was because Jack called his son William and Edith insisted on calling her son Clifford. The boy, needless to say, grew up an only child in a state of near schizophrenia and became known at the public school, where he had been sent as soon as Edith could get him there, as just Borley Broome.

He spent more time, until he was fifteen, away at school than he did at home as his mother had no maternal instincts whatsoever and would have sooner not have had a child in the first place. She constantly scolded her husband over the years for not withdrawing quickly enough after having his pleasure and he suffered the fate of never having such a pleasure ever again.

She had no time for looking after a child, she said, if she was going to climb the social ladder.

Borley Broome grew up not really knowing his parents so when they died within a month of each other from a mysterious illness (there was a rumour that Jack, having had enough of his wife's nagging, put rat poison in the stew but it was never confirmed by the authorities), he found it difficult to feel any grief. He was left the farm, a great many cottages in the village, which he hardly knew, having been living in a freezing dormitory at the school which took his parents money but didn't think it their duty to use it to pay for heating; he inherited the Elizabethan house, which was full of large antique pieces of furniture and very little in the way of creature comforts.

As so often happens, when a man comes into property, a clutch of young women from the district suddenly found the rather rotund and spotty Borley Broome exceedingly attractive. Having never really known the female gender throughout his young life, except Matron at school, he was rather confused as to what to do or say to these beauties who were now wishing to be in his company.

Individually they would all ask him, whilst stroking his arm, or if in complete privacy, other parts of his anatomy, whether he liked her the best. Borley liked them all at different times. In order to clinch the deal, Fay Parker, the boldest of them all, decided that to win the prize she needed to go all the way and damn the consequences, which indeed, she did. She announced to a bewildered Borley, two months later, that she was expecting his child and he would have to marry her. They duly married in the village church two months later. Five months after that, baby Toby was born. Unfortunately for Fay her plans to live in a manner in which she could only dream about expired when she died from an undetected internal haemorrhage about ten minutes after Toby had made his entrance into the world.

The remaining clutch of women came out of the woodwork and fell over each other to coo over the baby and offer to "help" dear old Borley out. But Borley, having had five months of marriage realised that he did not wish to suffer that state again.

Apart from a local woman who offered herself as a wet nurse for the child, Borley did not want another woman in the house. Bringing up the baby on his own, Borley continued with the task of learning how to be a farmer, a job that all his expensive years of public-school education had not taught him to be.

However, some of the genes from his father and grandfather must have come to the fore as he made a good, if not a sensational, fist of it. Working all day on the farm as well as trying to bring up the child on his own took its toll on him and he and his son became more and more reclusive and odd. When the time came for Toby to start school, Borley, remembering the pain of the institution, refused to let the boy go, maintaining that he would teach him his numbers and letters himself. Sadly Borley's grasp of the three Rs was hazy, to say the least, so Toby grew up with little or no education. This situation soon became known to the authorities and they insisted on calling at the farm every week in order to persuade him to allow the boy to go to school. However, the more they persisted, the more determined he became to keep the lad from their clutches. Writs were served and torn up; the police were sent in order to restrain Borley as officials arrived at the farm gates to whisk the boy off to a place of learning. Both times the Crown's agents were met with both barrels of a twelve-bore shotgun. Having been peppered with shot more times than they cared to think about, the powers that be decided the boy's education was not a good enough reason to get themselves killed, so they gave in and left Borley Broome and his son, to their own devices and ticked the official box against "Home schooling".

Freed from the shackles of authority, the goings-on at Broome Farm became more and more bizarre and extreme. They bred mostly pigs in the field opposite the house but now the pigs found themselves foraging around the odd old car or van. A rusty tractor appeared followed by other bits and pieces of rotting metalwork. Finally, a double-decker bus arrived. No one in the village witnessed its arrival and its placing on the overgrown drive in front of the old house.

Villagers made a point of walking past the farm to see what else had turned up and were surprised to see an electric cable extending from a bedroom window of the house and through the side of the bus. In the dark, a faint light could be seen in the vehicle and before long old sacks, which at one time had contained feed for the pigs, were hung up at its windows. Word was soon put out that it looked like father and son were now living on the bus and not in the house at all.

That very same evening, Borley and his sixteen-year-old son came into the public bar of the Leggett Arms and Borley ordered two pints of bitter. Sam, the landlord, poured one pint and then lent over to Borley and said, somewhat rashly:

'If the other pint is for Toby, then I'm sorry Borley, but he's underage.'

At which point Borley lent even further over the bar and grabbed Sam by the lapels of his shirt and hissed:

'I own this pub, not you, so if I want a pint of beer for my boy, I'll have a pint of beer for my boy, understand?'

Sam, realising that it would be futile to argue a legal point about selling alcohol to a minor when the man had no qualms about emptying both barrels of three shotguns at a van load of police officers only a few years previously along with the fact that any likelihood of a policeman coming into the pub being pretty thin, decided it was safe to serve a pint of beer to a sixteen-year-old without threatening his liquor licence. Also, he reasoned that, as no money changed hands, as Borley always put his drinks on the slate, which had now been going for over ten years with no sign of it being settled, it could hardly be said that he was really selling alcohol at all, merely giving it away.

Chantry Bowman-Leggett stood outside the double-decker bus. The stench from the pigs in the field opposite and from the bus in front of her filled her nostrils. She looked across the field at a large JCB digger which lay abandoned amongst the rusting vehicles. Toby Broome had, it was noticed, taken to digging large holes in the field for no apparent reason and then filling up the first hole with the soil which had been taken from the second hole and vice versa. No one had any idea why he did this but it was assumed that it helped him pass the time as he was not mentally equipped to do much else. Chantry felt sorry for Toby as he could neither read, write, nor add up. All he could do was spend his days digging deep holes and then fill them up again and it was this action which had given Chantry the idea which she was now, tentatively, going to put to Borley.

'What do you want here, you old witch?'

'We need to talk, Borley,' Chantry tried not to hold her nose against the stench that came off his clothes, but it was difficult.

'I don't want to talk to you. Why would I want to talk to you?'

Chantry did not flinch. The insults were true to form.

'Borley, the village has a problem and I need your help. So if you want to keep throwing childish insults at me, I shall say this double-quick; if you don't want to see your assets plummet in a thrice then we must get our heads together before any more time is lost.'

'What the devil are you on about?'

'This is very, very serious, Borley and we need to talk.'

'You best come in then,' said Borley, a little taken aback at the way the conversation was going.

'I'd sooner we had this little discussion out here if you don't mind,' Chantry was not asking.

'I do bloody well mind. I've been up since five this morning and I'm in the middle of doing up a bit of breakfast, so if you want to talk then you'll have to do it in here or shout it through the bloody doorway if you want to stay outside. I ain't got time to waste standing about listening to you, you uppity old bat.' And on saying this Borley stepped inside the bus. A moment later, Chantry heard him bang a frying pan down on the small gas hob.

'Borley, I need you to bury something for me,' Chantry tried to project without shouting. She edged herself onto the bus and tried not to breathe too deeply.

'What sort of thing?' grunted Borley as he slapped a bit of bacon into the pan.

'Well, it's a few things, to be precise,' said Chantry.

'Go on.'

'Well, its seven things.'

'What sort of things, woman?'

'Cars,' said Chantry quickly.

'Cars?' Borley looked at her. 'You want me to bury seven bloody cars?'

'Yes. Today. Now,' continued Chantry.

'And why would you be wanting to bury seven cars all of a sudden?'

'In order to get rid of the evidence.'

Borley held the sizzling bacon pan in front of him. 'Bloody evidence?'

'Oh well I suppose I'd best tell you the whole story,' sighed Chantry.

'Aye, best you had,' said Borley.

So Chantry started to tell him about the extraordinary events that had occurred during the morning.

'I take it you don't want a van load of policemen turning up in the village,' said Chantry, by way of rounding off her story.

'They'd know better than to come near here,' he growled.

'They wouldn't be local police, Borley, they'd be city police and probably armed with guns, and we wouldn't want you to start having a pot shot at them, not with all the media people with their television cameras pointing at anything that moved in the village.' Chantry folded her arms.

'So you want me to bury the cars?' mused Borley.

'Yes.'

'Why don't you just sell 'em? Make some money that way.'

'Because the police will trace them back to us here and we'll all end up in prison,' said Chantry.

'I won't go to no prison,' grumbled Borley, taking a bite out of his bacon sandwich, 'I'll shoot any bugger who tries to take me to prison.'

'We don't want any more shooting, Borley. There are enough dead bodies in this village today, as it is, we don't want any more, thank you.'

Borley ripped another mouthful from his sandwich.

'So all I'm asking,' continued Chantry, 'is that your boy, digs a few deep hole in that field, just as he's been doing of late and we can come along with the cars and drop them in and Toby can fill it in, again, afterwards.'

'You best bring them here quick then. I'll get the boy to dig at the far end of the field, that'll be the place for 'em.'

Chantry breathed a sigh of relief. She wanted to kiss Borley but thought better of it.

'Thank you, Borley. I'll never forget it,' she said, starting to leave the bus and not a moment too soon in her book.

The farmer grunted again and took a slug of his tea.

As Chantry made her way back up the road towards the Old Rectory, she could hear Borley shouting at Toby.

'Boy, take the digger up to the top end of the pig field.'

'Why?'

''Cos I told you too, boy, that's why.'

'Am I to dig holes at the top of the field, Dad? I thought you didn't want me to dig holes no more.'

'You're to dig a fecking great big hole, boy. Then we're going to dump some fecking posh cars in it,' shouted Borley, loud enough for the whole village to hear, 'And if you tell anyone about it, I'll dump you in the fecking hole with the fecking cars and don't think I won't.'

'Why, Dad?'

''Cos it's a secret!' bellowed Borley.

Chantry flinched as she turned the corner. She felt into her cardigan pocket and took out another pill to ease the pain in her head.

———————

Chapter 9

Back at the rectory, Sue had put herself in charge of emptying all the deceased's pockets and bags and laying them on the large dining room table, like with like, whilst Molly Cox and Jane Fox collected and folded all the clothes and put them in black plastic bin bags. At one end of the table was a pile of wallets; purses; watches; bracelets etc., and at the other were car key fobs. Picking up a set, Chantry called her allies together and told them what she had been up to.

'You're just going to dump all the cars in a pit?' asked Neil incredulously.

'What would you like me to do with them, take them to a garage?' barked Chantry.

'Chantry's right, I don't suppose there is anything else we could do with them,' said George.

'They need to vanish into thin air, just like their owners otherwise, sooner or later, one will turn up and that will do for all of us,' Chantry explained, 'so, first of all, we need to find out which fob activates which car in order for us to drive them to the farm.'

'I've got the key to Colin's car,' said Sue.

The others, apart from Chantry, looked at her. It was very difficult for any of them to understand how she could take the death of her husband so calmly.

'What else am I meant to do?' she said, reading their minds, 'He was a stupid, selfish little shit of a man. He brought this upon himself, so why should I be expected to suffer anymore? Christ, I took it for over twenty-five years, I'm just relieved it's all over. And I don't give a damn what you all think of me.' Sue stared at them defiantly. 'I'll drive Colin's car, Chantry. It will give me great pleasure seeing it dropping into a hole. It was just a ridiculous extension of his dick as it is. It'll save a fortune in fuel costs.' Sue then let out a little laugh; not manic, just a sound of relief.

All the locks of the cars were activated by remote control sensors. Chantry stood looking at them and pushed the remote button to see which one flashed its lights and beeped at her. Eventually, having identified which was which, she handed a key to each of her helpers; first Neil, then Penny; George; Molly Cox and Jane Fox.

'Oh, I can't drive one with gears,' said Molly.

'Nor me; I only do automatics,' said Jane.

'I know nothing about gears and clutches and things,' continued Molly.

'The only thing I know about a gear stick is that it is very near a lady's knee if she's sitting in the front passenger seat,' said Jane.

'Yes, my knee has been mistaken for a gear stick on many occasions,' said Molly Cox.

'And mine,' agreed Jane Fox.

The others stopped and looked at the two old ladies and almost shuddered at the thought.

'We can drive them.' The voice came from the corner of the house. Ryan and Kylie had been looking on in silence.

'I've driven my dad's car,' piped up Kylie, 'Not on the road, of course but on the old airfield.'

'You're both too young to drive. You need a licence and be insured,' said Chantry without thinking.

'A bit late to be thinking about the legalities, wouldn't you say, Chantry?' said George.

'Yes, I suppose it is, only I don't want these young people to become more involved than they have to.'

'But we are involved. It's too late now; you involved us. We know everything,' said, Kylie.

'And another thing,' said Ryan, 'you'll need someone to clean up Mister Bennett's computer. Take down his website and stuff.'

'Website, what website?' said Chantry.

'The one which advertises the parties,' replied Ryan.

'Oh yes,' said Chantry unsure.

'Incriminating evidence. It might have names and addresses. I can do that after we've got rid of the cars,' continued Ryan.

Chantry shook her head and handed them the last two key fobs. 'Neil, you lead,' she said, 'We'll go in convoy. Let's just hope that we don't see anybody coming the other way.'

'Shouldn't we go as if they were just leaving the house as normal?' asked Ryan, 'Then if the police come nosing about, someone in the village would be bound to see the cars leaving and say so. We need witnesses, surely.'

'Good grief, I think we've taken enough risks, already,' said Chantry, 'We'll be our own witnesses. I'll work out a timetable of when the guests left and let you all know so we are all singing from the same hymn sheet.'

'Maybe a couple of the cars should go the long way through the village Chantry, just as an insurance policy,' said Neil.

'But what if some nosey parker sees who the driver is?' asked Chantry.

'We'll race through like they usually do. No one will clock who it is,' said Penny, who was determined to at least have a bit of fun.

'Oh, very well, just the two of you, but for goodness' sake don't have an accident or we're all for the high jump,' agreed Chantry.

And so saying the drivers all took to their respective cars and started the engines.

'Ladies,' said Chantry to Molly Cox and Jane Fox, 'both of you can sort out the cleaning materials and we'll be back as soon as we can.'

'I'll get a mop and bucket,' said Molly Cox.

'And I'll get a broom,' said Jane Fox.

Chantry nodded towards them and then as if directing a wagon train, waved her hand out of the window, a cue that Neil and Penny, in their respective cars, decided was the start of a race and, gunning their engines flew down the drive throwing up the gravel and screaming off in a cloud of dust. After the dust had settled, the others drove off in a more sedate fashion towards Broome Farm.

In the field opposite the house, Toby Broome was happily digging the biggest and deepest hole that he had ever dug. He was in his element. Normally his father would stride across the field, pull him out of the cab and bash him around the head, but not today. Today, Borley Broome was standing by the side of the digger urging his son to dig deeper and longer. It was only the sound of the first two cars driven by Neil and Penny skidding off the road and into the field, followed by the others, slowly turning in, that took Toby out of his revelry.

'What are they doing in this field, Dad?' he asked.

'Never you mind about them, boy. You just dig the fecking hole,' yelled Borley over the cars pulling up and stopping nearby. The drivers got out and gathered into a group.

'What a bloody waste,' said Neil. 'That engine purrs.'

'Sounded more like a roar to me, Neil,' said Chantry, throwing him a withering look.

'I could hardly hear her,' continued Neil.

'Well, you're the only one; the whole of the village could hear you, but what's done is done.' Chantry shook her head.

'What I'd give to have this as a second car.' Neil stroked the top of it.

'How are we going to get them in that hole?' asked Penny looking over the edge, sheepishly.

'Push the buggers in,' said Borley, 'Give each one a good shove with this thing.' So saying he slapped his hand on the bucket of the digger.

Chantry tottered over to the hole.

'Will it be big enough to take all these, do you think?'

'I reckon,' Borley nodded.

'Well, let's get on with it,' said George gruffly, 'I want to get this over with as soon as possible.'

'Me too,' chirped in Penny.

'We'll all have a drink on me as soon as we're done here,' said Chantry, trying to keep their spirits up.

'Well, that's the best thing you've said all day,' said Neil as Borley strode up purposefully behind the first car,

'Well let's not stand around talking about it, let's get these buggers in the hole,' he growled.

Neil took off the handbrake and the villagers stared as the digger started to push the car towards the slipway. Down it rolled and into the trench, its weight and momentum taking it along the bottom.

One by one the other cars were consigned to their final resting place and when that was done the others looked on as Toby lifted the digger bucket and started dropping great lumps of soil on top of them. Neil, Penny, George, Sue, Ryan, Kylie and Chantry all looked on as earth and stones covered the once luxury pride and joys below.

'Let's hope nobody finds them,' said George.

'Oh, nobody will come near this hole by the time I've finished,' said Borley, 'Boy,' he shouted up to Toby in the cab of the digger, 'when you've finished with this hole, fill the trailer with the dung heap and dump it on top of this lot.'

———————

Chapter 10

Over in the Leggett Arms things were as they always were since the days when the government had taken the last pleasure out of going to the pub. The smoking ban had killed off the last few customers more than it was meant to save; not that it stopped Ronnie Randell from lighting up as he sat at the bar.

The ritual was the same: Ronnie would come in, bleary-eyed, five minutes after opening time, walk slowly around the bar to the barstool at the end, order a large gin and tonic, take his cigarettes and lighter out of his pocket and light up. Sam, the landlord, would tell him that he had to go outside if he wanted to smoke and Ronnie would look at him, point his finger and tell Sam that he'd been coming into this pub and sitting at this barstool drinking his G&T and smoking his cigarettes for over forty years. He would then follow that up by reminding Sam that he was eighty-four years old and he was fucked if he was going to stand outside on the pavement at his age and freeze his tits off. At this, Sam would sigh and put the gin and tonic in front of him and say no more. Linda, Sam's wife, would, at this juncture, enter the bar as she always did. She'd stop in the doorway, put her hands on her hips, cough theatrically and look at her husband. Sam would look back at her and shrug his shoulders. At this point, Linda would sidle up to Sam and say the same thing that she always did.

'Sam, for Christ's sake smoking is illegal in here, we could lose our licence.'

To which, Sam would reply, 'What am I supposed to do? He's our only regular. He puts fifty quid over this bar every session besides we're at the arse end of nowhere, so who's going to come in and nick us?'

Linda would then shake her head and retort, 'What about our other customers?'

Wherein Sam would hold his arms out and walk around the bar and stare at the empty chairs, 'What sodding customers?'

At this Linda would straighten the bar towels for no good reason and leave the bar and go into the kitchen ready to take orders for lunch or bar snacks should, by some miracle, someone other than Ronnie Randell, dare to enter the establishment.

Sitting at the end of the bar every lunchtime and evening drinking large gin and tonics and chain-smoking was now Ronnie's only pleasure apart from quoting his party piece which he did with boring regularity. Should a stranger enter the bar it wouldn't be long before Ronnie would catch his or her eye and a variation of the following dialogue would ensue:

Ronnie: 'I see you recognise me.'

Customer: 'Pardon?'

Ronnie: 'Think you've seen me somewhere before?'

Customer: 'I'm sorry but…'

Ronnie: 'I expect it's the voice. It usually is. The voice is the first thing that you all think you know.'

At this point, either Sam or Linda would intervene with a friendly smile.

'Come on now, Ronnie, leave these good people alone. They've just come in for a quiet drink, not to be bothered by you.'

Then the dialogue would continue:

Ronnie: (to the customer) 'Am I bothering you?'

Customer: (trying to be polite) 'No, not at all.'

Ronnie: (To Sam or Linda) 'There you are, you see. Not bothering anybody. Just making conversation, that's the glory of the public house. They may try and stop you from drinking with all those warnings of how many units are in an average G&T or say you're not allowed to smoke (at this point he would theatrically and pointedly pull on his cigarette) but the one thing they can't stop you doing in a pub is having a conversation; a jolly good old chin wag. Nothing like standing in the public bar putting the world to rights, wouldn't you say?'

The customer would then give a forced smile, pick up his or her drink and attempt to walk away without trying to give offence to the boring old drunk. But it would be to no avail. Ronnie had them in his clutches and when he had a punter in his clutches, he wasn't going to let them go until he had finished his act and the curtain had only just risen as far as he was concerned.

Ronnie: (continuing) 'Do please forgive the Bar Steward for all his interruptions.'

Ronnie would then give a large, theatrical wink towards Sam, who, in turn, would have to restrain himself from grabbing Ronnie by the lapels and throwing him, bodily, out of the bar. He knew that this was irrational but the "Bar Steward" line always made him want to commit murder.

Ronnie: (ignoring Sam's look of daggers) 'Now, where were we? Oh yes; the voice. I could see that it was niggling you so let me put you out of your misery.'

The following dialogue would be voiced by Ronnie, playing all the characters:

1st Villain: 'Watch out, it's the rozzers.'

2nd Villain: 'Quick, down this narrow alley. They'll never think of looking for us down there.'

1st Villain: 'Blimey, it's a dead end.'

Suave young Police Inspector: 'Yes, I'm afraid chaps that you have fallen into my trap. Constable, take these gentlemen and put them in the cells back at the station. Gently mind, we don't want them damaged, do we?'

1st Villain: 'Oh, bloomin' 'eck, of all the coppers to be nicked by. Just my bloomin' luck, eh, Inspector?'

2nd Villain: 'Inspector? Why he looks no more than a kid.'

1st Villain: 'Yeah, that's right. That's why I knows him. He's the youngest copper in the country to be promoted to Inspector.'

2nd Villain: 'Who is he then?'

1st Villain: 'You mean you don't know?'

2nd Villain: 'Nah.'

Inspector: 'Allow me to introduce myself in that case, I'm Inspector Scotland of the Yard.'

Ronnie would then raise his glass in triumph, take a large swig and bang his empty glass on the counter in front of the customer, saying:

'You see, you didn't realise when you came in today that you would be meeting a real star, did you?

Ronnie would give a modest smile and a friendly wink. The customer would sometimes articulate something like: 'No, most certainly not,' or just smile back, giving a knowing nod, as if to say, 'Crikey, I've just met the famous "Scotland of the Yard" and raise his or her glass and then hot foot it back to their friends or hide in the furthest corner of the bar and admire one of the hunting prints on the wall.

As can probably be guessed, Ronnie was an actor, or should that be, ex-actor? No, Ronnie would never say, ex-actor. 'One can never give up the theatre if it's in their blood. The art of the performer courses through your veins. When it stops doing so, you're dead.'

Ronnie had not worked for forty years or more. The only entrance he made now, was twice daily through the doors of the pub. Ronnie was a has-been, or as Sam the landlord would say, an almost been.

Ronnie could have quoted that immortal line of Brando's 'I could have been somebody, I could have been a contender,' but he was never a fan of Marlon Brando as he didn't believe in "The Method". Ronnie's attitude to acting was more pragmatic: Spend the day in the pub until "the half"; shove on a bit of slap; walk on stage; say your lines; put your day clothes on under your costume; take a bow; discard your costume for your dresser to pick up and return to the pub to finish off the day.

Ronnie's claim to fame was short, but he was determined that nobody would forget it. "Scotland of the Yard" was a daily radio drama series broadcast on the BBC's Home Service. In the 1950s, the fifteen-minute detective or thriller series was a must listen to event for every teenage boy. The most famous series was, undoubtedly, "Dick Barton, Special Agent", closely followed by "Paul Temple" and "Quatermass and the Pit". Hidden among these classics were two series of "Scotland of the Yard". At first, the BBC producers thought that a series featuring Adam Scotland, the youngest man to gain the rank of Detective Inspector in the Metropolitan Police, had the potential of being a huge hit alongside the others.

Calls went out to all the leading acting talent agencies that they were looking for a new, handsome, male actor to play the lead part. Ronald Normington had been at the Royal Academy of Dramatic Art for three years. In his intake at the RADA were such talents as Albert Finney and Peter O'Toole amongst others. Both these actors were appearing in "London's West End" within months of leaving the Academy whilst Ronnie Normington was playing in weekly Rep in Frinton. Being out of work most of the time, Ronnie could be found holding up the bar in the Salisbury Tavern, in London's St Martin's Lane.

The Salisbury was the haunt of actors in the nineteen-fifties. In those days before mobile phones and the internet, it was the place where those in show business found out what television and radio programmes were being cast. The bar was abuzz with the news that the BBC were looking for a new actor to star in a radio series. No sooner had he heard the news than Ronnie was hot-footing it to the public phone by the front door, calling his agent. Within a couple of days, he was standing in the foyer of Broadcasting House waiting to be called into his audition. Walking along the winding narrow corridors with the producer's secretary to meet the producer, Ronnie felt strangely confident. The reading of the script went well. He caught the producer and the writer looking across at each other and nod.

'We're looking for a new leading actor for our serial, Mister Normington,' said the producer. 'Someone with the presence of Paul Temple or Dick Barton. Are you that star?'

Feeling confident, he said, 'Yes, I think I am.'

'Good,' said the producer.

'If we were to give you the part of Adam Scotland, we would have to be sure that you could handle the pressure of being the voice of our intrepid hero,' said the producer.

'Your voice would be heard all over the country every Monday to Friday. And on the World Service. Your voice will be heard all around the globe,' said the writer rather proudly.

'I think we should concentrate on the situation here in Britain for the moment,' said the producer a little firmly to the writer. He turned back to Ronnie, 'Every time you utter a word in the street.'

'Or in a shop.'

'Or in a shop, it will be recognised,' warned the producer.

'Your life would never be the same again,' said the writer.

'Everyone would recognise your name,' said the producer.

'Ronald Normington,' said the writer.

Suddenly, they both stopped and looked at one another.

'Oh, that won't do,' said the producer.

'Won't do at all,' said the writer, 'There's no music to it.'

'Very flat,' said the producer, 'Imagine the BBC radio announcer reading out the names of the cast and getting to Ronald Normington?'

'I'm sorry, Mister Normington, but we can't have that,' said the writer. 'We have this young, intelligent, handsome Detective Inspector, who is in not just any old police force but the Metropolitan Police Force. The amount of time, weeks, months it took me to come up with the perfect character name,

Adam Scotland. I can't possibly have it played by someone called Ronald Normington.'

'Well,' said the producer, 'it's been very nice meeting you. We'll be in touch.'

'Randell,' blurted out Ronnie, putting the stress on the second syllable, rhyming it with "Bell". 'How about Ronnie Randell? I could register the name with Equity this afternoon.'

'Ronnie Ran-dell,' said the writer, stressing the second syllable even more than Ronnie had, 'The part of Detective Inspector Adam Scotland was played by Mister Ronnie Ran-dell.'

'I like it,' said the producer.

'It works for me,' affirmed the writer.

'I think we've found our man,' said the producer.

'I think we have,' confirmed the writer.

'I will telephone your agent right away, that is, of course, if you wish to play the part,' said the producer.

'I do,' said Ronnie, shaking both the producer and writer by the hand.

'We start recording the programmes in two weeks' time,' said the Producer, who had pressed a button on his primitive intercom, 'Mrs Halliwell?'

'Yes, sir?' came the voice of the producer's secretary through the machine.

'Mrs Halliwell, cancel the other auditionees for the part,' said the producer.

'You wish me to cancel Mister Finney and Mister O'Toole?'

'Precisely,' said the producer, 'we have found our Scotland of the Yard.'

'That is splendid news, sir,' said Mrs Halliwell, 'I shall call the other agents right away.'

And this was the story that Ronnie told anybody who would listen of how he landed the part of Adam Scotland. The truth? Only Ronnie knew the truth. The producer, writer and Mrs Halliwell were long since dead. It's likely that Ronnie's gin-soaked brain completely believed his own version of events but the facts cannot be changed in that he did play Adam Scotland; that was no word of a lie.

Sadly, however, fame was short-lived for Ronnie. The series failed to catch the imagination of the listening millions. They wanted Dick or Paul; Adam wasn't either. After two series, the programme was quietly dropped. Unperturbed Ronnie realised that he had to keep himself in the public eye.

During the early sixties he appeared in stage tours of Agatha Christie "Poirot" plays, although, even he had to admit that his performance was not up to snuff as he couldn't manage the intricacies of the Belgian accent and the bloody moustache kept falling off, somewhat spoiling the effect when delivering the denouement in the library.

During the long days on tour, he would sit in various pubs and read the "Lord Peter Whimsey" stories of Dorothy L. Sayers or G.K. Chesterton's "Father Brown". It was during these sessions and after about the fourth G&T that he came up with the idea of adapting Chesterton's priest-detective into a stage play and proceeded to set it out and send it to every producer he could think of. He did not get one answer. Finally, with more bravado than sense, he talked to his bank manager, who liked to see himself as a more than passing amateur actor and who Ronnie always furnished with complimentary tickets whenever he was in a play when it was touring nearby, into approving a loan in order for Ronnie to play the lead part of Father Brown and produce the play himself.

Expectations were high but, sadly, ticket sales were low and, in some towns, non-existent. Before too many weeks passed, worried theatre owners were telephoning and cancelling the date altogether. Ronnie's bank manager's interest in the theatre declined in about the same ratio as the demand for tickets.

Ronnie's application for an extended overdraft facility was met with stony silence. The tour of "Father Brown Investigates" collapsed after five weeks on the road along with Ronnie's standing in the business. Fellow actors and stage management were left unpaid as Ronnie applied for bankruptcy. The actors' union was sorely tempted to throw him out but he managed to convince them that the fault lay with the theatre owners for reneging on their agreement.

Bankrupt, Ronnie took on one- or two-line roles in television dramas like "Dixon of Dock Green" but he soon realised that his career as a TV or radio policeman, with his rather upper-class accent, was over when he saw the Zephyr Zodiac hove into shot and the sound of the tin whistle at the beginning of the new, up to date, cop show "Z Cars".

All, however, was not lost. Producers who he had worked for in the theatre over the years on the Agatha Christie tours took pity on him and threw him a lifeline and he started to go out on tour again. This time, though, he was contracted to be what is termed in the business as a "walking understudy". This consisted of him spending every performance in a cold dressing room, having learned the words and stage moves of all the middle-aged or older men in the play just in case one of the leading players fell ill or was too drunk to perform, which came to much the same thing in those days. For this, he was paid the minimum union rate per week. Ronnie's pride was hurt but the money kept him in food, rent and gin.

By the time this all came to an end, he had not played in every worthwhile theatre in the country, but he had walked through the stage door and dozed in a dressing rooms of most of them. His touring days ended when he was contacted by an aunt he didn't know he had and which, in fact, he hadn't.

According to a letter sent to a Mister Ronnie Randell at the theatre, his father's sister, Jessica, was rather a rich old lady and a rather lonely one. It was fortuitous that the letter arrived at all as it had been sent to one theatre from much earlier on the tour and had been delivered to at least five other theatre stage doors before arriving by the skin of its teeth on the last Saturday of the tour. Needless to say, after so many crossing out of addresses and entering of others it had been forwarded to, it was a miracle that it arrived at all.

In the dressing room that evening, Ronnie read and re-read the letter from someone signed Aunt Jessica.

The letter said that she was glad to have tracked him down, at last, and asked whether it would be convenient for him to visit her as she needed to talk to him on the utmost importance concerning certain financial matters. She would be grateful, she wrote, if Ronnie would be good enough to come and see her at his earliest convenience. Ronnie decided to write straight back and offer to pop along the next Wednesday.

Aunt Jessica lived in a lovely little cottage in the village. She was very old and very frail and when he knocked upon her door the first time it took her so long to answer it that, at first, he thought that she wasn't at home. Eventually though he heard a thin voice from behind the door.

'Who's there?' said the voice.

'It is your nephew, Aunt Jessica,' Ronnie whispered, as if in church.

'Who is it?' asked the voice again.

'It is your nephew, Ronnie, Aunt,' said Ronnie again, projecting his voice a little more.

'Is there someone there?' came the voice again, a little truculently this time, 'I shall call the police.'

'It's your nephew, Ronnie, Aunt Jessica,' Ronnie projected his voice so that it could reach the back of the dress circle of the largest theatre in the country.

'Nephew Ronnie?' came the voice, 'How do I know that you are my nephew, Ronnie?'

For a second, Ronnie wasn't sure how he could prove that he was her nephew, especially as he had no idea until receiving the letter that he had an Aunt Jessica. The letter. He quickly brought it out of his blazer pocket.

'I have a letter from you, Aunt Jessica,' he said, waving it in the air for no good reason.

'A letter?' she said from the other side of the door. 'What letter?'

'This one,' he said, waving it in the air again, 'I can put it in your letterbox if you like,' he continued, looking for the cottage's letterbox in the front door.

'Yes, put it in the letterbox,' said Aunt Jessica.

Ronnie stepped back from the door and looked again for the letterbox opening. 'You don't seem to have a letterbox,' he said stepping back towards the door.

'Of course I have a letterbox. I had a letter this morning from the electricity company,' the aunt retorted somewhat firmly. It was then that Ronnie noticed a box on the wall next to the door.

'Your letterbox is on the wall,' he said.

'Yes,' she said, 'Put it in there and then I can read it.'

'But if I put the letter in the box, you won't be able to read it until you come out of your cottage to retrieve it from the box, surely,' reasoned Ronnie.

'Yes,' said the aunt.

'But if you come outside, you will see me. I will be able to give you the letter myself.' The logic of his argument was seemingly unquestionable.

'You will have to go away until I've read it.'

'Go away?'

'Oh, yes. Post the letter in the box and then go away,' she said.

'But surely,' at which point he stopped himself. There was a chance, he now realised, that they could go around in circles like this for hours. 'If I go away, how will I know when to come back?'

'Come back when I've read the letter,' she said matter of factly.

'And when will that be?'

'When I've got it out of the box and read it.'

'Of course,' sighed Ronnie, 'I will put it in the box then.'

'Have you put the letter in the box?' she asked.

'I'm doing so now,' replied Ronnie with the letter half in and half out of the letterbox, 'I'm just dropping it in now. You will come out and get it, won't you?'

'You need to go away now,' she replied.

'I am going away. I shall go into the public house and return in half an hour,' said Ronnie stepping away from the door. As he started to walk down the street, he heard the old woman say something, so he returned to the front door of the cottage, 'Did you say something?' he asked.

'Have you gone, yet?' said the aunt.

'No, well yes. I had gone but I came back again,' said Ronnie confused.

'I haven't read the letter yet,' she said.

'I know,' said Ronnie.

'Then, why have you come back?' she asked, not unreasonably.

'I…' started Ronnie but then thought the better of it. 'I'm going to the pub and will be back in half an hour. Goodbye for now.' And on this, he strode off down the street and through the doors of the Leggett Arms for the first time. He ordered a gin and tonic, which he downed in double quick time in exasperation and then got himself another double which he was only able to purchase by emptying out his pockets and hiding some foreign coins in the middle of the pile as he handed them over the counter. Ronnie immediately felt strangely at home sitting on the bar stool in the Leggett Arms, which on the whole, was good thing as, little did he realise then, from that day onward he was to spend more time there than anywhere else.

So, half an hour later Ronnie was back outside the front door of the cottage of the old woman that called herself his Aunt Jessica.

'Who is it?' she said after Ronnie had knocked on the door.

'It's your nephew, Ronnie, Aunt Jessica.'

'My nephew Ronnie?' the old woman said bemused. Ronnie's heart sank. He had spent the last of his money travelling to the village and passing the time in the pub. He had posted to her the only bit of proof that he was who he said he was.

'Yes, remember? I put a letter into your letterbox half an hour ago,' he said, very slowly hoping that it might help it to get into the old bird's brain.

'Are you from the electricity company?' she asked through the door.

Ronnie wanted to cry.

'No, Aunt, you wanted me to put the letter you sent me into your letterbox.' He had all but given up hope.

'Are you Ronnie Randell?' asked the old girl.

'Yes, yes, I am Ronnie Randell.'

'Someone has sent you a letter. It arrived this afternoon,' she said, confused.

'Yes, Aunt, you sent it to me and I put it in your letterbox.' Ronnie wished he had the money to get another gin and tonic.

'But why did you put it in my letterbox when it was addressed to you?' she asked.

'Because you asked me to, to prove I was who I said I was. I also sent you a letter saying that I would be coming down to see you today.'

'What day is it?'

Ronnie closed his eyes and tried to stay calm. 'Wednesday,' he said.

'Oh, in that case, you had better come in,' she said taking the chain off the door and releasing the two locks and a bolt. As the door opened, Ronnie stepped back a bit. A little head appeared around the door.

'Hello Aunt,' said Ronnie, putting on his best smile, 'I am your nephew, Ronnie.'

'Yes, I've been waiting for you. Your letter said you would be arriving an hour ago,' said Aunt Jessica a little crossly.

Over a cup of tea, Aunt Jessica talked about Ronnie's father and how it was so sad that whilst serving in the navy during the Second World War, his ship had been torpedoed by a German U Boat and all hands, including that of her brother, Ronnie's father, were lost in the Atlantic. Ronnie sat sipping his tea fascinated but a little confused. Clive Normington, his father was, until he died of tuberculosis brought on by smoking sixty Capstan Full Strength a day (which was as near as he got to anything naval), a junior Clerk who worked all his life in a cold office in the Ministry of Defence, having failed to pass his army medical as he had a clubbed foot and wore a raised shoe. This fact was indelibly printed on Ronnie's brain as whenever he misbehaved as a child, his father would take the shoe off and hit him over the head with it.

Aunt Jessica continued her story. She recounted how it broke her heart when Ronnie's mother, Irene, went to live in Australia after the war, taking young Ronnie with her. Ronnie sipped at his tea and thought of his upbringing in Ruislip, West London, with his mother, Hester, who grew very fat. So fat in fact that when she died one evening whilst sitting in her armchair listening to "The Archers", the undertaker had to break the arms off the armchair to get her body out of it.

There was a part of Ronnie that wanted to correct Aunt Jessica on the facts of his childhood but something inside him commanded him to hang fire and let the dotty old bat waffle on. He sat before a roaring fire as she told him how her father, Ronnie's grandfather, had squirrelled his money away and it wasn't until he died at the age of ninety that it was discovered that he was worth a fortune.

'A fortune?' said Ronnie, using all his acting skills not to sound too inquisitive, 'And what you would say a fortune was in those days, I wonder.'

'Five hundred thousand pounds. He won most of it on the horses and in Monte Carlo.'

'Monte Carlo?' said Ronnie trying to hold back.

'I never knew until I went through his papers and found the receipt from the Casino,' said Aunt Jessica in a matter-of-fact way.

'So what happened to the fortune?' asked Ronnie. He said "the fortune" as if in inverted commas, to make it sound that five hundred thousand pounds wasn't a fortune at all really, well not in his eyes. 'Did you share it with the family? I'm sure they all had their fair share.'

'Oh, well, no. There was no family, you see apart from me and well, your father, but he was long dead, wasn't he. The only other family was your mother and yourself.'

'Me?' said Ronnie, holding on to his cup and trying to stop his hands from shaking.

'You see, you and your mother were in Australia, weren't you?'

'Yes, of course.'

'And I had no way of contacting you. I'm afraid Irene and I did not see eye to eye. I think she thought that we were below her in class. I shouldn't really say this and perhaps you are not aware but your father and mother were not, shall we say, married, when you were conceived. Of course, she had to marry your father although I don't think they loved one another. Perhaps that's why she took off to Australia with you after the war, to start a new life.' Jessica picked up the teapot, 'I'll make some more tea, shall I?' she said.

'Please,' said Ronnie. 'So Aunt, with Mother and I out of the way in Australia, I take it that you took all the money, I mean inheritance, and used it? Quite right,' he added the last two words to make it sound as if he had no hard feelings.

'Oh no,' she said, hobbling off to the kitchen to refresh the teapot.

'No?' called Ronnie, staying in the armchair and trying to keep calm.

'Cake?' asked Aunt Jessica, returning with a large fruitcake. 'Oh, I had no need for it. You see I had my little cottage and I'd saved a little bit of my own money,' she continued leaving the room to get the freshly filled teapot.

'Bugger,' said Ronnie banging the arm of the chair, 'Silly old biddie's given it all away to some cat's home or something,' he muttered under his breath.

'I put it in the bank and left it there in a deposit account so it could gain some interest,' she said returning with the tea.

'What, all five hundred thousand pounds?' He modulated his voice to sound calm again.

'Oh, yes. Well, you see, I hoped, one day that I might find you and pass it on to you.' She poured some milk into his cup.

'Me?'

'Can you imagine how thrilled I was when I was watching the television a few weeks ago and I saw your name on it.'

'On the television?' asked Ronnie.

'Well, you see, there are so many channels on the television these days and I was pressing the button thing.'

'Remote control.'

'And I came across this detective programme and then as it ended, I saw our name appear.'

'You saw my name.' Ronnie's voice was slightly higher than normal.

'Yes, I wrote it down on a piece of paper,' she said crossing over to a bureau and producing a crumpled old envelope. She read from it, 'Charlie Andrews: Ronnie Randell.'

Ronnie closed his eyes.

'Ronnie Randell. I was so surprised. Little Ronnie Randell. The little boy I had not seen since just after the war.'

Ronald Normington looked over toward the little old lady. Ronald Normington, who through all his faults, always thought of himself as an honourable man, sipped at his third cup of tea and pondered his options.

'I wrote a letter to the television people and they gave me the address of someone who said that you were travelling around all the theatres in the country. You see, I thought that if I could find you, I could let you know that your money was safe and sound,' continued Aunt Jessica proudly.

'My money?' said Ronald Normington.

'Yes, your inheritance. Well, it's only right that you should benefit from your grandfather's will, don't you think?'

Ronald Normington so desperately wanted to tell the old lady the truth about his past. His mind did a thousand somersaults trying to figure out what would happen if he came clean. Ronald Normington remembered that he had spent his last few pounds in the pub down the street and knew that his wallet and pockets were both now devoid of cash.

'Oh, Aunt Jessica, how can I ever thank you?' replied Ronnie Randell, after a moment's pause. He took the old lady's hand and kissed it theatrically.

Over the next hour, it became obvious that he could not just ask the old girl to write out a cheque and disappear into the night, no matter how much he wanted to. It was decided that Aunt Jessica should cook her newly found nephew dinner and put him up for the night. That night he could not sleep a wink. His head kept turning: *What if the real Ronnie Randell should turn up one day? Bugger him. Why on earth should he turn up? If the old girl was correct in thinking that his mother looked down on the Randell family then she would have surely airbrushed them out of existence. The real Ronnie Randell was probably no longer called Ronnie Randell anyway. Probably something suitably antipodean, whatever that might be.*

Ronnie stared at the ceiling and worked out a scenario and in the morning, started to act it out.

'Aunt Jessica,' he said at breakfast, 'your kindness in holding onto my inheritance should not go unrewarded, and, if you will allow me, I would like to stay here and look after you. Of course, I would need access to some of the money that has been put by, let's say...' and here he cleared his throat and hoped that he was judging his performance right, 'twenty thousand pounds, to be going on with, just to buy us a few luxuries. What do you think of that?'

Aunt Jessica thought it a very generous idea from her very generous nephew. And so it transpired that over the next years Ronnie Randell and his Aunt Jessica lived in perfect harmony together. Every morning Ronnie would make a pot of tea and take it into his aged aunt and wake her gently from her slumbers. This continued until one morning when he discovered that his aunt had breathed her last during the night. He made sure that he gave her a wonderful send off and buried her with full village honours in the churchyard. He then adjourned to the Leggett Arms and with a legitimate excuse, at least in his eyes, got spectacularly drunk. By this time he had safely managed to get his fraudulently obtained inheritance into his own bank account, having changed his name, legally, by deed poll to Ronnie Randell, sighting it, to the authorities, as it being, his stage name and one that he was now forever known.

The money in the bank was beyond Ronnie's wildest dreams. Aunt Jessica's presence of mind to put it into a savings account had meant the five hundred thousand had over doubled through interest and was continuing to do so. He thought about taking long exclusive cruises around the world or, perhaps, flying 1st Class to Paris or New York, or maybe Sydney, Australia, but then again, perhaps not Australia; no point pushing his luck. In the end he thought that it would be best if he just stayed put, in the village. He liked the fact that he could walk up the street to the pub and drink copious amounts of Gin and tonic and not worry about how he paid for them. The interest alone on the money would keep him in G&Ts for the rest of his life. He knew that no matter how drunk he became in the pub, and how boring he was with his stories of "Scotland of the Yard" the landlord was never going to throw him out because he put more money over the bar in a week than any of the other locals did in a lifetime. On a Sunday, Ronnie, at some point, would clear his throat and demand that he pay for a round for everybody in the pub at that time. He would then raise his glass and ask everyone to drink a toast to Ronnie Randell, and when all the others would be thinking that he meant himself, he would mutter, knowingly: 'Here's to you, cobber.'

So Ronnie was, as usual, holding up the far end of the bar when the burial party entered the pub.

'Landlord,' yelled Ronnie, 'a drink on Ronnie Randell for these good people, on this lovely Sunday lunchtime, if you would be so kind.'

'I'm sure that won't be necessary, Ronnie,' said Chantry, ushering her brood towards the large table at the other end of the bar, 'I'll take care of it, thank you.'

'I insist, dear lady,' said Ronnie waving his hand towards Sam. In truth, it was well known that he could not stand the sight of Chantry Bowman-Leggett. The feeling, it must be said, was mutual. To Ronnie, Chantry was an upper-class snob, whilst to Chantry, Ronnie was a common little con man. She had done her homework on Ronnie Randell and was more than au fait with his past. She had tried to warn Jessica, whom she had known for over sixty years but the old girl would have none of it. Perhaps Jessica was aware of the truth and just decided that her need for companionship was the lesser of the two evils. In the end Chantry decided to leave it be. It was really none of her business what Jessica did with her money, after all. She did, however, make a point of cornering Ronnie after Jessica's funeral and fired a warning shot across his bows. She knew everything, she told him, and she would forever keep an eye on him. He tried to brazen it out, of course, but in his heart he knew the truth and knew that Chantry knew it too. From that moment, he feigned being nice to her. She, in turn, made it her duty never to accept anything from him, including even so much as a dry sherry.

The seven villagers sat around the table in silence for a moment.

Chantry looked at her fellow conspirators 'We have to stay strong and focused,' she said, firmly and then clammed up as Sam called out that their drinks were on the bar, and he didn't run a waitress service. George and Neil went to collect the drinks.

'Have the perverts scuttled off then, Chantry?' called Ronnie.

Chantry jumped. 'What?'

'At the big house. Have they all had their wicked ways and gone off to their boring lives in suburbia?' he chuckled.

'However would I know?' said Chantry, overly affronted.

'Oh, come on, Chantry, I saw you earlier hovering about Church Lane, having a nose around,' Ronnie continued.

'Did you, indeed.' Chantry tried not to sound too worried, 'I was just taking in some air. Those deviants are of no interest to me, I can assure you.'

'Of course not,' said Ronnie.

'What else did he see?' whispered Penny, a little too loudly.

Ronnie chuckled.

'He knows. He bloody knows,' whispered Penny again rashly.

'Oh, do be quiet Penelope,' snapped Chantry, 'You know what Ronnie's like. He lives in his own fantasy world. He thinks he's a real detective. Any excuse to stir things up. It's his way of passing the day, apart from getting sloshed.' Chantry smiled across at Ronnie to show she was having a harmless little joke at his expense.

'Blimey you lot look as if you're planning to blow the place up. Is that what you're plotting?' said Sam, winking at Ronnie.

'Yes, you've cracked it, Samuel. They're going to blow the Old Rectory up whilst those inside are giving each other blow jobs.' Ronnie let out a loud barking laugh at his own joke.

'It'll give a new meaning to the phrase having a gang bang,' joined in Sam.

'You can both be so utterly vulgar at times,' said Chantry witheringly.

George put his head in his hands while Neil held Penny's hand. Molly Cox and Jane Fox got a fit of the giggles whilst Sue sat silent.

'Ladies please,' hissed Chantry over to them.

Neil downed his pint in one go. Penny drank her gin without putting any tonic in it and let out a yelp as the neat alcohol hit the back of her throat.

'Just ignore them,' cautioned Chantry.

'He's giving me the willies,' coughed Penny.

'Now, the next thing we have to do is make the place look just like any other home,' said Chantry, making sure she couldn't be heard from across the bar, 'We must take all the accoutrements off the walls and fill in all the holes as well as repaint the place. We will need to get rid of all those black satin sheets off the beds and put nice white cotton sheets on them, like normal people, have.'

'I have silk sheets on my bed,' said Penny.

'That, somehow, does not come as a surprise to me, Penny,' said Chantry, giving a wry smile between her and Neil.

'And let me guess who's going to be doing all this filling and painting,' said Neil.

'Well, you are the professional, dear,' answered Chantry.

'Yes, and I have a business to run. I've got a kitchen to fit before the end of the week.' Neil was not happy.

'In that case, the sooner we get started the sooner we'll finish.' Chantry was not to be put off her task, 'There can be no going back now. We're all in this together.'

'I'll remember that when some eight-foot gorilla is trying to bugger me in my cell and insist on calling me Mandy,' said Neil forcefully.

'Oh, stop being overly dramatic, Neil,' snapped Chantry, 'If we all stay calm and keep together and our mouths shut no one will be ever the wiser.'

'Of course not, a dozen people just disappear off the face of the earth and no one's going to come and look for them,' said Neil.

'If people do come looking for them then we are going to all make sure we have the story straight,' said Chantry firmly.

'Are we?' butted in George, 'And what will that story be, pray?'

'Leave it to me, George. First things first. A jolly good spring clean of the Rectory is the order of the day, so let us put our best foot forward and get on with it.' And so saying, Chantry took to her feet.

'You'd think that we were just going onto the playing field for a jolly good game of hockey,' whispered Penny in Neil's ear as they started getting up.

'We must hope they have a good supply of cleaning products in the house otherwise we will have to raid our own supplies,' said Chantry matter of factly and sweeping out of the door.

Sam cleared the table of the drinks glasses whilst Ronnie looked out of the window. He saw Chantry stop and give a sideways glance towards the pub. Their eyes met through the glass and he gave a little nod to her and raised his drink in salute. He could faintly hear Chantry say "Goodbye" to all the others rather loudly and then whisper something and the crowd suddenly started to disperse in different directions. Ronnie chuckled and sat down calling for Sam to get him another large one.

In the street, Chantry stopped and craned her neck back to see if Ronnie's face was still at the window of the pub. The coast, she reasoned, was clear and she waved her arms forcefully as she herded the separated conspirators back together again and headed off towards the Old Rectory gates.

Neil went back to his cottage to pick up his van and drove it onto the gravel and parked it up out of sight behind the house. Taking out his tool kit and an electric drill, he climbed up the stairs and into the first of the two bedrooms that had handcuffs and ankle chains along with other sado-masochistic implements screwed to the wall. Not wishing to make contact with these items for fear of what they might be covered with he donned some rubber gloves that he only normally used when pottering about under the bonnet of his van.

Downstairs in the lounge, Sue was looking at the remains of the suckling pig on the rotisserie.

'What are we going to do with that?' she said, turning to Chantry, 'I certainly don't want to eat it, but it seems a shame that the poor little thing died for no good reason.'

'We can chop it up and feed it to Borley's pigs, I suppose,' said Chantry.

'Oh, do pigs eat pig?' Sue was not happy with this solution.

'Who knows? Animal husbandry is not my strongest suit,' answered Chantry with a wry smile.

'Anyway, isn't that where the poor thing came from in the first place? The pigs might be eating their own piglet.' Sue shivered.

'Well, just chop it up and put it in a bin bag. I'll take it into the woods later and leave it there, the foxes will soon polish it off,' said Chantry.

Sue thought this a much more satisfactory idea, even though she had no time for foxes after they had killed all her chickens which she kept for their eggs. Colin hated the chickens and could not see why she wanted them. Colin's dislike of them made Sue want to have them even more.

———————

Chapter 11

Sue had to admit it, Colin was a mistake and she came to this conclusion approximately one hour after saying "I will" in front of all her family and friends over twenty years ago. She watched him chatting up the daughter of one of her friends in the corner of the marquee where they were having their wedding reception. He stood edging the girl, who was only about eighteen, into the canvas, touching her arm, whilst still in his wedding suit. Sue knew, even at that distance, that her new husband was wishing he and the girl were both in their birthday suits.

Sadly, this was not the first time than she had seen Colin behaving in this way. She had kidded herself that as soon as he had slipped the wedding ring on her finger his attitude to other women would change forever. She gently pointed out to him that she was not happy that he felt the desire to chat up anything that wore a skirt and had a pulse but he would laugh and say that he was just flirting; he couldn't help it; flirting was fun; nothing to be read into it; nothing came from it. He didn't think or even wish anything came of it. He loved Sue, or so he told her and everything else was just 'having a bit of fun, darling, nothing else'.

She knew when she tackled him on their wedding night at the airport hotel, before jetting off on their honeymoon in Mustique, that she had just married a lying bastard.

Colin was good at his job which consisted of convincing people that the best place to put their savings was not in a bank but in an investment plan that he had concocted. It wasn't a con and somehow most of the investors made a small profit on their money, most of the time. Colin, however, made a great deal of profit on all of their money all of the time. Sue had no idea how the scheme worked, she just knew that, as a couple, they were comfortably off. They lived in a house in the leafy suburbs of London. At least, she did. Colin spent all day in his office somewhere in the city and Sue stayed at home. In the evening, Colin would telephone her to say that he would have to meet a client in the West End later that night to tie up this and that and he'd probably be very late and, you know have a little drink to keep the discussion lose and that he'd more than likely sleep in the office on the couch there. He had brought a sleeping bag and travel wash kit, which he installed in the cupboard for such eventualities, he told her. Sue knew that he wasn't telling the truth but decided to go along with his little fiction as it seemed pointless not to at that time.

Things changed one day, however, when sitting at home in leafy suburbia and leafing through a copy of "Country Life" magazine she came across a lovely little cottage in a pretty village, which was up for sale.

When Colin came home, unusually for him that same night she, tentatively, broached the subject: It might suit them better if they had a little place in the real countryside as opposed to the pretend countryside of suburbia and perhaps it would be an idea if he got a small flat in the centre of London; save sleeping in that uncomfortable office. He'd feel a lot fresher that way to do his business. He could come down to the country at the weekends and they could spend some quality time walking the lanes and having a drink in the local pub on a Sunday lunchtime. Colin looked at his wife and she looked back at him. They were both more than aware of what was being said.

'Are you sure, darling?' said Colin, 'Won't you be dreadfully lonely out in the sticks on your own?'

'I'm lonely in bloody suburbia, Colin,' hissed Sue.

'Well, all right,' said Colin, probably a little too hastily, 'If you like, we'll sell this place, then, I suppose you'd best start looking for your rural idyll.' He couldn't resist a little dig.

'Oh, I think I've already found it,' said Sue, 'I thought I'd go down there and look at it tomorrow.'

'I'm not free tomorrow, darling,' said Colin, pouring himself a drink, 'I'll probably have a late one, in fact.'

'Oh, I don't need you to come. I'd sooner drive down on my own, anyway.' Sue gave a little smile.

'Right,' said Colin, a little hesitantly, 'Right well, you seem to have it all worked out; jolly good.' He poured another whisky. For once he felt that he wasn't in control of the situation, which made him feel uneasy. Sue felt his unease and gained, tremendous, pleasure from it. Colin thought it best not to protest too much. She knew he wouldn't. Perhaps it was for the best. *A jolly good thing, really,* he thought. Sue knew exactly what he was thinking.

And so, the next morning, Sue drove to the village and looked around the cottage. On an impulse, she put in an offer there and then, which was accepted immediately.

'Big mistake, darling, big mistake,' said Colin the next evening, shaking his head and sucking in air through his teeth. 'You should have left it a few days and then put in a low offer.'

'I didn't want to wait a few days, Colin. I liked the place, in fact, I loved it and I wanted to pay them what they were asking. We can afford it, can't we? I mean we have more than enough money,' she said.

'But that's not the point, honey, is it? They were probably asking a great deal more than it's worth. That's what estate agents do. Haggling is all part of the game.'

'I'm not playing a bloody game. I'm buying a cottage; my cottage,' snapped Sue.

'Your cottage? Our cottage, surely. My money paying for it.' Colin was back to the whisky.

'Don't be such a prick, Colin.'

'Darling, I just think,' he tried to take her hand but she pulled away.

'I don't give a fuck what you think. I've bought the cottage and that's that. Don't you understand? Buy yourself a little bachelor pad and you're free, my darling.' This "my darling" was said with a snarl, 'You're free to offer whatever price you like on your shag pad in Mayfair, or wherever, I don't give a damn.'

'Shag pad?' said Colin with all the hurt in his voice which he could muster, 'Shag pad? Is that what you think I'm going to get?'

'Colin, don't say another word, for God's sake credit me with a modicum of intelligence. You get your little place and stay up there all week. All I ask is that, at the weekends, we, at least, give the impression of behaving like a civilised married couple. Is that understood?'

'Whatever you say, darling,' agreed Colin, not quite sure that he liked the thought of being given "carte blanche" by his wife to play around. Surely part of the fun was fooling the old girl. It made the illicit more alluring.

'Oh, and by the way Colin, the cottage has two bedrooms. Yours is the smaller one.' And on this piece of news, Sue crossed to the drinks cabinet and helped herself to a large whisky.

And so the marriage continued, five days off, two days on. Or should that be two days making it look to all those around them that it was on? Not that it was really fooling anyone, because, apart from everything else, Sue never tired of telling the whole village what a philandering shit her husband was.

And then there was Colin's investment business. Sue could tell that all was not going well there but Colin, of course, denied anything was wrong when asked about it. She tried to do it gently; she tried to ask in a way that a perfect wife would ask. She could see that Colin was hurting inside and although she despised him for his behaviour towards her, she wanted to understand. She wasn't worried about the money. She had insisted when they married that he paid money into her own account which he was unable to have access to and this was in a very healthy condition. Financially because of her forethought they had nothing to worry about unless Colin found a way to raid it, which she had no intention of letting him do, while she was still alive, anyway. As for Colin's business account, she had no idea how healthy that was.

She found out however when he left his briefcase open one Sunday evening before driving back to London. On top was a letter. Its subject was the winding up of the company. It had gone under. Colin was going back to London for no other reason than to make it appear that there was still a job to go back to.

Sue decided to wait for him to bring up the subject. She would say nothing and try and be a sensitive wife, as far as she could. Who knew, perhaps the humiliation might change him; perhaps they would be able to put the past behind them and come together for the first time as husband and wife; perhaps? But he never came to her. He never told her. He would return to the cottage on a Friday evening, full of tales of this investment or that. *He must have spent all his time away thinking of the latest fiction,* Sue thought. She wanted to scream but she resisted. She didn't tackle him; she didn't pull him up on it; she didn't tell him she knew the truth. Perhaps she was hanging on to the belief that one day he'd come to his senses and tell her and say he wanted to make it better. He didn't and it wasn't.

They would go for walks in the countryside and Sue would tell him all the gossip in the village; just meaningless tittle tattle; she'd hardly come up for breath as she didn't want to hear Colin's lies about his week. They would go to the pub for a drink on a Sunday and mingle with the locals. It wasn't long before Colin would tell her that he was just going to pop out for a while on a Saturday evening. He would drive off to some place and not return until after midnight smelling of cheap perfume. Sue surmised that he'd found a bar or two to go to in the nearest town where a young woman would be prepared to listen to the exploits of this handsome and outwardly successful man. He would, undoubtedly, buy some drinks for which every female that attached herself to him and then be taken off for a little drive to somewhere secluded for a quick knee-trembler in the back of the car.

She had no qualms in imparting her husband's nocturnal exploits to anyone who'd listen. Soon everybody had heard about it for the umpteenth time and were no longer listening. Sue cried herself to sleep most nights, especially on a Saturday when he was supposed to be there.

It was around this time that Colin started talking to Philip Bennett, the new owner of the Old Rectory. They would chat away, downing a few pints and it was during one of these chats, when they were both well lubricated, that Sue overheard Philip admitting to Colin that he found her rather attractive. She was standing at the bar, a little away from them listening to Alice witter on about something or other. She didn't turn around but looked up at Colin's reflection in the bar mirror. At first it looked to her that Colin was a little put out by this but then she noticed her husband's head turn. She followed his gaze as it came to rest on Bennett's wife. He was looking at her backside as she leaned over to talk to someone or other.

'Well, your missus looks a real sexy little minx,' she heard him reply.

Sue threw back her drink and ordered another as the two men laughed behind her.

Rumour started to get around that Philip and Sarah Bennett were holding little parties at the house. The word "Swingers" started to be banded around the village. The village, in turn, tried to close its ears and eyes to such goings-on. Colin, who did not really feel himself a member of the village in any real sense, did not. He was intrigued. Then Bennett asked him one Sunday lunchtime; Sue had decided to give the pub a miss; whether he would like to come over to the Rectory on the following Saturday evening when they would be throwing another one of their little get togethers. Colin knew what he meant.

Colin broached the subject with Sue, at the last minute, on the following Saturday. She wanted to scream but, instead, stormed out of the cottage and into the woods to calm herself down. She genuinely wanted to kill him and not for the first time. She let her mind play on how she could do it without getting caught.

When she returned home, Colin told her that he needed to go out. She didn't say anything. She watched him get in his car and drive off and assumed that he had gone to the nearest town and tart in a bar. It hadn't dawned on her until the Sunday morning, when she was summoned to the village hall by Alice, that her husband had spent the night less than three hundred yards from her cottage and was now dead.

Sue finished cutting up the pig carcass and wrapped it in a black bin-liner.

———————

Chapter 12

In the study, Ryan and Kylie were looking at Philip Bennett's computer. As with most people Bennett had not bothered to put any personal security on it so Ryan was able to get online without any difficulty. This state of affairs rather peeved Ryan as he was looking forward to showing that he could crack the code, firstly because he was under the impression that he was good at cracking codes and secondly because Kylie was sitting next to him and he wanted to show her how clever he was. He needn't have worried though as, no matter what, Kylie already thought that Ryan was clever by just knowing how to turn a computer on. Kylie was really rather an old-fashioned girl who believed that it was the right thing for her sex to behave as if they knew nothing and allowed men to do things for them.

'The thing I'm looking for is the website which he used to advertise the orgies,' he told Kylie. He tried a few alternative web names like Bennettorgies.com or villageshenanigans.com but pornographic sites kept popping up and not the one he was looking for.

'What about oldrectoryparties.com?' asked Kylie.

'Oh, I wouldn't have thought it would be called that,' replied Ryan with a snort of laughter.

'But it says it here,' said Kylie, pointing to a post-it note stuck to the corkboard on the wall in front of them. Ryan looked up at the sticker and wished he had seen it first. He tapped in the address and within a second a photograph of the Old Rectory with the words: 'Old Rectory parties for people who like to have some fun with other people.'

'What happens now?' asked Kylie.

'I need to get into the administration part and see if I can clear down the account. It will have all sorts of security and passwords and stuff which I'll have to get past. This is going to be difficult, so I will need to concentrate.' Ryan turned to Kylie and put his hand up as if to say, 'Complete silence, please, a genius at work.' He typed in settings and found his way blocked with the phrase: enter password. He typed in "oldrectory" but that wasn't it. Then he entered "swingers" but, again he was refused entry. Also, the words that he hoped would not appear, appeared: "You have had two attempts out of four."

'What does that mean?' asked Kylie.

'It means that if I can't find the password by the fourth attempt I'll be locked out and I won't be able to close it down,' snapped Ryan then instantly groaned and banged his head with the heal of his hand, rather over theatrically, 'Of course,' he said, 'Idiot. It's always this.' And he proceeded to type in the word: password. He was blocked for the third time. 'Shit!'

'Ryan?' said Kylie. She had never heard him use a horrible word like that before. She didn't like horrible words, even though she knew that if she became an actress, she might have to say such words if the writer had put them in a play. She thought though she wouldn't have to say them if she became a nun. At least she didn't think so.

'Sorry,' said Ryan. His heart was beating fast now. He knew he had only one more chance. If he failed the others would realise that he was not as clever as he liked to think he was. His hand hovered over the keys of the computer.

'Shagfest,' said Kylie suddenly.

'Kylie!' said Ryan, shocked.

'I think the password is "shagfest",' replied Kylie, not thinking she had said a horrible word.

'Why would it be shagfest?' asked Ryan.

'Because it says it up there,' she said pointing to another post-it sticker.

Ryan looked to where her finger was pointing. The sticker bore the legend: "P/W shagfest". Ryan paused and then looked down at the keyboard and taking a deep breath slowly and deliberately typed the word: shagfest. The password prompt disappeared and he was allowed access to the website's settings.

'Phew!' he said, trying not to sound too relieved.

Kylie waited for a moment for Ryan to say "Thank you" to her, but he didn't, which made her heart sink a little. She so didn't want Ryan to be like other boys but at that moment she feared that he might be.

'Thanks,' said Ryan after a long pause.

Kylie wanted to kiss him but didn't. Ryan was hoping that she might give him a little kiss in the cheek, but she didn't. Both of them sat for a moment, deflated, staring at the screen and not sure what to do next.

106

'What happens now?' asked Kylie, breaking the silence.

'I have to tell the administration that I want to close down the site.'

'Do you mean that you have to talk to someone?'

'No, I just need to type in some instructions and just in case it doesn't clear properly I'm going to clear the pages of all the content first,' said Ryan, turning to Kylie, 'Get rid of everything which may give away the fact that this place was where the parties were held.'

And with that, his fingers dashed confidently over the keys. Page after page of the website appeared and then vanished into thin air. Photographs of bedrooms with manacles and black satin sheets were consigned to the trash can, in much the same way as, hopefully, the real contents of the rooms were being consigned to rubbish bags.

Within a couple of minutes all that remained of oldrectories.com was the name. Ryan typed in the last few instructions and the screen asked if he wanted to terminate the site permanently. Ryan typed "yes" and the legend "Goodbye" appeared then shrank away into oblivion.

To make sure that it had gone, Ryan typed in the website name again and was told that the domain name was free and not in use. Ryan punched the air and looked at Kylie. Would she kiss him on the cheek now? She did and they both blushed as Chantry entered the study.

'Do I take it that you've succeeded?' she asked.

'Yes,' replied Ryan, 'Easy.'

'He's very clever, Miss Bowman-Leggett,' said Kylie proudly.

'I'm sure you both are,' said Chantry with a smile.

───────────

Chapter 13

Alice lay in her bed. It was the first time in her life that she had lain in bed after eight in the morning, except for when she had whooping cough as a child. She felt tired, confused, a little ashamed and very happy all at the same time. Getting up she took a long deep bath, pouring in more bath cream than she ever done before and luxuriated in the bubbles until the water became too cold for her to stay in any longer. Changing into fresh clean clothes, she pottered off down to the Old Rectory. Her legs felt very light and floaty and she experienced a tingling sensation in regions which weren't polite to talk about.

She found Chantry around the back of the house hanging a rug over a washing line. Next to her was a broom handle.

'Ah, Alice,' said Chantry, not at all surprised to see her and straightening the rug, 'Just in time, give this a good banging will you and return it to the study when you've got all the dust out.'

'Yes, of course, Chantry,' said Alice, taking the broom from her.

'Oh, and Alice,' said Chantry as she started to walk back to the house, 'Jolly well done. You must tell me all about it later over a cup of tea.' Chantry gave her small friend a wink and was off. Alice bashed the rug hard and the dust flew up into her face and all over her clean clothes. She was, she feared, back in the real world and a morning in paradise just a memory.

Upstairs in one of the bedrooms, Neil had finished unscrewing the various manacles along with leather fur-lined straps and was busily filling the holes before applying a coat of paint.

'I don't know if I can match this red,' said Neil as Chantry entered.

'Oh, I think we should get rid of all these hideous vibrant colours, don't you?' said Chantry, 'Magnolia throughout I would say.'

'It'll take at least four coats of magnolia to cover this,' said Neil, waving his hand around a very red room.

'Well, I'm sure you must have gallons of the stuff.'

'And who's going to pay for it?' said Neil, 'I'm not a bloody charity.'

'Neil, a four-gallon tin of paint isn't going to break the bank; not at your usual hourly rate anyway,' said Chantry.

'It's going to take a couple of days to neutralise these rooms. I can't do it for nothing,' he said.

'But you're not going to be doing it for nothing, are you, Neil? You're going to be doing it for the good of the village.'

Neil closed his eyes in exasperation and Chantry wandered off downstairs to see how the rest of the clear-up operation was taking shape.

Penny was pushing around the vacuum cleaner in a half-hearted way. Molly Cox and Jane Fox, on the other hand, were removing every ornament and dusting every surface to within an inch of its life.

In the kitchen Sue was washing up all the wine glasses and tumblers along with the plates.

'I hope you are all wearing gloves. Penelope?' Penny was not wearing gloves. All the others were. 'We don't want to be leaving our fingerprints all over the shop now, do we? Should the police come snooping around, Penny, how would you explain your dabs all over that vacuum cleaner?'

Penny sighed and pulled the arm down on her cardigan and wiped the handle and continued pushing it aimlessly around the room with the sleeve stretched down over her hand.

Once the lounge was done, the cleaners moved into the next room and started again in an attempt to make the house spick and span.

Chantry took a last look around and declared herself satisfied that the room looked and smelt like a normal lounge where nothing unseemly could have happened. Everything looked in place, except a small rug in front of the fireplace which, Chantry noticed, was a little askew. She bent down slowly to adjust it by flicking the corner. As she did so something laying beneath it caught her eye. She picked it up. It was an envelope with the words "To whom it may concern" written across it, in rather a shaky hand. She looked at the envelope and then up at the mantelpiece above the fire. It occurred to her that the envelope had been placed against the ornamental clock and a gust of wind had blown it to the ground where it had worked its way under the rug as these things have a tendency to do. After looking at it for a moment or two, Chantry quickly pushed the envelope into her cardigan pocket, straightened the rug properly and continued her inspection of the room.

By the end of the afternoon, every surface, every doorframe and handle had been wiped down and polished. Every carpet, rug and curtain had been vacuumed. Every piece of evidence that the Old Rectory had been a den of iniquity, as Chantry saw it, less than twenty-four hours earlier had been consigned to black bin bags; a line of which were now standing like sentinels by the back door to be disposed of somehow. Neil had filled every hole in every wall and had started to magnolia the whole of the upstairs with the help of George. Ryan and Kylie, after they had finished emptying cyberspace of oldrectories.com, helped in any way they could to finish the clear up.

Clapping her hands, Chantry brought all the workers together in the fading afternoon light.

'You are all to be congratulated on an excellent job, so far,' she said.

'So far?' exclaimed Penny.

'I'm afraid we haven't quite finished yet and when we have, we will have to remember to be on our guard at all times until we know the coast is clear. Even then, I fancy, mum will still have to be the word,' stated Chantry, 'The bedrooms need a few more coats of paint so George and Susan, I think you should be in charge of that. I suggest you get on with it in the morning and then it will be out of the way. Neil will supply the paint. Neil tomorrow afternoon you'll be able to make a start on walling the Monks' Cell. Penny will help you.'

'I bloody won't,' said Penny, 'Do you honestly think that I'm going to heave bloody great stones about?'

'Yes, Penelope, I do.' Chantry's eyes bore into her. 'Frankly you have no choice unless you want to spend the rest of your days in Holloway Prison with a bunch of lesbians as you so succinctly put it earlier today.'

Penny looked at Neil for sympathy and he put his arms around her.

'I,' continued Chantry, 'will find the Reverend Martin in the morning when he comes down to the church and inform him what we have done and ask him to say a few, well-chosen, words over their remains before you consign the doorway to history, Neil.'

'You're going to tell the vicar?' asked George. 'Is that wise?'

'Probably not, George, but I feel that we owe the deceased a little dignity in death.' She looked over towards Sue.

'I'm not sure any of them deserve it,' said Sue, proudly.

'Maybe not, but we are not heathens, are we.' Chantry took a breath. 'Listen, everyone, I realise that what we have done today may not seem ethical and there is no point in pretending that it isn't totally illegal but you must understand that the good name and standing of this village was and is at stake here and we mustn't allow ourselves to doubt that now. What we have done today is for the best, no matter how much we might not feel that at this moment. We have gone too far on our journey to be able to turn back now. Thank you one and all. I, for one, need to have a cup of tea and a nap.' At which, Chantry ushered the workforce out of the house and taking a key out of her pocket, locked the front door.

'Where did you get that key?' asked George.

'Oh, I've always had one. The locks are the originals. This key has been in my family for centuries.'

She smiled and tottered off down the gravel drive. Her head was throbbing by the time she got back to her cottage and she poured herself a glass of water to pop a pill.

———————

Chapter 14

Jane Fox and Molly Cox walked back from the Old Rectory to the little cottage that they had shared for many years.

'Did we do something really bad?' said Jane.

'Well, it looks like we murdered thirteen people, Jane,' said Molly, 'I think that may count as very, very bad.'

'Worse than selling our bodies?' asked Jane.

'Even worse than that,' replied Molly.

Since arriving in the village, many years before, the locals assumed they knew everything about Molly Cox and Jane Fox's relationship to each other. At that time, of course, they were not old ladies but two very attractive women in their early to mid-thirties. Without fanfare, the two of them set up home and kept themselves very much to themselves. To the villagers it was obvious they were a lesbian couple and the less said about that the better.

Only the villagers were wrong. Jane Fox and Molly Cox had slept with, or at least had sex with, more men than all the other female inhabitants of the village had put together. They were prostitutes or were until they stole all the money from their pimp one night and caught the last train out of London before he found out.

They had both arrived in London in their late teens, runaways from unhappy home lives. Sleeping in hostels or on more occasions than they each cared to think about on the streets or on the benches of Kings Cross or Paddington stations, they were eventually spotted by prospective pimps. Innocent of the ways of the world Molly and Jane were quickly and easily taken in by the kindness of these male strangers and, before long, stood open mouthed, as rivals fought over which of them had more rights over the girls' futures. The winner in both of their cases was a short, bald-headed Italian called Tony.

The cover for Tony's "business" was a mini-cab service run out of a shabby building opposite the stage door of the Palace Theatre, off the Cambridge Circus in the centre of London's West End. Tony would stand outside the door, at the bottom of its rickety stairs, clipboard in hand, taking names and destinations from punters who had missed their last tube home or lived too far out of the centre of town for the black cabs to want to take them. Every night men, and it was mostly men, stood chain-smoking waiting for Tony to call their name as one of his beaten-up fleet of cars pulled up to take him off at a pre-agreed rate.

In this Tony had a reputation amongst his regulars of being fair; the more you used his service the better the rate; tourists got fleeced. On a ledge, just inside the door was a telephone, which he would answer when it rang. He'd grunt into the mouthpiece; note down a name and address; state an amount; put the receiver back on the hook and shout up the stairs.

Upstairs was a dingy room, writhing in cigarette smoke. In the corner was a makeshift counter with a large teapot, a few tea-stained mugs and a spoon on a chain. Around the edges of the room the girls sat on hard, upright chairs, waiting for the call, dressed to titillate their clients tastes. Occasionally, a man would sidle up to Tony and whisper something in his ear.

The pimp would nod and mumble something back. This was usually followed by a dumb show where the man would fane outrage at what Tony had said; Tony would shrug his shoulders and turn his back on the man; the man would then take the pimp's arm and whisper something else. After repeating the pantomime one or two times more, Tony would shake the man's hand and point a finger towards the stairs, whereupon the man would make his way up and take a look at the girls, who would look back at him with various degrees of enthusiasm. Having made up his mind which one of the girls he wanted to take away, he would come down the stairs again and inform Tony of his choice. Then as soon as the next car arrived, Tony would call the name of the girl required and she would totter down the stairs in her high heels and clip-clop across the pavement into the waiting car, the man getting in after her. Both Molly and Jane had been taken away like this many times.

As they became more experienced, Tony realised that Molly and Jane had the potential to be hired out to more discerning clients, foreign businessmen who stayed at hotels such as the Dorchester or the Hilton. These higher castes, as he liked to think of them, were spared the indignity of sitting in the upstairs room. They whiled away the night in Tony's second-floor flat which boasted such luxuries as a sofa and armchairs, a flickering black and white TV and a record player. It was here that the girls got to know each other better and would fantasise about stealing Tony's money until their revelry was broken by the telephone ringing and one of them being summoned to go off and meet a stranger. Every so often, however, the pimp would call both of them down and they would be sent off in one of the cabs together to perform what they termed as a "man sandwich". The clients, in most of these cases, were from the more exotic climes and they liked to watch the girls perform various acts on each other. At first, both of them were repulsed at such requests but the clients usually paid over the odds and they learned very quickly to squirrel away some of the extra earnings without Tony finding out. They both agreed that neither of them particularly liked cavorting around with each other on hotel beds, but they found a way of making it look convincing to the clients; so convincing, in fact, that they quickly got the reputation of being the best in London. Before long they were in great demand as a twosome. This worked in their favour on two counts, one: they were paid a great deal more money than the other girls (including generous tips) and two: the men very rarely had sex with then, having satisfied themselves and their fantasies while watching them roll about the room fondling each other.

It soon got around to the other pimps in town that these girls were a gold mine and Tony knew that to hang onto them he had to keep them sweet. They demanded that the second-floor flat be re-decorated; one of the brand-new colour televisions installed plus soft leather sofas. Between jobs they spent their time in the lap of luxury, drinking chilled champagne, smoking marijuana, snorting cocaine and plotting their escape.

They perfected the art of stealing from the clients: one of them would grab his attention whilst the other lifted various bits of jewellery, or cash that was lying about. But this was small fry. Their eye was on the main prize, the cash in the safe in Tony's office. Before credit cards all transactions were strictly cash in hand. A rate was agreed; the girls were told what they had to have in their hands before they got down to business and that cash was to be brought back and put in Tony's hand before the girls were allowed to relax.

The key to the safe was always in his pocket on a chain attached to his belt. There was no way that they could get hold of it without him knowing – except one. Sometimes around three in the morning when it was a little quieter on the street, Tony would get Peter, his rather simple-minded minder, to man the clipboard while he took a nap on one of the leather sofas. It was very rare that either Molly or Jane would be in the flat at the time.

However, one night business was slow, even for them and Tony burst into the room and threw himself onto the sofa and within seconds was snoring loudly. It was their chance. Having had a line of cocaine only ten minutes before, they were both buzzing and up for anything.

Months before Molly had purchased a packet of plasticine for this very eventuality. The two women looked at each other and took up pre-planned positions; Molly by the door, as lookout, and Jane to ease the key out of Tony's pocket and press it into the mould.

'Tony?' cooed Jane.

Tony snored loudly.

'Tony?' she said a little louder.

He snored even louder.

Slowly and delicately, Jane started to pull at the chain.

Molly had the door ajar keeping her eyes peeled for any movements downstairs. In no time, the key was in Jane's hand. She pressed it into the soft plasticine to produce a perfect imprint.

Tony shuffled.

Jane froze.

A loud snore came out of Tony's nose and Jane slipped the key back in his pocket as quickly as she could.

The next day, the two women made their way down a side alley to a locksmith who they knew would ask no questions. Within two days, they had a copy of the safe key in their hands. All they had to do now was wait; not rush; bide their time until the safe was at its fullest, a Saturday night after a big football match at Wembley Stadium. Checking the sports pages, they saw that the ideal one was only weeks away, the yearly home international match between England and Scotland. The West End would be heaving with drunken fans needing to get home; the corporate fans, staying at one of the capital's hotels, wanting sex. By the end of the night the safe would be full to overflowing and they knew that Tony wouldn't be emptying it until Monday morning. Tony's operation was seven days a week; like *The Windmill* he never closed.

Sunday was usually a slow night for Molly and Jane; their type of client tended to go off home on a Sunday morning to play "Happy Families". Hearts in their mouths, they knew the time had come to make their escape. They snorted a long line of coke for Dutch courage and making sure that Tony was busy downstairs in the street and Peter was asleep in the smoky room below, they crept into Tony's office and over to the safe. Taking a deep breath, Jane put the key in the lock and tried to turn it. It didn't budge. Molly and Jane looked at each other. The key didn't work. Molly bent down next to her friend and tried again. It moved. It was very stiff but it did move. She held the key in both hands and tried again. Success. The door opened and piles of banknotes stared them in the face. Trying to keep their cool, they placed the money in the large handbags that they had bought for the purpose. When all the money was safely hidden away, Molly locked the safe and put the key in her bag. Now was the time to make a run for it. There was a door to the fire escape down to the side alley on the first floor. They needed to get past Peter and any of the other girls sitting around. Jane went off to recce. They were in luck; all the girls were out on jobs and Peter was fast asleep. Taking off their high heels and padding their way down the stairs in their stocking feet they reached the smoky room. Gingerly they tiptoed over to behind the counter and opened the door. A cold breeze swept in stirring Peter from his slumber; they froze; Peter moved in his chair and slumped forward. They made the exit as quickly as they could.

They crept down the metal fire escape and into the side alley. They paused and looked around the corner from where the alley met the street. Popping her head around, Molly could see Tony only twenty feet away; his back was turned. Beckoning to Jane they stepped out of the alley and walked as fast as they could away from the building and turning the corner, they found themselves in Shaftsbury Avenue where they hailed a black cab and told the driver to take them to King's Cross Railway Station. Paying the cabbie with a wadge of notes from their ill-gotten gains, they bought two train tickets and hopped on the sleeper to Edinburgh.

Having spent over ten years north of the border and investing some of the money in various stocks and shares, they found that they were rather wealthy. They had bought a small house on the outskirts of the city, which, when they got it, wasn't fashionable. In the ten years, however, it trebled in value.

Neither Molly Cox nor Jane Fox had any desire for any form of relationship. They both had had quite enough sexual encounters to last them a lifetime and found that they liked to just sit around; cook; read or wander the countryside in each other's platonic company.

It was during one of these walks that Molly admitted that, although she liked Scotland, she had always dreamed of living in a cottage nestled within a little English village. Jane took her friend by the arm and agreed that she, too, would love to settle down in just such a place. And so it was, with some trepidation that they got in the little car that they had bought between them and set off back into England for the first time since that fateful night. Although they had not heard a thing and had no idea whether Tony had ever tried to look for them, they were more than a little nervous.

After touring the country for a few weeks, they found themselves in the little market town which lay about five miles from the village. In the estate agents window, they saw a photograph of the most charming little cottage and less than half an hour later found themselves in the lovely little beamed front room. Looking about the cottage, the two ladies clung to each other in excitement and before the estate agent could start his sales pitch, they stated that they would purchase the property for cash that very afternoon and asked when they could move in.

———————

Chapter 15

The Old Rectory was spick and span but still Chantry and Alice popped in to make sure they hadn't missed anything and then did another sweep around with the vacuum cleaner and wiped every surface again to make sure that no fingerprints had been missed.

'Chantry,' said Alice, 'If the police should come around and they dust for prints,' Alice watched a lot of detective dramas on the television and so knew the jargon, 'won't they find it suspicious that there isn't even one to be found, including the owners?'

'Let us just hope they think that Mrs Bennett was a fastidious cleaner,' replied Chantry, 'but we mustn't worry about that for now. Better for the police to think that than to find our fingerprints all over the shop.' And with that, she closed the front door with her hand wrapped in a handkerchief.

They walked out into Church Lane and breathed in the clean country air.

'Now Alice, I see the vicar hasn't arrived yet,' said Chantry with a smile, 'so I think it's time we had that cup of coffee and you can tell me all about your morning with Constable Dealey.'

Alice blushed and they walked arm in arm down the lane towards Chantry's cottage.

That afternoon, The Reverend Jonathan Martin was tidying the hymn books in the choir. There was really no need as they very rarely had a choir these days, except for weddings when brides insisted on hearing angelic voices on her wedding day – a luxury could cost anything up to fifteen pounds an angel.

Alice, wearing an apron and rubber gloves, was washing the church floor, but anyone looking on could tell that her heart wasn't in it today, and she nearly jumped out of her skin when the main door opened noisily and Chantry strode in.

'Ah, Vicar. I'm glad to have caught you. I was wondering if I might have a quiet word.'

The Reverend looked up to see her coming towards him. 'A quiet word, you say?'

'If you would be so kind?'

'Silence,' he said, smiling.

Chantry looked around her.

'What is it, Vicar?' she said in a hushed voice.

'What's what, Miss Bowman-Leggett?'

'What is there to be silent about?'

'Nothing. Oh, I see what you mean.' Rev. Martin let out a loud snorting laugh, which made the highly strung Alice let out a scream.

'Are you all right, Alice?' he asked kindly.

Alice nearly fainted 'I'm perfectly all right, Vicar. Thank you.'

'I'm so sorry, Miss Bowman-Leggett, I'm afraid I was having a little joke with you. I was just having a play on your words. You asked if you might have a quiet word and I said "silence". But no matter, I don't think I'm cut out to be a comedian, do you?'

'I see,' she said, not really seeing. 'Well, is now a good time?'

'Yes, of course. I was only pottering about really. Beverley has gone away for the week to see the grandchildren and I seemed to be rattling about at home, on my own. So what can I do for you?'

'Well, Vicar,' she confided, taking him by the arm and leading him towards the alter, 'I need to talk to you in your capacity as Father of our flock.'

'Shall I stand in my "Father of the Flock" pose?' he said, folding his hands like a medieval monk in prayer. 'Does this look fatherly?'

Chantry was by now a little flustered and replied, probably a little too loudly, 'Vicar, I need to make a confession.'

Alice looked up from her bucket and gave a little whimper.

'Are you sure you are all right, Alice?' said the Vicar.

'She's perfectly all right, Vicar. She's just overcome with a little too much religious fervour,' said Chantry, throwing a cross look towards Alice.

Reverend Martin gave Alice a smile.

'You keep the church spick and span, Alice, I don't know what we'd do without you. We missed you yesterday at the service. Yes, I heard you spent some time in bed.'

Alice whimpered again.

Miss Bowman-Leggett cleared her throat, noisily, to get the Martin's attention back to her.

'A confession, Miss Bowman-Leggett, I see. Well come through into the vestry. I'm afraid we don't have those boxes like our catholic friends.'

He chuckled as he took Chantry gently by the arm and led her through into the vestry, 'I know it's naughty to say it,' he continued, 'but I'm always a little amused by their little cubicles, with the priest not being able to see who is unburdening themselves. It's all meant to be secret, of course, but I'm sure in a small community the priest is bound to recognise the voice.' Here he assumed a very bad music hall Irish accent, 'Oh dear, what's Missus O'Brien been up to now?' He gave another little chuckle.

Chantry did not.

'I'm afraid, Vicar, what I have to confess is of a serious nature,' said Chantry, a little too haughtily.

Fearing he had slightly overstepped the mark The Reverend Martin gathered himself and pointed to a bench against the wall which was lined with hanging cassocks and surplices.

'Well, Miss Bowman-Leggett, you sit yourself down there and I'll sit here, next to you behind these cassocks, so I won't be looking at you.'

Chantry gave him yet another withering look, which, this time, the Reverend was unaware of as he was now obscured by a row of surplices that stank of rather stale boy.

'So tell me, what is your confession?'

Chantry clasped and then unclasped her hands and took a deep breath. Up until that point, she'd felt confident about telling the Reverend Martin everything, but now, on the point of letting it out, her confidence failed her for a moment. Sensing her unease, the Reverend tried to reassure her.

'You mustn't feel at all concerned about shocking me,' he said kindly, 'I'm very long in the tooth. In all my years as a parish priest I think I've heard just about everything.'

Chantry took another deep breath and spoke.

'Well, Vicar, there are bodies in the crypt.'

He breathed a sigh of relief. Nothing serious.

'Well, of course there are bodies in the crypt, it is the resting place of your family.'

'I am well aware of that,' said Chantry, curtly, her reluctance completely evaporating, 'what I'm trying to tell you is there are other bodies in there, also.'

Reverend Martin was a little puzzled.

'Really, I had no idea. When were they put there?'

Chantry said it quickly: 'Yesterday.'

There was an eerie silence from behind the surplices. Slowly one of them was pulled back to reveal the Vicar's worried face, 'Whatever do you mean?'

'We buried thirteen in there yesterday morning,' said Chantry, turning towards him.

Outside the vestry, Alice had made her way down the nave and was now pressed against the door trying to hear what was going on within.

'Good God. This is dreadful!' she heard the Vicar exclaim loudly.

She jumped back so far, she crashed into the altar and knocked the crucifix onto its back. Whimpering she, gingerly, stood it upright again. If nothing else had happened today, she thought, she was clearly on her way to hell.

Back in the vestry, Reverend Jonathan Martin was pacing the room in a very agitated fashion.

'What are we to do?' he muttered.

Chantry was now back on top of her subject. She knew it was time to re-take charge of events.

'I think, as the Vicar, you should give them a Christian burial.'

Martin stopped and shook his head.

'We must call the police, surely?'

'No, Vicar,' said Chantry, sharply.

'No? Why ever not?' He looked down at her, somewhat at a loss.

'Think of all our reputations, Vicar.'

'I don't understand what you're saying?'

Chantry stood and faced him.

'Think of the gossip that will go around if we are descended upon by all the police. Think what they'll dig up.'

'I'm tempted to say the thirteen bodies, but I'll refrain,' the Vicar answered almost despite himself.

Chantry continued, ignoring him.

'Do you really want the place overrun with journalists and those dreadful television news people?'

He was by now very confused.

'I'm afraid, I can't see how that matters, under the circumstances.'

Chantry looked at him. 'Can't you?'

The Reverend Martin looked back at her somewhat puzzled. Suddenly Chantry straightened herself and seemed to change her whole demeanour.

'No, Vicar, I understand your point. I'm sorry that I even thought it,' she said.

Hearing this outside, Alice became very perplexed. What was Chantry doing? Had she had a change of heart? Was she now going to the police after all?

In the vestry, The Reverend Jonathan Martin breathed an inward sigh of relief.

'That's very wise of you, Miss Bowman-Leggett.'

'Yes,' continued Chantry, 'I'm sure that Beverley will stand by you, whatever happens and dismiss all the rumours as idle tittle-tattle.'

'What? What rumours?'

'No, no. I don't know what came over me. I must do the right thing and inform the police at once.'

'Wait a moment. What are these rumours?

'Regarding you and Neville, the gardener,' she said, leaning against the cassocks.

'Me and?'

'In the potting shed.'

'In the potting shed? Miss Bowman-Leggett, I'm surprised at you. I've never...'

'Oh, I don't believe a word of it myself but these rumours have a tendency of getting out of hand. I'm sure that you'd be willing to swear on the Bible that the whole thing is nonsense.' As she said this, she placed a book into Reverend Martin's hand. 'Would you swear on the Bible?' she asked.

'This is a hymn book,' he said, looking it.

'Yes, but were it to be a Bible, would you be confident that you hadn't done anything in your life that you wouldn't want banded about the tabloids?'

The two of them exchanged glances. Chantry gave a little smile.

The door creaked open and the small two sixty-watt light bulbs were switched on to reveal: Chantry, The Reverend Martin and Alice. The Reverend, Bible in hand, was dressed in his full funeral regalia.

'I'm not sure that you needed to dress up, Vicar,' said Chantry.

'A funeral is a funeral, Miss Bowman-Leggett, however little I approve of it.'

'Will we have to sing any hymns?' asked Alice.

Chantry shook her head.

'I am the resurrection and the life: he that believeth in me, though he were dead, yet shall he live,' intoned The Reverend Martin, solemnly.

Chantry and Alice looked at each other.

'We have come here today to remember before God our brothers and sisters; to give thanks for his, I mean, their lives; to commend them to God, our merciful redeemer and judge; to commit their bodies to be buried, and to comfort one another in our grief.'

Alice sniffled.

'Steady the Buffs,' said Chantry, sternly.

Chapter 16

The village seemed to return to its normal, genteel, unassuming self. At least on the surface. Chantry and Alice met every morning after Alice had finished her bicycle ride around the boundary. When she passed the gates of the Old Rectory, she purposefully kept her eyes on the road as she did not wish to see any more dead bodies, 'Thank you very much.' Over the many cups of tea, the two women would discuss all and sundry but what neither would bring up was what had happened on that fateful Sunday, except, for one thing.

'Well, I must say, Alice, recent events have brought a certain colour to your cheeks.'

Behind closed doors of the Alexander house, George was worrying; not about bodies, but about himself. About what Chantry knew of his past. He was in two minds as to whether he should tackle her about it.

He had passed off the Sunday morning meeting of the council to his wife as just one of those ridiculous ideas that Chantry came up with from time to time. His wife knew better than to pry into any of George's affairs, so she let it be. She knew George to be a strange and secretive man when he wanted to be. George mulled over his situation and decided to leave it for a while.

'Just going for a little leg stretch,' called out George, changing his mind, almost immediately. He hadn't slept a wink all night. He just had to find out what that bloody woman knew.

'I wondered how long it would take you,' said Chantry, having waved at George to come in when he turned up at her kitchen door, 'Tea?'

'Yes, yes, thank you,' answered George, a little preoccupied.

'Make yourself comfy in the front room, dear. I'll be with you in a moment.' Chantry gestured towards the far door. He nodded and, giving a weak smile, he did as he was bidden. It wasn't, by no means, the first time that he had been in there as Chantry had convened many a village council meeting there, but he had never really taken it in. Today, however, was different.

He had, of course, noticed the shelves either side of the chimney breast that were crammed full of books. He had even commented on the fact that Chantry was an avid reader. But today a number of the spines from the books drew his attention with titles such as: "The Cold War Diaries", "Beyond the Berlin Wall", "The Cambridge Traitors" and many others. He gave a shudder.

'Here we are,' said Chantry, entering with the tea tray set out with cup and saucers, teapot and milk jug plus a sugar bowl and two plates with a slice of cake on each.

George turned and watched her as she, suddenly, faltered; her knees buckling slightly and the tray tipping at a dangerous angle. George ran to catch it as Chantry attempted to steady herself.

'Would you mind?' she said, handing over the tray. George put it on the coffee table. Chantry followed him with her eyes. He turned to her.

'Are you, all right, old girl?'

'I have these dizzy spells, but no matter, dear. You didn't come here to talk about me, did you?' answered Chantry.

'No, right. Yes, you're right.' He took a deep breath. 'Do you know everything?' he asked, rather slowly.

'I know you're Freddy Pollard.'

Hearing the name again made his blood run cold.

'And I know that you served ten years of a twenty-five-year sentence, in prison, for handing secrets over to the Soviets.'

He stared at her. His past loomed up in front of him.

'Yes, I was a spy,' confirmed George, 'that's what I was, and not a very good one at that.'

'Do take a seat,' Chantry sat herself down in one of the armchairs.

George followed by sitting in the chair opposite her.

'How did you find out?'

Chantry looked up at her bookshelves. 'As a girl I was always fond of a good yarn: Dornford Yates; John Buchan; Kipling's Great Game; The British Lion against the Russian Bear and how they both played with the Persian Cat. My reading matter was a mix of intrigue, both fact and fiction. Later in life, I became very fond of Mister Le Carre's Cold War novels, which in turn led me to delve a little deeper into the real world of espionage and Burgess and

Maclean's treachery. I came across your name many years ago; you must have still been in prison. You weren't up there with the big boys, I know that, but I remembered reading what there was about you.'

'I was only a footnote,' said George, rather wistfully. In his mind he was back many years: 'I joined the RAF, you see, because I wanted to be a pilot but my eye-sight has never been good enough. Instead, I became a Signals Officer and then was promoted to the position of a Telecommunications Officer with the Ministry of Aviation.' He looked across at Chantry.

'Go on,' she said nodding.

'After a few years they offered me a senior post in the Scientific and Intelligence branch in Germany. It was there the intelligence service recruited me. Hardly very strenuous; my job was to wine and dine the minor scientists who had jumped the Berlin Wall. The service wanted me to pick their brains for anything that might come in useful later. I was given carte blanche on the old entertainment allowance. I'm not proud of the fact, now, but I think I visited every strip joint and brothel in Bonn many times over.' George looked shamefaced.

'Sugar?' said Chantry, leaning over the tray.

'No, just milk. Thank you,' said George taking the cup from her. 'I never had a very strong character. Temptation was never that far away and I could never resist it. Most of the defectors I met had no knowledge of any use to the service and I was afraid that the top brass would eventually cotton on that they were wasting their time and money on these people and send me on my way rejoicing. So I started making information up. Inventing things. Nothing big, just a few snippets. I had enough knowledge of the sort of stuff, I knew they were looking for, to make it all sound quite genuine. So more clubs; more tarts; more booze. Then, crash. Sent back to London with no notice. Nothing was said. I wasn't pulled in and asked if I was fabricating the whole thing. The service didn't work like that. They would have had to have admitted that they had been taken in and the last thing the "powers that be" wanted was to be thought of as mugs. An airline ticket handed over in a plain envelope along with a message to report to some faceless office in Whitehall, Monday morning, that was all: A desk; a mountain of pointless paperwork; no entertainment allowance and a monstrous drinking habit that had to be satisfied.' He took a sip of his tea.

Chantry raised hers to her lips, drank and settled herself for the next instalment. George understood that he was in the confessional and that Chantry was the priest. He had never told his story to anyone and as it came out now, it seemed to him to be about someone else.

'I started drinking in a pub just off the Strand; it was up a side ally. Tiny place. Straight in there as soon after five-thirty as I could and not fall out until closing time. Money was tight, so I stopped eating and just drank. Then, one evening, Marcus introduced himself to me; Mark he called himself at first. He bought me a drink and we talked about this, that and nothing at all. Then he offered another. I protested, "My round old chap," and scrambled around in my pockets for some money. Before I could count out the loose change a large one was on the counter in front of me. "No problem, my friend," said Mark, "you can buy next time." But I never did and I started drinking with him every evening. He took me out for dinner. "Don't worry, my friend, I have a good expense account." I never really noticed the slight accent. I was too drunk, most of the time, to care. Then he hit me with it. I was insisting on buying a round and had squirrelled enough money away over a few days in order that I could pay my way, at least once. Mark nodded and allowed me to hand over the money to the barman. "We should talk, I think," he then said. "We're always talking incessant chat," I said. "I think we need to have a serious talk, my friend," he said and he pulled me over to a corner table. "You are embarrassed, I sense, that you are unable to buy me as many drinks as I buy you. Is that not so?" He smiled, I remember. It was rather a sinister smile. "We could change all that." He looked at me. I felt his eyes piercing into my head as if he was trying to see if I was going to be receptive to what he was about to say. "Yes," he said. "What do you earn a week in your job at the Ministry?" he asked. "Twenty-five pounds?" "Something like that," I said. "How would you like to double that?" He did not take his eyes off me. "How could I do that?" "Oh, it won't be hard. We'll just sit and chat just as we have done for the past few weeks, only you'll tell me what you know." "I don't know anything," I said. "Oh, I'm sure you know a lot of things." And that's how it started. What I didn't know I made up, just like I had before. Every week, Marcus, he had told me that he was Russian by now, and I would meet; every week I would chatter on about what I knew of British military intelligence and he would scribble it down in a notebook. A couple of hours a week; twenty-five pounds in an envelope; thank you very much. Then Marcus started asking for more. He asked for documents, plans; not just any old plans but specific ones. I wavered a bit, I can tell you. He said he'd up the money. Two hundred and fifty pounds, upfront. He handed over an envelope. In it was the cash and a list of what was wanted in return: It was all classified material, documents detailing missile systems and radar, stuff like that. All I had to do was photograph them and deliver the negative. They would process it. I said I doubted I could lay my hands on them but he wouldn't hear of it. I was given a list of ten drop boxes and was instructed to listen to Radio Moscow every Tuesday and Thursday evening. Each dropbox number had a song that corresponded: Number one was "Kalinka" I remember. That meant the gents' toilets at Waterloo Station, opposite platform two. "Tonkaya Ryabina" was number five, behind a large potted plant in the foyer of the Ritz Hotel. Marcus was very amused by that one; A British intelligence officer betraying his country in the middle of the opulent, bourgeois, Ritz. After a slow, tentative start, I was amazed by how easy it was to get my hands on the stuff. Filing cabinets left unlocked; offices unmanned for hours on end. I suddenly realised how much I was left in that gloomy little office on my own. As Marcus said, it was like taking candy from a baby. I would lift the documents in the morning, mostly, and then go off to lunch, briefcase in hand. Marcus had booked a room for me at a hotel around the back of the British Museum under the name of John Bull; his little joke. I would get the key; snap away at the documents; eat my sandwich and pootle off back to the office and put the material back where it came from. After a while, Marcus told me that his people were so happy with what I was giving them that they upped my money four-fold. A thousand pounds; an enormous amount of money. It was to be my downfall: I spent; I gambled and I whored.'

George looked at Chantry, 'Sorry old girl, no need for that language.'

Chantry shook her head. 'No matter. Go on.'

'It just seemed to get easier. Documents were left lying about on desks. I just took them; went off to lunch; snap, back in the office at two; documents back where I found them by quarter passed. Then I was arrested. MI5 had been watching me. They'd had a tip-off about my nightlife. How could I afford to go to the clubs I was seen at on twenty-five quid a week? "The Flamingo", "Ronnie Scott's", "The Cromwellian". Of course I hadn't been that discreet about my night-time activities to the other men in the office. The alcohol gave me a loose tongue.'

George took a sip of his tea.

'Then they set a honey trap for me at The Flamingo. Pretty girl. Very tall, I remember. All arms and legs. We drank champagne and then I invited her back to the hotel. She was reluctant at first, or made out she was, then gave in. We made love, least I did, she was being paid to make it look like she was. And I fell for her. It was the first time. I honestly thought that she might be the girl for me. Love at first sight, I suppose. She played along. She was good. She played me like a fish on a hook. Out it all came in a champagne and sex induced haze. "I'm a spy," I told her. "Not like James Bond. I steal secrets. Photograph them in this very hotel room, on this very bed." She giggled and asked me to tell her everything. She made out that she didn't believe me; told me that she thought it was all part of a game to arouse her. She said it was working and I, of course, threw caution to the wind and blurted the whole thing out: Marcus; the drop boxes; Radio Moscow, the bloody lot. She called me a fibber and we made love again. I woke up the next morning and she was gone. Before I could get up, there was a knock on the door. I threw on some clothes and answered it. I was flung to the other side of the room before the door was half open. Four men stood over me.'

'More tea, George?'

'They'd recorded the whole thing. Played back the tape to me. I tried to laugh it off. I was boasting to impress her, but they had other evidence. They had fitted some form of mini transmitter on some of the clips on the documents and tracked them to the hotel room and back, although that was kept secret at the time as they didn't want the Soviets to know that such a device had been developed. The room had been bugged for around four weeks before the sting. They had me and as you say, I got sent down for twenty-five years.'

'But only served ten,' said Chantry.

'I was a good boy inside. Completely cleaned up my act. Saw the error of my ways. Did as I was told as well as giving the authorities everything they wanted, so they let me out with a new identity and a Civil Service pension. They told me to disappear so I bought a small car and drove around the country looking for the best place to start afresh and ended up here.'

George took a sip of his tea and looked at Chantry, 'But you knew all this, didn't you?'

'Some of it. There was some article in one of the newspapers about spies and your full name was mentioned, Frederick George Alexander Pollard. It said that you had been given a new identity and were living somewhere in England.

The George Alexander caught my eye and I wondered whether if it could be you.'

'Yes, the name change wasn't very original, but I couldn't think of any better,' he agreed.

'You arrived in the October that year having been released in August. The dates fitted. I remember you were very jumpy at first and then you met Elizabeth and you seemed to relax more. Does she know all this, by the way?'

'Elizabeth? Good God, no,' he chuckled, 'She thinks I was a pen pusher at the Ministry of Defence, stamping expense chits for Junior Clerks.'

'Will you ever tell her the truth?' asked Chantry, leaning in towards him.

'What good would that do? No, I think it best to let sleeping dogs lie, don't you?' George stood up. 'Do you think very badly of me, Chantry?'

'Why ever should I?'

'I was a traitor to the country.'

'You were young and foolish. Let's put it like that. We all do things we might regret, George. We all have our secrets.'

George nodded and gave Chantry a kiss on the cheek.

'Thank you, dear lady,' and started to make his way to the door.

Chantry closed her eyes and swayed slightly.

'Are you all right?' he asked.

'Yes. Well, actually as you've been honest with me, it would only be fair for me to be honest with you.' Chantry sat back in her armchair.

'Whatever is it, Chantry? Are you ill?'

'Mortally wounded, I'm afraid,' she answered.

'How so?'

'I have a brain tumour. It's been growing a while now.' She smiled and nodded her head.

'Oh, Chantry,' exclaimed George, 'can't they do anything?'

'Yes, yes. I've been told I could go on a course of steroids, but I have no intention of doing so.'

'Why ever not, if it will help,' he reasoned.

'Delay. That's all. And the side effects, well I've read all about them and I'd rather not if you don't mind.' She held up her hand as if to say she was not moving from her decision so there was no point arguing.

'So how do you control it? Is it very painful?'

'Excruciating at times. I take a form of morphine tablets but I'm afraid their effectiveness is beginning to wane. I don't think that I'm much longer for the world.' Chantry gave a smile as if trying to reassure George that she had comes to terms with it.

'Chantry, I am so sorry,' said George.

'Well, now you know my little secret. That's one each, so we shall call it a draw?'

On his way back to his cottage the thought of telling his wife the truth kept nagging at him. Something inside his head kept telling him to unburden himself once and for all. Telling his story to Chantry was the first time that he'd actually said it out loud. The words had swum about his head a thousand times since being incarcerated in Wandsworth Prison for those ten years, but now he had aired it, he felt strangely liberated. Yes, he had said he would let sleeping dogs lie as far as Elizabeth being told was concerned but now he wondered why. *Let it go*, he thought, *she has a right to know. Yes, she has a right to know.* 'Elizabeth!' he called.

'Yes, dear?' she answered, dutifully.

'Do you have a moment?' he asked.

Well, that was a first; everything he said to her tended to be an order.

'Yes, of course, George,' she answered.

'Come into the front room if you would, dear,' he continued.

Now she was confused. This was so unlike him.

He opened the door and ushered her in. 'Now, I'm not sure how to start this, my dear, so you must forgive me if I take a run at it, so to speak.'

'Anything you say, George, dear.' She was intrigued.

'Elizabeth, this will come as a bit of a shock to you and, I don't expect you to understand straight away but,' he took a deep breath, 'I was a spy.'

His wife looked at him. She tilted her head slightly to one side and let out a sigh.

'Yes, I know, dear,' she said quietly.

'I was a traitor,' he started to say, then stopped. 'You know?'

'Yes, dear.'

'But how do you know? Did Chantry tell you?'

'Chantry? Does she know?'

'Yes. What?' George was at a loss, 'Then how?'

'You told me, dear.'

131

'Told you? When did I tell you?'

'Oh, most nights for the last 20 years, I'd say.'

'Most nights?'

'In your sleep. The whole story, over and over again.

'In my sleep?' George was aghast.

'The whole story; chapter and verse, I think the saying goes. All those nightclubs and ladies of the night and the mysterious Marcus.'

'Good God, you *do* know,' exclaimed George, 'but why have you never pulled me up on it?'

'It was all before my time. All in the past. I saw no point in worrying you about it.'

'My dear, Elizabeth.' Tears filled his eyes.

'Although there is one thing I've always wanted to ask you, now you have brought the subject up,' she said.

'What?'

'The lady in the honey trap. The one who was all arms and legs. Did you really fall in love with her at first sight?'

George looked at her. He thought for a moment then: 'Come to think of it, no. No, I don't think I really did.' He looked across at this woman he had taken for granted for twenty years and realised something. 'There's only one person I've fallen in love with and she's standing opposite me now.' He crossed over to his wife and took her in his arms. He hadn't done that for many years and, feeling her warm breath on his neck, he wondered why.

Chapter 17

In Penny Bright's cottage, Penny found it very difficult to keep her mind off events. She would watch the news and half expect her husband, the newsreader, to report that thirteen people had gone missing in a small English village and that certain members of the community were suspects in their disappearance. He didn't of course, but she could not shake off her paranoia. She lay in her bed alone, having had many vivid dreams which involved her walking down long dark corridors dressed in a grey serge suit; her hair cropped short carrying a coarse blanket with the voice of her husband echoing around her head. Around three in the morning, Neil Hardy's mobile phone would ring. It was Penny: Could he come around; she was frightened?

The first time it happened Neil tried to reason with her. 'Everything was okay. Nothing to worry about baby girl.'

He didn't really want to climb out of his bed at this time in the morning and creep along the street to her place. He knew she'd keep talking and there would be no chance of sex. He'd get up exhausted in the morning and have to do a full day's manual work. Eventually, of course, she would wear him down and he would slip on his clothes, and bleary-eyed, shuffle off down the street. As expected, she would just gabble on and it was at times like these that he was grateful that he was not married to her. *She's a great girl in the sack*, he thought, *but her conversation is somewhat limited.*

Penny had met Dan when she was an air hostess on one of the major airlines. On the long-haul flights, the "Trolley Dollies" would lay bets with each other on who could be chatted up the most by the eligible men on the flight. Penny liked to think that she possessed a certain feminine charm which appealed, and, apart from when Joanna Copstick was on her shift, Penny would win hands down. Joanna, although no great beauty, had a way with her that men liked: she was petit with short hair and rather gamin. Penny always wondered why men fancied girls who looked like boys.

On a flight to Sydney, the gloves between the two air hostesses came off. Sitting in First Class was a very attractive man. Both took a bee-line for him. Both recognised him but couldn't figure out why until Malcolm, one of the male "Dollies" filled them in.

'He's one of those reporters with the BBC. Used to be "Our Man in Washington". He would stand there talking to the camera with the White House poking over his left shoulder. He's off to do the same thing in Australia now, only this time it'll be the Sydney Opera House. I read somewhere that he's still single,' reported Malcolm, 'Ooh, look his light's flashing. He'll be wanting another whisky and soda; my turn.' And they watched as Malcolm minced down the aisle towards the man from the BBC. Both girls looked at each other. Single?

'Well,' said Malcolm on his return, 'I got the cold shoulder. The field's open to one of you two now.'

'The first one to get a date with him, wins,' said Joanna.

'You're on,' replied Penny.

At first, Joanna seemed to be getting the upper hand. He was very chatty with her, asking her how long the flight crew stayed over before flying back to the UK, that sort of thing.

'Four nights on the Oz flights,' said Joanna, 'We stay at the Sydney Hilton.'

'Really. Four nights, and what do you do during those four nights?' he asked, looking up at her. She bent down to his level.

'Shopping, mostly. Relaxing by the pool; eating out.' She gave him a wink.

'Lucky you,' he said and smiled and took his drink.

He's playing it cool, thought Joanna. *Next whisky and he's mine.* Only he wasn't. One of the other passengers who had partaken far too readily of the free champagne was feeling the after-effects as they flew at thirty-five thousand feet over the Indian Ocean. Having seen it, Penny decided to ignore it and stuck her head onto the flight deck, instead, to check whether the Captain needed anything. Joanna saw her doing this but could do nothing about it as another passenger caught her eye and pointed over to the unfortunate, who was vomiting violently into an ever-disintegrating sick bag.

Coming off the flight deck, Penny saw her chance and sashayed down the aisle towards her prey. 'Would you care for another, sir?' she asked.

'No, I'm fine at the moment,' answered the BBC man. At which point, Penny "lost" her balance and landed in his lap. As she did so, she put her hand down to save herself, right on top of his crotch. She felt it immediately stir beneath her.

'Oh, I'm so sorry. These heels,' she smiled and lifted her hand slowly off his groin. He took the hand in his and squeezed it.

'No problem.' He gazed up at her. 'I hear you all have four nights off before flying back.'

'That's correct, sir,' she answered.

'I was just wondering whether you would be free to have dinner with me tomorrow evening?' he continued.

'I'm not sure about that, sir,' she answered coyly.

'Please,' he said.

'I don't even know your name,' she said.

'Dan, Dan Baker.'

'Well, Mister Baker, on second thoughts, I'd be delighted.'

As soon as she got behind the little curtain which separated the cabin from the tiny service area, she punched the air. 'Yes, yes, yes!'

'Somebody's going to be a very tired bunny on the flight back,' said Malcolm pursing his lips.

'I certainly hope so,' said Penny, as Joanna reappeared, her hands covered in the passenger's vomit.

Penny and Dan married three months later and they settled in a smart two-storey apartment in Sydney while he did a stint as the BBC's Australian Correspondent. Every weekend was party time and Penny did not want it to end. The situation lasted for a couple of years and then Dan was asked whether he would like to take over as "Anchor" on the flagship news broadcast back in London. He said yes without consulting her. A month later they were on a flight back to the UK. Penny never forgave him and started using her maiden name and embarked on a series of casual affairs in retaliation.

They bought a flat in Kensington to be near the BBC's Television Centre and on a whim, Penny insisted that they have a little cottage in the country. To shut her up, Dan agreed and sent her off to choose one. Penny, being too lazy to look far saw the cottage in a copy of *Country Life* magazine and drove down to look at it. She could see that it needed some work done on it but the estate agent assured her that finding someone to renovate it would be no problem and introduced her there and then to Neil, who was doing some work a few doors down the street. Penny put in an offer straight away and Neil was employed on the spot. Within a couple of days of starting work, Neil was doing overtime in the bedroom.

A few weeks after the fateful weekend, Dan was due to be back in the village. Only he didn't arrive. What did arrive, however, was a letter from him which stated that, what with one thing and another, he would not be coming out to the country anymore as he had become involved with another woman and felt that it was time to stop living a lie. He informed Penny that he was not a fool and was fully aware of her relationship with Neil. It was no use denying it, he continued, and stated that it would be in her own interest not to make a fuss over the separation. He was aware, he continued, that as he was in the public eye that she could sell her story to some Red Top newspaper or another for a tidy bit of cash, but if she did this, he would fight her all the way sighting her long-standing infidelity and leave her without a bean. He finished off the letter by saying that if she kept her council, he would make sure that she was kept in the manner that she was accustomed to.

Although Penny had been cheating on her husband, she did not like the fact that he had got his retaliation in first. Penny always liked to think that she was the captain of the ship and controlled life the way she wanted to. She immediately rang Neil, who was at work trying to finish off the kitchen which had been held up because he had been busy bricking up a twelfth-century doorway, which was now, duly, concealing nearly two dozen dead bodies, and told him that she needed him back straight away. On hearing that Penny had been abandoned by her husband, Neil felt a little uncomfortable. Let's face it, he didn't want to be lumbered with her forever.

Chapter 18

It was about three weeks later that events took a turn for the worse.

Chantry was taking her mid-afternoon walk when she turned into Church Lane and saw a car outside the gates of the Old Rectory. She stopped a moment and wondered whether she should turn back but her curiosity got the better of her and she walked over to the car. It was empty. She looked towards the house and saw two men standing in the driveway, looking up at the house.

'May I help you?' said Chantry. Both men turned towards her.

'Would you be Mrs Bennett?' said the much older of the two men, in a distinctly Scottish accent.

'Certainly not,' said Miss Bowman-Leggett.

'In that case, would you know where I might find Mrs Bennett or, indeed, Mr Bennett?'

'I'm sure I have no idea as to their whereabouts,' said Chantry, rather too curtly. 'May I enquire who is asking?' She took a step towards the gates.

'My name is Inspector Lore, with an R,' said the older man, rolling the R in his name. He produced a leather wallet from his inside jacket pocket and waved his photo warrant card at her.

'I see,' said Chantry, attempting to hold off the wavering in her voice.

'And this is Sergeant Paget,' at which the younger man pulled out his ID as proof.

'Indeed,' said Chantry. 'And what would you be wanting with the Bennetts?' she asked.

'Have you seen either of them recently, Mrs...?' He stopped.

'Miss Bowman-Leggett,' said Chantry forcefully and pulling herself as upright as she could. 'No, I can't say that I have, but then again, I very rarely see them. They keep themselves to themselves,' she continued a little haughtily.

'I see,' said the Inspector.

'Why do you ask?' said Chantry, probing a little.

'I would like to have a little chat with them, that's all,' said Lore.

'They could, come to think of it, be on one of their holidays, I suppose,' said Chantry, attempting to be a little more helpful.

'On one of their holidays, you say. Now why would you think that?' Sergeant Paget chipped in.

'Merely that, if they are not at home and haven't been for a while then, I assume that they may be, that's all.' Chantry gave a smile.

'Haven't they been seen for a while?' asked the Inspector.

'I beg your pardon?' said Chantry.

'You said they hadn't been at home for a while, yet you say that you very rarely see them. So why would you think that they haven't been seen for a while?'

Chantry pulled herself together, 'I don't think that, Inspector, I was merely presenting a scenario to you that is all.'

'I see.' Inspector Lore nodded. 'Do they go on a lot of holidays?'

'However would I know?'

'You said earlier something about one of their holidays.'

'Did I? Well, they do go skiing I believe.' The vision of mummified bodies being lowered downstairs on a pair of skis came into her head

'Do they and how would you know that?' asked the Inspector, raising an eyebrow.

'I have no idea, someone must have told me,' said Chantry, attempting to wave the question away, 'It probably came up in conversation in the pub, as these things do.' She clasped her hands together as if to put in a full stop on the subject.

'Yes,' said Inspector Lore, elongating the word with his Scottish burr,

'Yes, I suppose they do.' He nodded towards Paget, and his sidekick took over for a moment.

'Could you tell me, Miss...?'

'Bowman-Leggett.'

'Miss Bowman-Leggett, did you notice anything untoward on the evening of Saturday the fourteenth or morning of Sunday the fifteenth of last month?' Paget put on his serious inquiry face.

'Untoward? In what way untoward?' asked Chantry.

'Did you notice anybody strange in the village over that weekend?'

'Strange?' Chantry gave him a withering look.

'What my Sergeant means,' cut in the Inspector, 'is did you see anybody acting strangely in the village?'

'Do you mean one of the villagers acting strangely or a stranger acting strangely?' wondered Chantry.

'Either, Miss Bowman-Leggett.'

'Well, most of the villagers, here abouts, act a little strangely at some time or another. As for a stranger doing so, I really would have no idea whether they were or not,' riddled Chantry, on purpose, with a smile.

'I am asking whether you saw a stranger or strangers here, in the village over the weekend of the fourteenth.'

Chantry paused as if to think back.

'No,' she said eventually. 'No, I can't think that I saw any strangers in the village then.'

'You see,' continued the sergeant, 'we understand, that the Bennetts threw a house party on the evening of the fourteenth.'

'Why was it someone's birthday?' Chantry was secretly rather pleased with that reply.

The Inspector gave a small laugh. 'No, it wasn't a birthday party, or so we're led to believe.'

'Oh, so what sort of party was it?' asked Chantry, with as much innocence as she could muster.

'Shall we just say it was more of an adult party,' chimed in Sergeant Paget.

'Oh, come now Paget,' said the Inspector chidingly. 'There's no need to be coy in front of the lady,' he turned to Chantry, 'Have you heard the phrase "swingers party", Miss Bowman-Leggett?'

'No, Inspector, I can't say that I have.' Chantry looked him straight in the eye.

'You mean to tell me that there's been no gossip in this tight-knit community concerning the type of parties that are supposed to have been going on in this house for quite a while, on a regular basis?'

'Oh, there's always been gossip around the village, Inspector, but even though I might look to you like the classic village busybody; a spinster who has nothing better to do than peer from behind the net curtains and whisper malicious rumours about the village, I can assure you that we are not all Miss

Marple and that I have better things to do with my days,' Chantry peered back hard at the Inspector and produced a loud 'hmm' as a full stop.

'Yes, yes, I'm sure you do, Miss Bowman-Leggett; forgive me if you thought, for a moment, that I was accusing you of being an old busybody; nothing could be further from the truth, I assure you.'

Neither she nor the Inspector believed a word of it. They exchanged weak smiles. Eventually, the Inspector looked back at the Old Rectory. 'Well, we mustn't keep you any longer. You have been most helpful, Miss Bowman-Leggett, thank you.'

'I fear I have been of little help, Inspector.' Chantry nodded.

'Good afternoon, to you,' and the Inspector would have doffed his hat, had he been wearing one. He paused and waited for Chantry to walk on, but she stayed rooted to the spot.

'Well, we must get on, eh, Paget?' Inspector Lore turned and started to walk off, back towards the house, 'We'll just take a quick look around the place,' he said sotto voce to Paget, but, obviously, not sotto enough.

'To what end?' came Chantry's voice from behind them.

Lore turned around slowly and looked at the old girl.

'Just to satisfy ourselves that all as it should be, that is all,' he answered slowly. 'Nothing specific.' The Inspector had had enough of Miss Bowman-Leggett.

Chantry grunted a wordless acknowledgement and continued on her way down Church Lane. Lore watched her until she had disappeared around the bend and then, pulling Paget by the arm, continued towards the house.

As soon as she had turned the bend, Chantry craned her neck back to see if she was clear of the piercing eyes of the Inspector. She decided that the coast was clear and made her way over to the Rectory's garden wall and peered through a gap in the hedge, which shielded the house from the lane. She could see the two detectives making their way back towards the house. There was, she knew, nothing she could do at this stage apart from warn the other conspirators to be on their guard. Her head had started to throb and she reached into her cardigan for a pill and popped it expertly. She could see that the two policemen were talking but her hearing was not as good as it was so decided to continue on her way back into the village.

'So, what do we have, Sergeant?' asked Inspector Lore slowly and deliberately.

'Sir?' said Sergeant Paget.

The Inspector did not respond immediately but started walking slowly around the outside of the house, putting his hand up to his face and looking into each ground floor window as he passed.

'I said,' he said, eventually, 'what do we have? Meaning, where are we in this investigation?' He pushed his face against the window glass and peered into the kitchen. 'We have two separate reports of married couples, whom, we are informed, separately, were supposed to be attending a party in this very house on Saturday the fourteenth of last month. We have also been informed that this was no ordinary party. Not a birthday party or an engagement party. No nothing as proper as that, but a naughty party; a swinger's party,' he turned to Paget, 'so what does that make it, Paget?'

'A bloody orgy, sir.'

'A bloody orgy, Sergeant. A bit of debauchery in the countryside.'

'Drugs, sir?' said Paget.

'Sex, drugs and rock and bloody roll, I shouldn't wonder.'

'And that nosy old cow knew nothing about it,' stated Paget.

'Aye, so she says,' mused Lore, 'So, we're informed, again by two separate sources and as far as we know, sources who have no knowledge of each other, that neither couple has been seen since they left their homes to come here for some communal "humpy pumpy". Are you with me so far, Paget?'

'Yes, sir,' said Paget.

'Good, so we pop down from the big city to this lovely quiet village to have a little chat with the owners of the house and, we surmise, the organisers of the said orgy and find,' he stopped, 'what do we find, Paget?'

'No one at home, sir,' said the Sergeant.

'No one at home, indeed, and, from what I can gather, they haven't been for some time.' The Inspector and his sidekick were now outside the French windows, both with their faces hard against the glass and peering in. 'What do you see, Paget?'

'A sitting room,' said the Sergeant.

'A lounge, Paget, is what you see, and a suspiciously clean and bloody tidy one,' said Lore, 'what does that suggest to you?'

'I've no idea, sir,' said Paget, eventually having racked his brains, wondering what his superior was getting at.

'No, Paget, nor have I, and I don't like it.' Inspector Lore stepped back from the French windows and looked up and then away towards the lane, 'A step ladder is required, Sergeant,' continued Lore, which seemed like a non-sequitur until Paget, following the Inspectors gaze, saw a roof of a van with a ladder on the top, going down the lane towards the village.

'Stop that van, Paget, in the name of the law,' said Inspector Lore with theatricality.

Paget looked at his Inspector.

'Run Paget, run Paget, run, run, run,' said Lore.

Sergeant Paget trotted off to try and acquire the said stepladder. The Inspector followed on at a more leisurely pace. Luckily for Paget, the van pulled up in the village outside one of the cottages and Neil Hardy got out.

'Hello,' called Sergeant Paget from some considerable distance, as Neil walked around to the back of the van.

'Excuse me, sir,' said the voice, getting closer.

Neil froze as he looked up. His blood went cold as he saw two suited figures approaching him. He could recognise a plainclothes copper a mile away. As a young lad, he had come across many, on account of being an incessant, but not very successful shoplifter as a little lad. He had the urge to make a run for it but didn't.

'Good afternoon,' said the elder of the two with a Scottish accent, who was bringing up the rear. 'My name is Lore, Detective Inspector Lore, with an R and again he rolled the R in his name to emphasise its existence, 'from the city police. This is Sergeant Paget.' They both produced their warrant cards. Neil felt sick. 'I wondered whether you may be able to help us, Mister…?'

'Hardy. Neil Hardy,' Neil replied a little too loudly.

A face appeared at the pub window. Ronnie Randell had staggered over from his barstool to see what all the noise was about.

'Policemen, Samuel,' he called across to the landlord, 'Two plainclothes coppers. I thought they'd get here sooner or later.'

'What the bloody hell are you talking about,' said Sam, crossing to the window.

'It was only a matter of time,' said Ronnie as he staggered back to his stool and held up his empty glass, 'Refill, Bar Steward, I think we might need it.'

Sam shook his head and returned to behind the bar. Ronnie, he thought, was uttering more nonsense than ever these days.

Back outside, Neil was trying to compose himself.

'I have a small problem, Mister Hardy that you may be able to help me with,' said Inspector Lore.

'Me? How?' said Neil, as nonchalantly as he could.

'I am in urgent need of a ladder, the like of which as I see on the top of your van here.'

'A ladder?' Neil wasn't expecting that.

'Aye. You see, I need to look at something high up. That is to say, not at ground level. I won't bother you with the whys and wherefores at this juncture, but the loan of your ladder for ten minutes, or so, would be much appreciated.' Lore gave a little smile.

Neil felt considerable relief, at least, for a moment. He started to reach up to take the ladder off the roof when he was brought up short.

'Do you know the Bennetts at the Old Rectory, by any chance, Mister Hardy?'

Neil almost dropped the end of the ladder but caught it just in time.

'No, not really. I spoke to him a couple of times in the pub. Never spoken to her as far as I can remember. Why?' said Neil, trying not to make it sound like a speech he had rehearsed in his head a thousand times over the last few weeks.

'So you've not been invited to one of their parties, then?' inquired the Sergeant.

'Parties, what parties?' said Neil a little too hysterically.

'No, Sergeant, I don't see Mister Hardy at one of those sort of parties,' cut in the Inspector.

He said no more as Neil handed over one end of the ladder to the Sergeant.

'Have you seen Mister Bennett in the pub recently?' asked Lore, in what he liked to think of as his conversational voice.

'No, not for a few weeks,' Neil replied trying to sound just as conversational.

'No, that's right, I believe they are having a holiday – skiing, is that right?' continued the Inspector.

The words "skiing and holiday" alerted Neil to the fact that these two coppers had spoken to one of the others, and that was more than likely Chantry.

'What makes you say that?'

'Oh, only something someone else said that's all.'

'Miss Bowman-Leggett,' said the Sergeant.

'Aye, that's right, Miss Bowman-Leggett. She said that she'd been told, by someone in the pub, that the Bennetts took skiing holidays. I was merely wondering whether it was you who told her that,' continued Inspector Lore.

Neil shook his head. 'Me? No. I had no idea he went skiing, we've only passed a few words, pleasantries over a pint. Someone else must have been talking to the old girl. She knows everybody.'

'Yes, I'm sure she does,' Lore mused, almost to himself, 'Oh, by the way,' said Lore looking at the side of Neil's van, 'You have a bit missing on the "n".'

'The what?' asked Neil.

'On the "n" here. Where it says "The Handy Man" it actually reads, 'The Hardy Man.'

'That's what it's meant to say. That's my name, Hardy. It's a play on words.'

'Oh, I see,' said the Inspector, 'Each to his own, each to his own.' And so saying he grabbed the front of the ladder whilst Sergeant Paget got hold of the back and they marched off down the street towards Church Lane. 'We'll return these within half an hour, Mister Hardy,' he called, not looking back.

As soon as they were out of sight, Neil hot-footed it around to Penny's cottage to warn her and make sure she stayed calm and didn't do anything stupid.

The Inspector and his Sergeant marched into the drive and up towards the house.

'What are we going to do with the ladder, sir?' asked Paget.

'Start a window cleaning business, what do you think we are going to do with it, Paget?' replied Lore sarcastically. 'Now, I'll foot the bottom while you put them upright.' And so saying he placed his end on the ground in front of the house.

'You're going to look through the upstairs windows aren't you, sir,' said Paget, pushing the ladder into the upright position under a first-floor window.

'It's easy to see how you got your promotion to Sergeant,' said Lore through his teeth, 'If you get any cleverer, you'll overtake me in rank in no time.'

Paget decided to ignore the Inspector's sarcasm and finished making the ladder safe against the wall.

'Right, Paget, in order to conform to all the health and safety regulations that land on my desk with annoying regularity these days, place your feet on the ground at the bottom of this ladder, while I go aloft and take a shoofty through the bedroom windows.'

The Inspector was getting into his stride and was starting to enjoy himself. Sergeant Paget dutifully placed himself at the base of the ladder a little too quickly.

'Move your arse, Paget. Let me get on the bloody thing first.' And so saying the Inspector pushed Paget gently to one side and placed his feet on the first rungs and proceeded to climb. Paget duly placed his feet at the base of the ladder for the second time.

'Should we be doing this, sir?' asked Paget.

'Should we be doing what, Sergeant?' asked the Inspector, putting his hand to the side of his face and pressing his nose against the bedroom window to see in.

'Snooping around like this, sir.'

'And is that what you think we are doing, eh?'

'Well, yes, sir. Don't we need a warrant or something first,' asked Paget.

'I don't know, Sergeant, perhaps when we get back to the nick, you could look it up in the rule book and let me know; I would hate to be doing something unlawful,' said Lore, descending the ladder and pushing Paget out of the way again. 'Now stop your blathering and help me move this bloody thing over to the next window.' And on this, he grabbed hold of the ladder. Sergeant Paget followed suit deciding it was best if he kept his mouth shut and let his boss get on with it his way.

For the next half an hour or so they moved from upstairs window to upstairs window; the Inspector climbing up and down and looking through each one trying to build a picture of the house in his mind.

From what he could see every bedroom was clean, neat and tidy; beds made with what looked to him at a distance through the glass with plain white cotton sheets. Rugs were neatly placed by the side of beds. Everything just so. No clutter; no mess; no fuss.

'What did you expect to see?' inquired Paget as they lowered the ladder and made their way down the drive one of them at each end of the ladder.

'I'm not sure, Sergeant,' mused the Inspector, 'All so clean and tidy. Boringly normal, some would say. Not the sort of place by the looks of things where a bacchanalian romp would take place.'

'So where does that leave us, sir?' asked the Sergeant.

'Where does that leave us, you ask? Well, I'll tell you, my dear Paget, a trifle confused and a little bit suspicious,' said Lore, sucking at his teeth.

'Suspicious of what?'

'I have no idea, Paget and that's what's nagging me. It's all so perfect in there and from where I come from there's no such thing as perfection.'

'But surely if they've gone away on their holidays, they'd have given the house a good tidy up before they left. Wouldn't want to come back to a mess,' reasoned the Sergeant.

'Is that what you would do, Paget? Is that what you and the good Mrs Paget do before you pop off for a fortnight in Tenerife?'

'The Greek islands, usually, sir.'

'Wherever.'

'Well, yes we do. Well, my wife does,' said Paget.

'Yes, my wife does too.'

'So what's the problem, sir?' said Paget.

'We have a mystery: Two couples go missing after, we are told, they had come to this house for an evening of "how's your father?" The owners of that house have also gone absent without leave and abandon the place looking immaculate.'

'And?' Paget was at a loss.

'Too immaculate if you ask me. It's all too immaculate.' Inspector Lore was not happy. 'Paget, I feel a pint is in order,' he continued as they stood on the pavement outside the pub, 'What about you?'

'I'm driving, sir.'

'A pint won't hurt you,' said Inspector Lore.

'We're policemen, sir. I don't think it's a good idea to drink and drive,' answered Sergeant Paget.

'Noble,' said Lore as he stepped over the threshold with Paget following on behind, shaking his head.

The two plainclothes policemen walked into the Leggett Arms and up to the bar, which, not surprisingly, was empty except for Ronnie who was by now nursing his umpteenth G&T of the day.

'Good afternoon,' said Inspector Lore, as he entered.

Ronnie looked over both of them and took a sip of his gin, at which point Sam entered the bar.

'I'm so sorry gentlemen, I didn't hear you come in. What can I get you?'

'Two pints of your best if you'd be so kind,' said the older of the two.

'Not for me, sir,' whispered the younger, 'Driving.'

'Worry not, Paget. I shall drive you back for a change,' said Lore.

'In that case, should you…?'

'Shut up, Paget.'

'Yes, sir.'

Suddenly, Ronnie piped up. Sam knew that he wouldn't be able to resist, so let out a snigger as soon as Ronnie started to speak.

'I believe, gentlemen that you and I share the same profession.

'Indeed, and what would that be?' asked Inspector Lore.

'Now let me guess,' continued Ronnie. He stood, which at this late stage in the day, was not that easy. Never the less he was not to be thwarted in his desire to launch into his well-rehearsed routine.

'Watch out, it's the rozzers. Quick down this ally, they'll never think of looking down there. Blimey, it's a dead end.'

His voice changed from chirpy cockney to that of the suave young man.

'Yes, I'm afraid chaps that you've fallen into my little trap. Constable, take these gentlemen and put them in the cells at the station.'

Ronnie returned to the cockney voice,

'Oh blimey, of all the coppers to be nicked by. Just my luck Inspector. Inspector? Why he looks no more than a kid. Yeah, that's why I know him, he's the youngest ever copper in the entire country to be made Inspector. Who is he? You mean you don't know?'

Ronnie assumed the suave voice, 'Allow me to introduce myself. I'm Inspector Scotland of the Yard.'

'That's very good, sir,' said Inspector Lore, 'Well, Inspector, Scotland, is it? It's a pleasure to meet you.'

'What's all that about?' whispered Paget out of the corner of his mouth.

'I haven't a clue,' whispered back the Inspector.

'You're plainclothes boys from the city if I'm not very much mistaken,' said Ronnie, eying them up and down.

'Well done, sir. Very good, again,' replied the Inspector.

At this point Sam thought he should explain,

'This, gentlemen, is the famous Ronnie Randell, actor extraordinaire.'

Ronnie threw him a look; he didn't like being mocked.

'Mister Randell. I'm Inspector Lore, with an R and this is Sergeant Paget. So, an actor, is it?'

'A hundred years ago.' Sam smirked.

'Once an actor, always an actor, Samuel,' answered Ronnie.

Lore looked at Ronnie. 'If I'm not mistaken, you actor types can be very observant, is that correct?'

'Acting is all observation, observe, observe, observe,' said Ronnie, getting into his stride 'All life is theatre.'

'Indeed,' said Lore, 'and so, what did you observe in this village on the fourteenth and fifteenth of last month?'

Ronnie took a swig from his glass and mused a moment. 'One sees great things from the valley; only small things from the peak.' Ronnie raised his glass, as if in a toast and downed his gin.

'What's he talking about?' whispered Paget, taking a swig of his beer.

' Let a man walk steadily on a hot summer's day, along a dusty English road, and he will soon discover why beer was invented.' Ronnie winked at Paget.

'All very interesting, sir, but let me ask you again; did you see anything strange or untoward on the fourteenth or fifteenth of last month?'

Ronnie stared into the mirror across the bar at the reflections of the two policemen.

'Let me ask you gentlemen and consider what I ask you most carefully. What I ask you is this: Where does a wise man kick a pebble?' Ronnie rose from his stool.

'I don't know, sir, where does a wise man kick a pebble?' asked Lore, humouring him.

'You are the detectives, gentlemen. I shall leave you to try and work that one out, whilst I go for a jimmy-riddle,' waved Ronnie, as he staggered off towards the gents.

'I don't think we'll learn a lot from that drunk, sir,' said Paget, watching him go.

Lore sucked his teeth and looked thoughtfully into the middle distance. 'No. I'm going to have to sleep on this one, Paget.'

'You're going to have to excuse Ronnie, he tends to talk a lot of nonsense when he's had a few,' butted in Sam from across the bar.

'Is there any time when he's not had a few?' asked Lore.

'Not that I can remember,' answered Sam.

'Come, Paget, homewards,' called Lore downing his pint, almost in one and making his way to the door.

Paget took another swig of his beer and followed his superior.

Moments later Ronnie came out of the toilet still pulling up his flies. Making his way back to his stool, he looked around.

Sam watched him take his seat.

'Honestly, Ronnie, you do talk some bollocks.'

'You think so, Samuel? Let me tell you something, Bar Steward, Chesterton was right, truth is sacred, and if you tell the truth often enough, nobody will believe it.'

As the car left the village, Chantry and Alice stepped back into the street alongside, Sue, Neil and Penny.

'Let's hope that's the last we see of them,' said Penny.

It wasn't.

———————

Chapter 19

A week later, Chantry picked up a folded sheet of paper that had been put through her door. At the top was the crest of the City Police and below was typed the following message:

'It may have come to your attention that various persons who were said to have visited this area on the weekend of 14th 15th of last month have been reported missing. The Investigating Officer, Detective Inspector Lore requests your assistance in this matter and is, therefore, chairing a meeting at the Village Hall this evening at 7pm. Your attendance would be appreciated.'

Since leaving the week before, Lore had not stopped pacing around his office pondering the case, and at the same time telling Paget to keep it close to his chest.

'No idle gossip in the canteen, Paget,' he muttered.

'What do you mean, sir?'

'We don't want every Tom, Dick or Harry crawling over that place,' he continued, 'I need time to work this one out, so if anybody asks what you're working on, invent something boring.'

Before he knew it, Paget was driving Inspector Lore back to the village.

'Why are we going back there, sir?' asked Paget.

'Another couple reported missing, last seen heading off to the place. No record of the Bennetts going through any port or airport. Your own eyes, Paget, on storks from staring at CCTV footage of all the main roads in the area and no sign of their cars heading off into the sunset,' said Lore, 'and you ask me why we are going back there, Paget?' Lore's voice rose to a crescendo. 'We are going back because I'm of the firm opinion that those eight people; at least eight people; who knows how many more, were in the house doing the Hokey Cokey that weekend and didn't leave. They're still there, somewhere.'

'This isn't normal, sir,' said Paget as he started un-stacking the chairs and putting them in rows in front of the Village Hall stage.

'What's not normal about it?' asked Inspector Lore and he attempted to put up one of the trestle tables up on to the stage.

'I mean, sir, that we should have a whole team of Bobbies knocking on doors and asking questions, shouldn't we?' reasoned Paget.

'God forbid, Paget. Ouch!' yelled Lore as he trapped his finger trying to undo one of the legs on the table.

'You all right, sir?'

'Come and help me with this bloody contraption, Sergeant; it's trying to kill me.'

Paget leapt up onto the stage and unclipped the table legs and stood it upright.

'There we are; done,' said Paget.

'Don't look so smug, Sergeant.'

'And Scene of the Crime, boys. Forensics; Dogs,' continued Sergeant Paget.

'The whole bloody circus you mean,' said Lore disdainfully.

'Surely we should be combing the area?'

'With all those vans parked along the street each with their communications equipment chattering away into the uniform boy's headsets. A cacophony of squawks and white noise along with two-tones blaring in and out of the village every five minutes for no reason. Helicopters flying around and kicking up the dust. Not to mention all the television wagons with their be-suited hacks churning out their inane drivel,' Lore stared at his Sergeant. 'I prefer to do it my way, Paget. Just the two of us. You've not been with me long Sergeant and, no doubt, you'll ask for a transfer as soon as possible; everybody does. I'm a maverick, you see. The Chief knows that. Every so often he pulls me into his office and gives me a good old bollocking, but the one thing he doesn't do is sack me. Do you know why that is, Paget?'

'No, sir.'

'Because I get results. He hates to admit it; he'd much prefer it if I toed the line and played by the book, but he knows I solve cases my way, so he turns a blind eye,' explained Lore.

'But shouldn't we, at least, have some backup?' asked the Sergeant.

151

'Why, do you fear that the boogie man will come out and get yer?' The Inspector laughed.

At dead on seven o'clock, Sergeant Paget opened the Village Hall doors and looked out. There was no one in sight.

'Patience Paget,' said the Inspector, 'They'll come. Curiosity will get the better of them, you mark my words.'

In Chantry's cottage, the members of the Village Council were listening to the words of their leader:

'It is very important that we all stay calm,' said Chantry. 'The way I see it is this: the Inspector is adopting the tactic of divide and conquer. If one of us crumbles then all will be lost. Be prepared to be intimidated and bullied. Be prepared to be looked in the eye and asked about what you know. Remember, you know nothing. Remember that the Bennetts were outsiders and behaved as such. Remember that the village had no interest in their parties. Most importantly, remember that we are here to uphold the name and integrity of this village above all things.'

It was a rallying cry worthy of Churchill. Palms sweated; hearts beat faster. No one in that room doubted that they were facing the most difficult hour or so of their lives. If they could get through this evening, perhaps all would return to normal. Perhaps.

'Now I suggest we go over there in dribs and drabs. We don't want to arrive en-masse,' advised Chantry. 'Penny and Neil, you go first.'

'Are you kidding?' exclaimed Penny, 'Bugger that. I'm not sitting there any longer than I have to. Last one in; the first one out.'

'I'll go over first, Chantry,' said George, 'I'll fetch Elizabeth on the way.'

'I'll go next and take the children,' said Sue.

'We're not children,' Kylie yelled at Sue, rather hysterically. 'My breasts are almost as big as yours.'

'Sorry, yes,' said Sue, not really sure how to react to that outburst. 'Well, Ryan and Kylie, perhaps you'll come with me.'

The two teenagers nodded. Kylie blushed. Her nerves had got the better of her.

'I don't think these two should be allowed anywhere near that hall,' said Penny, looking over at the teenagers.

'They are part of this, so they have every right,' answered Chantry.

'And whose bloody fault is that?' Neil retorted.

George held up his hands. 'Now is not the time for arguments. What's done is done. Let's all save our strength for this meeting.'

'Thank you, George,' said Chantry. 'Right. Let's get on with it.'

Slowly the room emptied until it was just Chantry and Alice left.

'Oh, Chantry, I am so frightened that I'll break under the pressure,' said Alice.

'Stiff upper lip, Alice,' said Chantry, 'but if you feel your resolve slipping, I shall be very cross with you.' Chantry smiled at her friend. 'You'll be all right, dear, just stick with me.'

By the time that Chantry and Alice had made their way into the Village Hall, most of the villagers were already there. The place was far from full.

Chantry and Alice took their seats near the front in a blatant refusal to be intimidated while the others had hid away as near the back as they could.

On the stage, Inspector Lore was looking down at some typed notes. Sergeant Paget fidgeted next to him.

'How are we doing?' asked Lore, not looking up from his notes.

'Not full, sir,' said Paget.

'I think you'll find, Inspector, that those who are coming are already here,' said Chantry looking about the hall and then back at the detective.

'Really?' said Lore, looking up at her and smiling at her.

'So many are not here throughout the week, you see. This is your nucleus, so to speak. I think you'll find that we have a quorum,' continued Chantry, helpfully.

Inspector Lore got to his feet and cleared his throat. He looked about the hall. The place was stilled.

'Ladies and gentlemen, I don't intend to detain you long this evening, but I do have to speak to you on a matter of some urgency. I am sure that you are all aware that my Sergeant and I are attempting to ascertain the whereabouts of the owners of what I believe is called The Old Rectory. I understand that the owners' names are Mister and Missus Bennett. Would I be right in that?'

Nobody answered. Seats scraped on the wooden floor.

'Come now; am I right in that?' said the Inspector, a little more firmly.

'You are right, Inspector,' answered Chantry from the floor of the hall.

'Jolly good,' said Lore, almost to himself. He looked down at his notes and then walked slowly around the table and sat on the corner of it in the most casual way he could. 'It has come to my attention that three couples have gone missing since the weekend of the 14th and 15th of last month. These three couples, we have been informed, were all due to meet at the Bennetts house on the Saturday evening to take part in a "swinger's party".' He stopped and let the word swingers seep in. ' "A swinger's party". Do all of you know what that is?'

Some people nodded; others cleared their throats.

'Come now, don't be shy. We are all adults here.' As he said this, his eye caught sight of Ryan and Kylie sitting in the middle, 'Well, nearly all.'

'We're adults too, Inspector,' said Ryan defiantly. Kylie nodded in agreement. Their parents, next to them, glanced at their children.

'Of course you are,' said Lore, 'so, in that case, perhaps one of you could tell me what you understand by the word, swinger, in this context.'

Ryan thought that this was like some strange, liberated, school lesson.

'Sexual deviants,' said Ryan. His mother looked at him uncomfortably.

'Yes, I suppose that's one way of describing it,' said Lore.

'Well, they were,' piped up Kylie.

The Inspector looked down on them.

'Why do you say that, young lady?' he asked slowly.

'What?' Kylie started to blush. Her confidence was ebbing away fast.

'You said "were". Why did you say that?' Lore stared at her. Kylie's face was on fire.

'Are. I meant are. I just said "were" by mistake.'

'Are you sure about that?' pressed Lore.

'Oh, Inspector, leave the child alone,' Chantry said standing up.

'I'm not a child,' yelled Kylie somewhat hysterically. Ryan grabbed her by the arm.

'What are you getting at, Inspector?' asked Chantry, trying to pull his attention from the girl.

'What am I getting at? I'll tell you what I'm getting at. What would you say the feeling is, in this village, to the fact that sex parties take place here?'

'Are you addressing me?' asked Chantry.

'If you wish,' answered Lore.

'Whatever do you mean by that question?' asked Chantry haughtily.

The Inspector leant forward and stared at Chantry.

'Oh, come now, Miss Bowman-Leggett. Let us not pretend that this village hasn't its fair share of prejudice and prudery.'

'And what if it has, Inspector? Does that make us murderers?' Chantry stared back.

'Murderers? Have I accused anyone here of murder?' asked Lore, raising an eyebrow.

'You may have skirted around the subject, but it is clear to me that this is what you are thinking,' said Chantry.

'Eight people have gone missing; three couples from outside the village plus the Bennetts. My Sergeant here has been studying all the CCTV footage on all the major routes out of the county,' Lore beckoned Paget to look up. 'Look at his eyes, ladies and gentlemen. Look at the bags under them. That's from staring at his computer screen checking the registration numbers of thousands of vehicles, for hours on end, day after day and do you know what conclusion he's reached? That not one of the vehicles belonging to all four of these couples have been seen on any major road in the district since Saturday. He has noted them coming into the area from various directions, on the Saturday afternoon, but not leaving. Now they could have all decided to pootle off down minor B roads, I grant you, and all just fallen down a black hole, but what do you think is the likelihood of that?'

The villagers shuffled in their seats. Chantry refused to look away but she could sense that some of the co-conspirators were feeling uncomfortable.

'Miss Bowman-Leggett, I believe it was you that told me that you thought that the Bennetts had, perhaps, gone on their holidays. Skiing, I remember you saying,' said Lore.

'Well?' said Chantry.

'Well, Philip Bennett's employer granted no such leave of absence to him. In fact, Philip Bennett failed to turn up to a very important meeting on the Monday morning following the party; a meeting that Philip Bennett was meant to lead.'

Chantry smiled weakly. 'In that case, Inspector, I must have been mistaken. I'm sorry if I inconvenienced you.'

Inspector Lore grunted, stepped down from the stage and started to walk around the edges of the room.

The villagers could feel his eyes burning into the backs of their heads.

'The Wilsons Toyota vanished, the Stevens Volkswagen vanished, the Lloyds Mercedes vanished, and last but not least Philip Bennett's Porsche vanished.'

Each name dug into the soul of all the village council members. It was the first time that names had been put to the naked bodies.

The innocent villagers around the hall looked uncomfortably at each other. They, of course, had no idea about any of this. This was all most distressing.

'These people were fathers, mothers, aunts and uncles, children of aged parents.' Lore stopped by the side of Kylie and Ryan and leant down between them. 'Sexual deviants they may be, but they were also human beings.'

The two teenagers looked straight ahead. Lore paused a moment and then continued walking back to the stage.

'Let me make this very clear to you, ladies and gentlemen. It is my opinion, based on many years in the police service, that these eight people, eight people that we know of, so far that is, there may be more, that these eight people are still hereabouts. Maybe they are still alive but more than likely, they will be lying in makeshift graves somewhere.'

The innocents looked at each in shock. The guilty did their best to follow suit with various degrees of success.

'Ah, Inspector,' barked Ronnie, as he almost fell through the double doors. 'Am I too late? Have you solved the case yet?' They all turned their heads.

Lore studied Ronnie for a moment.

'Why, have you come to help, Inspector Scotland?' he asked factitiously.

Ronnie took a breath. 'Well, that depends.'

'On what?' Inspector Lore asked.

'That depends on whether you have solved my little riddle, Inspector,' said Ronnie, holding onto the back of one of the chairs to keep his balance.

'And what riddle was that?'

'Oh, honestly, Inspector. Let's try again.' He was slurring quite badly and stepped forward unsteadily. 'Where does a wise man kick a pebble?'

Chantry froze. She knew this quote.

'Oh, really, Ronnie, now is not the time for your party piece,' she said scornfully.

'Oh, shut up, you silly old cow,' he answered and made to take a step forward.

Unseen by the others, George, who was sitting on the end of the row, put his leg out into the aisle right in Ronnie's path. Ronnie fell, poleaxed, to the floor.

'Ronnie, oh dear,' said George as he leant down to help him up.

Ronnie lay on the floor of the Village Hall. His head was spinning.

'He's blotto, I'm afraid,' said George, 'Neil, old chap, help me get him home to his bed, would you?'

Inspector Lore looked on as the two men physically dragged Ronnie out of the hall.

'So what was that about?' asked Lore.

'What?' said Chantry.

'The pebble on the beach?' asked Lore.

'Oh, pay no attention to that. It is just a speech from one of the many plays he was in years ago. Some murder mystery nonsense. He comes out with it when he's drunk. He gets confused between fantasy and reality, I'm afraid; he seems to think that he's a real policeman sometimes; I have no idea what any of it means; I doubt he does. Pay no heed to him, Inspector. He's in a world of his own when he's had too many gins. We try to ignore it.' Chantry gave a weary smile.

'I see,' said Inspector Lore. *She was probably right*, he thought, *no point in wasting any more time on that.* 'So, to continue, I believe that the party goers never left this village. I believe that someone here, in this room, could very well be harbouring information as to their whereabouts and I strongly recommend that, if that is the case, they come forward as soon as possible.'

The innocent villagers looked at each other. They truly were at a loss. The village council members again tried to follow suit.

Inspector Lore looked around the room. He knew that something was being hidden. He just knew that the answer was in front of him. It was literally staring him in the face.

'Right, well, I'll not detain you any longer, ladies and gentlemen, apart from to say that my mobile telephone number is on the bottom of the letter that we put through your doors earlier.'

He stared at them menacingly:

'Should any of you wake in the night with a guilty conscience, just call me. I will have the phone on the pillow next to my ear. Call any time, I'm a light sleeper; you won't disturb me. Call me and ease your conscience. Confess what you know; you'll find I'm a good listener.'

———————

Chapter 20

'No one called then, sir?' said Sergeant Paget as he drove the two of them back to the village the next morning.

'No,' said Inspector Lore curtly.

'So what are we going to do then?' asked Paget.

'The gloves are coming off, Paget,' said Lore, as the Sergeant pulled the car into the Rectory driveway.

'If they won't come to me, I'll show this village that I mean business,' said Lore in a business-like manner, 'How are you at breaking and entering, Paget?'

'Sir?'

'A side window I think,' continued Lore firmly.

'Do we have a warrant, sir?'

'Well, I don't; do you?' Lore touched around all his pockets mockingly.

'I really don't think I can be a party to a forced entry without the relevant documentation, sir.' Sergeant Paget looked at his Inspector.

'I'll make a deal with you, Paget, I'll not think badly of you if, when we get back to the nick when you report me for unprofessional conduct or whatever the phrase is, if you just shut up, for now, about warrants and push your elbow through that pain of glass there.' Lore's spittle hit Paget in the face.

The Sergeant wiped his face with a handkerchief and looked at him. He could see that the Inspector was not in the mood to be reasoned with so he reluctantly took up a position to break the window-pane. He brought his elbow back.

'Oh, don't do that Sergeant.'

Taking his eye off the target at the last, split second, his funny bone made contact between the window frame and the edge of the wall. 'Shit.'

Inspector Lore turned around to see that Chantry Bowman-Leggett was not three feet away.

'Oh, Inspector,' continued Chantry curtly, 'there really is no need to break the window. I can locate the key for you. All you need to do is ask.'

Lore stared at her a moment.

'A key you say; and where might that be?' he asked more than a little irritated.

Sergeant Paget danced around in pain.

'Stop whimpering, Paget,' said Lore gruffly.

'Well, if they haven't moved it, it will be in the garden shed where the tools are kept,' answered Chantry, 'I'll fetch it if you wish.'

'Sergeant, stop dancing up and down like a girl and go with Miss Bowman-Leggett and see if you can find the key,' said Lore.

'Yes, sir,' groaned Paget.

Chantry led him around to the back garden and over towards a small shed. She opened the door and put her hand inside. 'Now it used to be kept hanging on a nail under this ledge.

'Yes, yes,' she said producing the key which, she had palmed out of her cardigan pocket and into her hand making it look like she had taken off one of the many rusty old nails which protruded from the under the ledge. 'Here you are, Sergeant, I think you'll find it will do the trick. This old key has been here longer than I can remember. I doubt if the Bennetts knew, know, of its existence. It would have been such a shame to damage that window; I think you'll find it is the original Georgian glass; over three hundred years old. It would be a shame to shatter it after all that time.' She handed over the key to him as he rubbed his elbow.

'Thank you, madam,' he said, between gritted teeth as Chantry grabbed him by the arm.

'Sergeant, does the Inspector really think that someone in the village has killed these people?' Chantry asked in a hushed, sincere voice.

Paget thought for a moment. He wanted to tell her that he thought Lore was losing it mind but stopped himself.

'Inspector Lore is a very experienced officer, Madam. It really isn't for me to say,' he answered diplomatically.

'Oh, it is too absurd, Sergeant,' barked Chantry convincingly. Paget secretly agreed.

'We've found what looks like the key to this door, sir,' said Paget, calling over to the Inspector.

'The proof of the pudding is in the eating, Sergeant,' said Lore. 'Well, stick it in the hole; like Cinderella's glass slipper, let's see if it fits.' Inspector Lore eyed Chantry up and down.

Paget put the key in the lock and turned it. The door un-locked.

'Thank you, Miss Bowman-Leggett, I am much obliged,' said Inspector Lore. *What's your game?* he thought. 'May I ask how you knew where to find this key?'

'As I informed your sergeant, it's been there years, untouched, as far as I know. The previous owners told me about its existence just in case of an emergency. They used to pop off to Australia to see their son every winter,' lied Chantry in a matter of fact, but completely convincing, way, 'I have a feeling though that the present owners were not, or should I say, are not aware of it being there.

'But you were, Miss Bowman-Leggett,' said the Inspector, 'You most certainly were.'

'Oh yes,' replied Chantry, looking straight back at the Inspector. Inspector Lore held Chantry's gaze for a moment.

'Gloves on Paget,' said the Inspector, 'we don't want to put our prints all over the shop. Don't move or even touch anything unless I tell you to. Understood?'

'Sir?'

'Understood?'

'Of course, sir.'

Inspector Lore sucked in his breath, 'Carry on.'

And with that, they crossed the threshold. Chantry took a step forward but Inspector Lore spotted her out of the corner of his eye.

'I'm afraid, Miss Bowman-Leggett, this house may have been a scene of a crime and I must ask you not to go any further.'

'Yes, of course,' said Chantry.

Their eyes locked for what seemed an eternity. *She's trying to play me, the old bitch*, thought Lore.

Chantry eventually nodded and made her way down the drive.

At this very moment, PC Michael Dealey had decided to make a detour to the village to take a walk around and, perhaps, pop in to see Alice. As he came down Church Lane, he spotted Chantry and pulled over and wound his window down.

'Good morning, Constable,' said Chantry.

'Miss Bowman-Leggett,' replied PC Dealey politely.

'I was surprised not to see you at that meeting last night,' said Chantry.

'What meeting?' asked Constable Deale.

'The one with the Detective Inspector. He was throwing all sorts of outrageous suggestions about,' continued Chantry, mischievously.

'Detective Inspector? Who? What sort of suggestions?' he asked.

'Oh, it's best you ask him yourself; he's in the Old Rectory now with his Sergeant nosing around the place, looking for clues.'

Constable Dealey frowned. Two plainclothes boys? 'Local detectives?' he said, having not heard there was a problem on his beat.

'City Police, I think you'll find,' said Chantry.

'City?' said Dealey. *What was City doing on his patch?*

'Something about some people going missing after visiting the Bennetts.' Chantry was sailing close to the wind but she couldn't help herself.

Constable Dealey sucked his teeth and thought for a moment. 'I'd best go take a look,' he said, a little too self-importantly. Chantry nodded and continued up the lane towards the village.

PC Michael Dealey made his way up the gravel drive and peered through the open front door.

'Hello. Hello,' he called.

'Get your bloody hands off that door frame,' bellowed a voice from inside the house which was unmistakably Scottish.

'Who the hell are you?' said Lore coming towards him.

'Police Constable Dealey, local police,' said PC Dealey.

'Well, I'm Detective Inspector Lore, City Police. So that trumps you, Constable Plod.'

The Constable could feel his gorge rising but did his best to hold it back.

'May I ask you what you're doing here, sir?'

'No, you bloody well may not,' yelled Lore, 'now bugger off.'

PC Dealey wanted to say something but thought the better of it.

'Very good, sir,' he said and turned to go, his face flushed with anger; his ears burning.

'Wait,' said Lore, 'Hold on a moment.'

PC Dealey turned around.

'Is this your usual beat?'

'Yes, sir.'

'What was your shift over the weekend, fourteenth and fifteenth of last month?' snapped the Inspector.

Dealey stopped to think for a minute. 'Early turn, sir, I think. six a.m. to two p.m.'

'Did you visit this village over that weekend?' barked Lore.

'Why sir?'

'Never mind why, just tell me.'

'Yes. The Sunday morning. I always take a tour around on a Sunday,' answered Dealey.

'Did you notice anything fishy that Sunday?' asked Lore.

'No, I don't remember anything.' Then he remembered. He was talking about that Sunday. That wonderful Sunday. That blissful Sunday.

'Well?' shouted Lore.

'No, nothing, sir,' he said, coming out of his revelry. It wasn't a lie. The fact was he hadn't driven around the village that Sunday. The only part of the village he had seen was the inside of Alice's cottage, the inside of Alice's bedroom.

'Are you sure, Constable? Did I detect a moment's hesitation before you answered me?' Lore approached him.

'Just trying to remember, sir, that's all.'

'And you remember nothing. Nothing untoward; nothing suspicious? You got out of your little panda car and wandered the mean streets of this village and you saw, nor heard, anything out of the ordinary?' Lore was now toe-to-toe with him.

'No, sir.' PC Dealey looked straight into the Inspectors eyes and said it.

'Thank you, PC Plod. You've been very helpful.' Lore turned and made his way towards the house.

'Dealey, sir.'

'What?' said Lore turning back to him. 'It's Police Constable Dealey, sir. Not Plod.'

'Thank you, Police Constable Dealey, I'll remember that.' And with this, he turned back into the house and slammed the door.

'Alice, do you remember the weekend of the fourteenth and fifteenth of last month?'

Alice was making a pot of tea and PC Dealey was sitting at the kitchen table fiddling with a biscuit. Alice had the kettle in her hand and was pouring boiling water into the pot. She screamed and put the kettle down quickly.

'What is it?' said Dealey getting up and going over to her.

'Nothing, Michael, dear. Silly me; missed the pot and poured the water over my hand. I'll just rinse it under some cold water and it'll be as right as rain in no time,' she answered plunging her hand under the cold tap as Constable Dealey kissed her on the top of her head. Alice smiled up at him. She hated lying to him but when he mentioned that weekend, she didn't know what to say. Scalding herself with boiling water was a small price to pay.

'The City boys are swarming over the Old Rectory for some reason,' said Dealey, with his arms around Alice's waist.

'City boys?'

'City police. Some obnoxious DI called Lore.'

'Oh yes, him,' said Alice staring at her hand which did appear a bit red.

'He was asking about that weekend,' he said.

'That weekend?' said Alice sounding as innocent as she could.

'Our weekend.' Constable Dealey smiled.

'Oh, yes,' said Alice.

'He was asking whether I'd seen anything suspicious. Well, I hadn't, had I; I couldn't have, could I? I was…'

It was then that Alice lunged at him and pressed her lips forcefully over his. He instantly shut up, which was the idea. She didn't want to hear about the silly City Police, she'd had enough of that last evening. She had no idea how she hadn't broken. The kiss lasted longer than any kiss that PC Dealey had ever experienced.

'Now, you don't have to dash off, do you?' she said.

'No, why?' he said.

'Silly,' she said taking him by the hand and leading him towards the steep narrow staircase. Having tasted the forbidden fruit from the tree, Alice realised that she rather liked the taste.

———————

Chapter 21

Inspector Lore came out of the house with his Sergeant behind him weighed down with the computer that Ryan had so successfully hacked into and a pile of folders with files of paper stacked, precariously, on top. The Inspector was not in a good mood.

'Right, that place is as clean as a whistle which is suspicious in itself,' mused Lore.

'And the cars are nowhere to be seen,' said Paget, 'The car registered to Mrs Bennett is still here, well there,' he said pointing over to the bright red sporty number at the back of the house.

Lore looked at him. 'As I said last night; vanished. Now, supposing my theory is right and our innocent little villagers aren't as innocent as they like to make out and they wanted to get rid of something as large as a car or four cars in this instance, somewhere around here, where would they put them?'

'Under some tarpaulins in an old barn somewhere?' said Paget, non-committedly.

'And where would you find such things, young Paget?' posed the Inspector.

'On a farm, sir.'

'Now you're working with me, Sergeant. On a bloody farm. So what do we do now?'

'Go poking about the local farms, sir?'

'And if I'm not very much mistaken and my nostrils are not deceiving me, I'd say that the one we passed down the road earlier is as good a place to start. Come, Paget.' And with this Inspector Lore made off down the driveway.

The two plainclothes policemen strode along Church Lane away from the village and towards the stench coming from Broome Farm. It would be fair to say that Sergeant Paget was not convinced by any of this.

'Do you really think that the locals have something to do with the disappearances? I would have thought that you'd put the fear of God up them last night. Surely one of them would have come forward by now?' asked Paget.

'This is a close-knit community,' said Lore, 'Which suddenly finds itself with orgies taking place on its doorstep.'

'But you can't, honestly, think they would kill a bunch of swingers, can you. I mean that's a bit drastic?' reasoned Paget.

'Ask yourself this, Sergeant, how would you deal with sexual deviation in a small English village?'

'Not by murdering people.'

'Why ever not?

'Sir?'

'When you've been a copper as long as I have Paget, you learn to discount nothing. The more outrageous the theory the more likely for it to be the truth.' And with this Lore walked on.

Paget shook his head and thought that this was becoming more like a perverted version of Sherlock Holmes story by the minute.

Turning the corner, they came to a halt and stared at the sight in front of them.

'Bloody hell,' said Paget.

Ahead stood the crumbling Elizabethan Manor House; the rotting double-decker bus and on the other side of the road a large, steaming, pile of dung.

'Come, Paget,' said Lore as he marched off towards the farm track.

'Go another step and you'll find your balls splattered over half the next county.'

A large double-barrelled shotgun was pointing straight at them. Borley Broome stood at the other end of it; his finger hovering over the trigger. Sergeant Paget stopped in his tracks but, to his surprise, Inspector Lore did not.

'Sir?' exclaimed Paget as his boss planted his stomach against the end of both barrels.

'You were saying sir?' said Lore staring straight into the eyes of the farmer.

From the farmyard Toby Broome looked on, nervously, wondering what his father would do next. He had never seen him defied before; he doubted that the old man had ever been so; would he shoot the stranger?

'My name is Inspector Lore, with an R,' he said and rolled the R dramatically to make the point, 'and this,' he continued half turning towards his side-kick, 'is Sergeant Paget.'

'I knew you were coppers, I could smell you over the stench of yonder dung heap,' growled Borley.

'You really must take a bath more often, Sergeant,' chided the Inspector again turning slightly towards Paget, who could not but wonder at his boss's calm demeanour, 'I too have noticed an odour when he is in the car with me.' He turned back to Borley, 'Now, who do I have the honour of addressing?'

'This is my land; get off it,' said Borley.

'Would that be your boy?' said Lore, looking across at Toby, 'How do you think he'd fair with his father in prison for the rest of his life for shooting a policeman at close range?'

Borley looked around at Toby.

'May I humbly suggest that you put this weapon down in order for us to have a wee chat in a civilised manner? Do that and we'll say no more about it. Deal?'

'What do you want?' said Borley, lowering the gun.

Paget made a dive to grab it but was stopped in his tracks by his Inspector grabbing his arm.

'No, no, Sergeant; trust. Trust is the name of the game, wouldn't you say, Mister...?' Lore looked over to Borley who had raised the shotgun once more and was waving it between both men. 'You have Paget's word, doesn't he, Sergeant?'

'Sir,' said Paget, not at all convincingly.

Inspector Lore smiled and Borley slowly lowered the gun once more.

'Good,' said Lore, looking from one to the other. 'Now we would like, if you would be so kind, Mister?'

'Broome. Borley Broome.'

'We would like, Mister Broome, to take a look around your farm or, more precisely, your barns,' said the Inspector.

'You got a warrant?' growled Borley.

'Do we have a warrant, Sergeant?' asked Lore turning towards him.

'Err,' said Sergeant Paget, fumbling about his person looking for anything that could look like a warrant.

'No, we don't,' stated the Inspector, bringing Paget's charade to an end.

'Then you can bugger off,' said Borley.

'But we will have one tomorrow and with a great deal more officers, to boot.' Lore gave a smile.

Borley looked between them both. 'What do you want to see?'

'Just a little poke about, that's all,' said Lore.

'Boy,' shouted Borley to Toby, 'show these two around the barns. Don't answer any of their questions, do you hear?' Toby nodded and the two detectives followed him into the first of the three large barns on the farm. They discovered that they contained a great many old tarpaulin's covering many old tractors; piles of wooden pallets; rusting metal of various shapes and sizes and even a pile of dried-out chicken dung, but no cars or bodies.

As they came out, Paget turned to his Inspector. 'You were very brave earlier sir.'

'Brave, Paget? When was I brave?' asked Lore.

'With the shotgun.'

'Oh, that wasn't bravery that was recklessness.'

'Sir?'

'If you'd have said to me this morning that I would press my stomach against a loaded shotgun, I would have laughed at you. The fact is I have no idea why I did it. I just did, which in retrospect was very stupid. You see, Paget, human beings do things all the time for reasons they don't understand. For an intelligent creature, we Homo Sapiens can do some pretty silly things, which is why, you and I, to a large extent, are in a job. If all humans behaved rationally, they wouldn't commit crimes.'

Lore put his hand on Paget's shoulder, 'As you may have noticed, Paget, I don't toe the line; don't do things by the book. I carry on, regardless of the consequences, and it gets me into all sorts of trouble but I can't help myself. I'm reckless and, no doubt, very, very stupid and one day it will rear up and bite me in the backside; one day; let's just hope that it's not today, eh? Now best foot forward, Paget,' he said stepping out along the track.

Then, as they reached the road, the Inspector stopped. 'Will you look at that, Sergeant?'

The Sergeant followed Lore's eyes and saw that they rested on the field opposite, which contained various rusting vehicles, some snuffling pigs and the huge dung heap.

'A bloody mess, sir.'

'Aye, but what do you see in the middle of that bloody mess? 'Sir?'

'What the bloody hell you staring at?' came the booming voice of Borley Broome from behind them.

'Ah, Mister Broome,' said Lore half turning to Borley, 'apart from your very large and perfectly formed pile of animal excrement, I could not help but notice a piece of your machinery.'

Borley grunted, 'What you talking about?'

'It's just the thing I'm looking for.'

'What is?' said Borley.

'Your digger, Mister Broome.'

'What you be wanting with that?'

'To borrow it if I may?' smiled Lore.

'Why?' mumbled Borley a little too defensively.

'To help me with my enquiries,' said the Inspector.

'Can you drive one of them things?' asked Borley.

'Er, no, I can't say that I can,' said Lore, 'I was rather hoping that either you or your young laddie might be able to help me there.'

'I ain't got time to do your work for you, nor's my boy. You want to borrow it, you can work the thing yourself.'

'Oh, well, never mind, it was just a thought,' said Inspector Lore before turning to his sidekick. 'Tell me, Paget, have you ever driven one of those monsters.'

'No, sir. Forgive me, sir, but what do you intend using it for?' asked Paget.

'I thought we might take up a bit of gardening,' said Lore.

'Excuse me sir, but am I right in thinking that you intend digging up the Bennetts garden with it?'

'That's what I admire about you, Sergeant, your speed of thought,' mocked the Inspector.

'Oh, come on, sir, with the greatest respect, you can't just go around digging up gardens. We need back up, sir, the forensic boys. The least we need is a bloody warrant.'

'Ah, warrants, warrants all everybody keeps asking me about are warrants. When we get back to the office, you really must look up all this legal stuff, meanwhile,' he turned to Borley, 'would you mind showing my Sergeant how to work that machine?'

'You want to borrow it, you work it out for yourself. The keys in the ignition,' answered Borley before turning and making his way to his bus. 'Put as much as a scratch on it and I'll sue the arse off you.'

'Thank you, Mister Broome,' said Lore, 'Well Paget, don't just stand there, you heard the man, the keys are in the ignition.'

The Sergeant started to open his mouth to say something but thought better of it and opening the five-bar gate made his way into the field towards the digger. He had no sooner got halfway across when he heard the farmer's voice coming from the bus doorway.

'And you be careful of my pigs.'

'I won't harm them, sir,' called Paget after him.

'You may not, but they're savage bastards, they'll have you if you're not careful,' chuckled Borley, disappearing back into the bus.

Sergeant Paget turned back to find himself surrounded by grunting pigs.

As his Sergeant struggled with the controls of the digger, Inspector Lore took in the scene that lay in front of him. He scanned the rusted wrecks for a moment and then he felt strangely drawn towards the dung heap. It wasn't just the smell. He stared at it and felt uneasy. He walked up to it and pondered for a moment, then shook his head and wandered off back to the lane.

From inside the bus, Borley Broome looked on from behind the sacking curtains. 'This copper could be dangerous,' he said, half to himself and half to his son who was standing behind him, 'we're going to have to watch this bastard.'

'I'm really not happy about this, sir,' yelled Sergeant Paget over the noise of the digger's engine as they made their way down Church Lane towards the Old Rectory.

'I duly note your concerns, Sergeant. Now shut up and concentrate on where you're driving,' yelled Lore back at him from where he was precariously perched on the footplate of the machine.

'Now if seeing us doing this doesn't put the fear of Christ through the guilty party, nothing will.' Lore laughed at his own audacity. 'Right,' he continued, as they stopped around by the back garden, 'take her up to the far corner there, I noticed there's a lot of loose soil in that area.' Lore jumped off the machine and waved Paget on.

Sergeant Paget knew that it was useless to protest so he drove the digger to the top end of the garden and after many false starts at trying to get the bucket of the machine to do what he wanted, started to dig down into the herb garden.

'I don't like it, Chantry,' said George, as they hot-footed it up Church Lane having heard the racket from their cottages.

'Now, it's important that we all stay very calm,' replied Chantry, 'and try and act as naturally as we can.'

Without stopping she marched up the Rectory driveway, with George bringing up the rear. Inspector Lore turned at their approach.

'I'm afraid you can't come onto these premises, madam,' shouted Lore over the din of the digger destroying the Rosemary and Thyme, along with all the other herbs.

'Inspector, I demand to know what is going on here,' shouted Chantry as best she could.

'Police business, madam. Please move along now,' replied the Inspector.

'I will most certainly not,' said Chantry, 'until you give me an explanation as to what you think you are doing.'

'Miss Bowman-Leggett, I must warn you that if you don't leave these premises immediately, I will have no alternative than to have you arrested.'

'On what grounds?' piped up George.

'Obstructing the police in the course of their duty.'

'Very well, but as soon as I get home, I shall be calling your Chief Constable and putting in a formal complaint regarding your behaviour,' said Chantry, as Paget paused in his digging and looked on at the ensuing argument.

'You do that, madam. I'm sure the Chief Constable would love to have a little chat with you,' said Lore, as Chantry and George made their way back down the drive.

'It's bloody working,' chuckled the Inspector to himself as he watched them stride off, 'They're bloody cacking themselves. Don't just sit there, Paget, find those bloody bodies,' he yelled. At this Chantry and George stopped in their tracks and looked at each other.

After two hours of digging up various patches of the Bennetts back garden, Inspector Lore and Sergeant Paget stood and looked at their handy work.

'Nothing sir, apart from a few potatoes,' said Paget after a pause.

Lore was in a filthy mood.

'I can smell them,' said the Inspector. Paget was certain he saw him twitch as he said it. 'I can smell them as strongly as I can smell that pile of shit down the road.'

'That's as well as maybe,' started Paget, but he didn't get a chance to finish the sentence.

'As strongly as I can smell that pile of shit down the road,' repeated Lore, but this time very slowly. 'Of course,' he chastised himself for his stupidity. 'Mount up Paget, mount up,' he continued pushing his Sergeant back up into the cab of the digger.

'Where are we going now, sir?'

'To shovel some shit, Paget, to shovel some shit.'

Paget looked at him as if he were a madman. 'I really don't think that's a good idea, sir.'

Lore stopped in his tracks, 'Why ever not, Paget?'

'That farmer's a nut case, sir. And he has a double-barrelled shotgun,' replied the Sergeant.

'That's as maybe, Sergeant, but he could be concealing that which we are seeking,' answered Lore.

'What under a pile of cow dung?'

'The perfect place to bury bodies, don't you see? A pile of steaming dung would rot a corpse in double quick time,' reasoned Lore.

'But whatever makes you think he'd do that?' asked Paget.

'Many reasons: Greed, jealousy or because he's completely bonkers,' Inspector Lore responded.

'But...' But Sergeant Paget didn't really have a but. He was just trying to delay the inevitable.

'Stop arguing and fire up that engine, Sergeant, the flesh could be falling off the bones like casseroled oxtail. We have no time to lose.' And with that, he hastened a beaten Paget into the cab of the machine.

From behind the wall of the Church, Ronnie Randell watched as the digger threw up the gravel from the drive and started on its way down Church Lane. Ronnie smiled and crossed the road towards the pub just as George was walking along the other way.

'Do you know, George, I thought that Inspector was clever, but he's not,' said Ronnie, chuckling.

George looked at him. 'What the devil are you talking about, Ronnie?'

'Do you know what? He thinks there are stiffs under Borley's shit heap,' he sniggered

George froze. 'What?'

'Just saw them driving along to dig it up,' Ronnie answered.

'Oh, God,' muttered George as he turned and made his way, hurriedly, towards Chantry's cottage.

Chapter 22

'The game's up, Chantry,' exclaimed George as he burst into her kitchen.

Chantry Bowman-Leggett woke with a start.

'Is that you, George?' she said struggling to her feet as George entered her front room.

'I'm so sorry, Chantry, but this is serious.' And he filled her in with what Ronnie had told him.

'Oh, what have I done?' she said quietly.

'What have we all done?' said George. 'When he finds those cars, we'll have the whole kit and caboodle thrown at us.'

'Oh well, in for a penny, in for a pound,' said Chantry making her way towards the door.

'You're not going down there, surely?' said George.

'Well, I'm not running away, that's for certain,' answered Chantry as she opened the back door, 'if the shit is going to hit the fan, we might as well take it full in the face.'

'Don't stop, drive straight in and get moving that lot,' bellowed Inspector Lore over the noise of the engine as they approached the gate to the field.

'What if he shoots at us, sir?' bellowed Sergeant Paget back.

'Duck!' said Lore, chuckling.

'It's not funny, sir,' replied Paget, 'I wouldn't put it past him, especially if you're right and there are bodies underneath it.'

'Then you'll die a hero, Paget and policemen from all over the country will be lining up to carry your coffin.'

Paget threw his eyes to heaven as he swung the machine into the field and towards the dung heap.

'Dig for victory,' yelled the Inspector as he jumped off the digger.

Paget plunged the digger into the steaming pile and started moving it to one side, bucket by bucket.

Borley Broome poked his head through the bus window and watched what was going on for a moment. He did not pick up his shotgun but wandered out and across the lane and into the field. Inspector Lore watched him out of the corner of his eye.

'What the fuck you think you're doing?' bellowed Borley.

Lore ignored him.

'This is private land; my land. Where's your warrant? You got a warrant?'

'I'm afraid we are fresh out of warrants for shit shovelling,' answered the Inspector, not taking his eyes off the diminishing pile of dung.

'Whatever is going on Borley,' shouted Chantry as she arrived with George bringing up the rear.

'Chantry?' said George, not wanting to draw attention to their presence.

'We're already in the shit, George,' said Chantry out of the corner of her mouth.

Inspector Lore glanced over to them and allowed himself a slight smile. He'd got them on the ropes; he was sure of it. The dung heap removed to one side, Paget started to dig the bucket into the soil.

'What do we do now, Borley?' asked Chantry.

'Wait and see,' answered Borley, unusually calm.

They watched the digger as it removed the earth and burrowed further down into the ground. Both George and Chantry flinched every time the bucket disappeared into the hole expecting any moment to hear the clang as it hit the roof of one of the cars.

And then it happened. Lore walked over to the edge of the large trench and looked down, and Paget, turning off the machine's engine jumped down to join him. George and Chantry closed their eyes and waited for the inevitable.

'I must have gone down twelve to fifteen feet, sir. The bucket won't go any deeper; nothing,' said Sergeant Paget.

'Bollocks!' Lore looked up at the onlookers, who stood stunned.

'Come, Sergeant,' he said, storming out of the field. 'They're bloody here somewhere,' he said stopping and looking Chantry in the eye, 'and I intend to find them.' He marched off down the lane, with Sergeant Paget at pains to keep up.

Chantry and George watched the two policemen disappear around the corner before turning back to Borley, who, by this time, had a huge grin across his face.

'But where are the cars, Borley? Why didn't he find the cars?'

'He's a clever bugger that Inspector,' stated Borley, 'but I can read him like a book.'

'What are you going on about?' asked George gruffly.

'You all think I'm thicker than that pile of shit over there, but I tell yer, I outwitted that bastard.'

'For crying out loud, Borley,' exclaimed George, exasperated.

'My old guts told me that he'd come and have a look under that lot, so the boy and me moved it along a bit whilst he was buggering about at the Rectory,' Borley laughed. 'That sidekick of his has put the whole lot back on top of the motors.'

They both looked at him and almost collapsed in relief. 'But how did you move it, Borley. They had the machine?' asked Chantry.

'Shovels girl, shovels. Like we used to,' grunted Borley. Chantry then did something she never thought she would ever do to Borley Broome; she hugged him and gave him a kiss on the cheek. His bristles pricked her and he stank of rotting manure but she did not care; their bacon had been well and truly saved and she was grateful, although she made a mental note to go home to wash and change as soon as she could.

―――――――

Chapter 23

The Reverend Jonathan Martin was just coming out of the church as the Inspector and his Sergeant arrived by the Old Rectory gates. He looked across and noticed that Ronnie Randell, who seemed to have been hovering around the place for the last hour or so, was making his way towards them. Curious as to what Ronnie was doing, as it was unusual for him not to be in the pub at this time, the Reverend Martin, made his way, nonchalantly, through the churchyard, looking at the aged and worn gravestones whilst keeping his ears pinned back to overhear what Ronnie was saying to the policemen.

'Ah, Inspector, just the man,' said Ronnie as they hove into view. 'How's the old investigation going? Got any clues?'

'Plenty to be going on with, sir,' answered Paget.

'Worked out my little riddle, have you?'

'I'm sorry, sir, we need to get on now,' said Paget attempting to move Ronnie, gently, out of the way.

'Where does a wise man kick a pebble? Remember?' continued Ronnie undeterred.

The Reverend Martin froze. *Oh, no,* he thought.

'Not now, sir, thank you,' said the Sergeant.

'On a beach, you silly bugger. Easy.' Ronnie laughed and took a pull on his cigarette.

Paget looked at him. 'Very good, sir. Now if you'll excuse us?'

'All right, second one. You should get this now you've got the idea. Where does a wise man hide a leaf?' asked Ronnie, smiling.

The Reverend looked on in horror. *What the hell was the silly old fool trying to do?*

'Hello, Ronnie,' called the Reverend Martin, quickly making his way over to the churchyard wall.

'Ah, Vicar, help these gentlemen out. You'll know this,' said Ronnie.

'Enough now, Ronnie. Actually, I would love to have a little chat with you if I may?' continued the Reverend.

'Nothing I'd like better, Vicar, but a little busy with the old police matters at this moment in time,' answered Ronnie before turning his attention back to the Inspector. 'Well, any idea, Inspector? Let me give it to you again, old chap. Where does a wise man kick a pebble, on a beach, where does a wise man hide a leaf?'

'I really think you should come with me now,' said the Reverend Martin rather hysterically, trying to grab Ronnie by the arm over the wall.

The Inspector looked up slowly and took in the spectacle. 'One moment, Reverend,' he said slowly.

Martin froze.

'It seems to me that you may know the answer to this gentleman's question.' Lore looked him in the eye. 'Perhaps, you could help me out here?'

The Reverend Martin wished that God would send a thunderbolt down from the heavens and blast Ronnie and the two policemen into eternity; he didn't.

'Well, sir?'

'Ah,' started the Reverend, 'I believe I do know this.'

'Really?' said Lore.

'It's a quote from a story,' Martin continued trying to string the answer out in the hope that he could think of a way of not answering the question fully. 'By G.K. Chesterton if I'm not mistaken. Isn't that right, Ronnie?'

'Absolutely, Vicar; dear old Gilbert Keith.' Ronnie smiled while pulling on his cigarette.

'Go on,' said Lore, his eyes boring into the Reverend Martin's head.

'I believe the quote goes something like, "Where would a wise man kick a pebble on a beach? Where would a wise man hide a leaf in a forest?" Yes, that's about it. Nothing more than that. Now come on, Ronnie, let me buy you a drink,' he said trying to appeal to Ronnie's natural instinct of never refusing to have a drink if he could help it.

'Wait a minute, Vicar. You forgot the last bit,' said Ronnie.

Reverend Martin's heart sank.

'No, that's all there is, Ronnie. There isn't any more,' he said trying to make a grab, once more, for Ronnie's arm.

'Don't be a silly arse, of course there is. The last bit's what the whole bloody case rests on.'

Jonathan Martin knew that a man of the cloth should not want to strangle anybody but he felt an urge to throttle Ronnie Randell there and then.

'You're mistaken, Ronnie. That's the end of it.'

'Case?' said the Inspector.

'It's how Father Brown solves the case, Inspector. It's the most important clue, without which the case wouldn't be solved,' said Ronnie pulling himself away from the Reverend and walking up to Lore, waving his finger dramatically.

'I see,' said Lore, looking over to the Reverend, 'So, Mister Randell, riddle us the last part of the clue if you'd be so kind?'

'And if a man had to hide a dead body.'

Ronnie looked over to the Reverend. 'Come on Vicar, you know this bit.'

'Yes, come on, Reverend,' said the Inspector, staring straight at Martin.

He knew there was no way out. He knew he had to answer. Pulling on all his reserves of strength he answered:

'And if a wise man had to hide a dead body, he would make a field of dead bodies to hide it in.' The words stuck in his mouth as he said them.

'A field of dead bodies,' repeated Inspector Lore, slowly as he took a couple of steps towards the churchyard wall and leant on it looking at the gravestones before him, 'to hide them in.' He sucked his teeth. 'Paget!'

'Sir?'

'Go and get that bloody digger!' he shouted letting out a laugh, which made the Reverend Martin's blood run cold.

'Why sir?' asked the Sergeant.

'To dig this lot up,' answered the Inspector with an almost maniacal gleam in his eye.

'What?' said the Reverend Martin, disbelievingly?

'Surely...' Paget did not get the chance of finishing the sentence.

'Do it!' yelled Lore, as he climbed over the wall and started pacing amongst the gravestones. 'They're here somewhere. They're staring me right in the face, aren't they? In plain bloody sight. I've got you, you bastards.'

'I really must protest most vigorously,' said the Reverend. 'This is consecrated ground.'

'Bollocks,' said Lore, turning around and grabbing the Reverend by the lapels of his jacket. 'Where are they? You know, don't you?'

'Really Inspector, I…'

'They're in this churchyard, aren't they?'

'Who are?' asked Martin as calmly as he could.

'You know damned well who.'

Paget started to climb the wall. 'Sir, I really think you should calm down a bit.'

'Be quiet, Paget,' replied the Inspector.

'No, sir, I'm afraid I can't do that.'

'Sergeant, I order you to get that digger!' screamed Inspector Lore, so loudly that his voice echoed around the village.

George and Chantry, who were making their way back up Church Lane, stopped and looked at each other.

Alice who was giving Constable Dealey a farewell kiss on the cheek as he was about to climb into his Panda car, let out a scream.

Neil Hardy, who was doing some odd jobs for Penny, stopped sawing and walked around the front of the cottage.

Mary Cox and Jane Fox, who were taking their usual afternoon constitutional, after smoking a rather satisfying joint, looked over to the policemen and then at each other:

'Should we, do you think?' asked Jane Fox.

'Do you think it a good idea?' answered Mary Cox.

'Well, we are, more than likely, responsible for this mess,' said Jane Fox.

And with that, they turned and made their way back to their cottage.

Ryan and Kylie, who were engaged in a romantic clinch in the vestry, un-entwined themselves when they heard the noise from outside.

Within minutes the whole of the Village Council was starting to converge upon the churchyard.

'Inspector, from what I can make out, you have no evidence that those poor souls, whoever they are, are still in the village,' argued the Reverend Martin following him around as he picked his way through the graves.

'True but I also have no evidence that they are not,' said Lore, noticing some loose soil in the corner near the fallen part of the wall. He knelt down and picked up a clump of earth and let it run through his fingers.

'Sergeant!' he yelled.

'Sir?' called Paget as he climbed the wall from the lane.

'Have you got that bloody digger yet?'

'No, sir,' replied Paget as defiantly as he could, making his way across to his Inspector.

'Inspector, you can't just go around digging up graveyards. They are protected by law,' argued the Reverend.

'But I am the law,' answered the Inspector, with a twinkle in his eye, 'I'm the law twice over: Lore in name and Law in deed. I am a Lore unto myself.'

The Reverend Martin stared at him. Had the Inspector gone completely mad?

'You need a licence to exhume human remains,' he explained, 'Surely you know that?'

'A licence you say? And where would I get one of those, pray? The local Post office?' asked the Inspector facetiously.

Paget looked around and noticed that half the village was now standing staring at them, 'Sir, you're making a fool of yourself.'

But Inspector Lore was in his element. He smelt victory and was determined to push his theory forward to see where it would take him. Someone would have to break.

'Making a fool of myself, am I?' he said at full volume, turning to face the crowd that had gathered by the lych gate. He slowly started to walk towards them, defiantly. 'A fool of myself,' he repeated, staring straight at the throng of villagers. 'Is that right, eh? Well, let me put this scenario to you, ladies and gentleman. What would you say if I informed you that I was of the firm opinion that it's you who are trying to make a fool out of me? What if I said that I know that you know where those people have disappeared to?' He looked from one face to another. 'Come on now. Let's have it. No point in prolonging the agony. Let's get it over with.' Lore turned to his Sergeant. 'I've got them, Paget; I've bloody got them!'

Penny dug her face into Neil's shoulder rather than meet the policeman's gaze as George looked at his feet and Sue stared back at him. She had gone from strength to strength and refused to be cowered.

Alice let out a whimper as her eyes met the Inspectors and she clung onto P.C. Dealey's uniformed arm, for dear life.

Chantry met Lore's steely gaze with defiance.

'Excuse me, sir?' Constable Dealey stepped forward. Inspector Lore whipped his eyes back to stare at him.

'Why, and if it isn't P.C. Plod?'

'P.C Dealey, actually sir,' replied the Constable, fixing him with a look, 'Do I take it, sir, that you're suggesting that the residents of this village have been complicit in murder?'

Lore stepped towards him. They were standing toe to toe. 'And what if I am Constable?'

'On what evidence, sir?' asked Dealey.

'The evidence of my gut man and the fact that they are all here looking as guilty as sin.'

The man's mad, thought PC Dealey. 'And do I also take it that you intend digging up this graveyard?' he asked.

'If I have to, yes, unless one of these good people has the sense to come forward and give me the information that I require. Do you have a problem with that, Constable?'

Chantry resisted the urge to look around at her fellow villagers.

'I must advise you, that you'd be very unwise to take such an action, sir,' PC Dealey was attempting to keep his voice from wavering.

'You must advise me, eh? Well, I'm obliged to you for furnishing me with you unsolicited advice, Constable,' Inspector Lore pulled himself up to his full height, 'And in return, let me give you some advice: Why don't you go and help an old lady cross the road and let the big boys get on with some real policing, eh?'

The uniformed Police Constable and the plainclothes Inspector stared at each other.

By this time, Chantry had made her way over to Alice. 'Alice, dear, you must get Constable Dealey away from here, immediately,' she whispered.

'Oh yes, right,' wittered Alice. 'Michael, dear?'

Constable Dealey turned to her. She gave him one of her little girl lost looks. He looked back to the Inspector and then to Alice. Haltingly, he walked back over to her. The Inspector sniggered.

'What is it, Alice?' he whispered a little crossly.

Alice looked at him. 'I really think you should get off on your rounds, dear. There's nothing to worry about. Don't get yourself involved.' She touched his arm. 'Think of your pension, dear. There's no point in getting yourself into trouble.'

'Yes, Constable,' heckled Lore, 'you pop off now.'

Constable Dealey was torn. He wanted to go over and punch Lore on the nose but knew it would be a futile gesture. He scowled at the Inspector and smiled down at Alice. Should he kiss her? He half bent towards her then thought better of it and stumbled off. Alice gave a half-smile in embarrassment. The others watched Constable Dealey as he got into his panda car and drove off.

'Gentlemen.' It was Mary Cox. She and her friend, Jane Fox were walking towards the throng; Jane was carrying a tray of empty glasses, empty that is apart from two of them and a jug of cloudy liquid.

'We were wondering,' said Jane Fox as they approached, 'whether you would all care for some refreshment.'

'Yes, it's been such a long day so we've brought you some lovely cordial,' said Mary Cox.

Jane started pouring the drink into the empty glasses and offered them around to the gathered throng whilst Mary took the two full ones and walked over to the two detectives.

Inspector Lore was at a loss at how to react to this kindness. 'That's very good of you ladies but, I'm sure we'll manage without,' he said.

'Oh, that's a shame,' said Jane Fox, 'We've squeezed the lemons ourselves.'

'And added the sugar and water,' continued Mary Cox, 'it seems a shame to have it go to waste.'

'That's very kind of you,' said Sergeant Paget, smiling, seeing this as an opportunity to defuse the situation a little, apart from the fact that his throat was as dry as a bone. 'I could certainly do with a little refreshment.'

'Oh good,' said Mary Cox, as she handed a glass to the Sergeant.

'Inspector, are you sure?' said Jane Fox.

'Oh, aye, go ahead then,' agreed Lore, rather off guard.

Both detectives downed their drinks while the village looked on. Jane Fox and Mary Cox smiled.

Chantry stood, her eyes on stalks. *Had the old girls done it again?* she thought. Chantry had sworn them to secrecy after they had told her about the fruit punch so none of the other villagers could be aware of what might be going on.

'You bloody fool, Ronnie,' whispered the Reverend Martin.

'Why's that, Vicar?' asked Ronnie, pulling on yet another cigarette.

'Why did you tell them where to find the bodies?' Ronnie stared at him a moment.

'What bodies?' he said frowning.

'The bodies in the vault. The ones you were giving him clues about,' said Martin crossly.

'What?' said Ronnie, confused. 'You mean there are dead bodies in the graveyard?'

The Reverend Martin stared at him.

'Oh, well I'm buggered,' chuckled Ronnie, 'I was just playing about, seeing if they knew Father Brown. I was only playing detectives, Vicar. Can't help myself, you see? Just having a bit of fun. I had no idea...'

The Reverend Jonathan Martin threw his eyes up to heaven as Ronnie shook his head and let out a barking laugh:

'Well, I'm buggered,' he repeated.

Mary Cox and Jane Fox took the empty glasses off the two detectives and started to make their way back to their cottage, only pausing for both of them to throw a wink at Chantry as they passed her.

'We only put three berries in this time, didn't we Molly?' said Jane Fox.

'Oh, yes. I think I must have overdone it last time,' said Molly Cox.

'We thought that if we make them feel poorly, they'll go home,' continued Jane Fox. And with that they tottered off, muttering to each other. 'Actually, Jane. I may have used four; I lost count,' said Molly Cox.

'Oh dear,' said Jane Fox.

'My memories not as good as it was, but I don't think I put any cocaine in this time.'

'Oh, that's all right, then.'

Molly stopped a moment and thought again, *Or did I?*

Chantry watched the two old women go and tried to work out what to do for the best.

Inspector Lore turned away from the group and looked across the churchyard. As he was doing this, Chantry took a deep breath and made up her mind. She summoned Ryan over to her and whispered in his ear whilst at the same time putting something in his hand. Ryan nodded and snuck off.

'Any new burials here recently; official ones, I mean?' the Inspector was asking the Reverend Martin, as he and his Sergeant started to wander about the graves, surveying the ground.

'Er, no,' said Reverend Martin, 'as you can see, we are full to overflowing. There is no more room. Sadly, over the last few years every villager we've lost has had to go to the town's cemetery.'

'So no fresh graves. In that case, where do you think we should dig first, Sergeant?' said Lore looking up at Paget. Sergeant Paget did his best to avoid the question and the Inspector's stare as he continued walking between the grave stones.

Paget belched and felt a little light-headed.

Meanwhile, Ryan had made his way out of the church, making sure that the Inspector hadn't seen him, and back over to Chantry.

'Done,' he said in his best conspiratorial voice.

'Good,' answered Chantry as quietly as she could. 'Now, you understand what you have to do?'

'Oh, yes,' said Ryan.

'Well, get yourself set up and wait for my cue,' returned Chantry, who then sidled towards Alice and whispered in her ear.

'Oh, no, Chantry, I couldn't possibly do that,' Alice whispered back to her friend.

'Nonsense, Alice. Just do as I say and everything will be sorted out,' Chantry whispered back to her.

'Oh,' whimpered Alice.

'Inspector?' Chantry stepped forward.

'So, Miss Bowman-Leggett?' started the Inspector. At first he thought he could see two of her. He blinked to regain his focus.

'The thing is, Inspector, I have to inform you that there are more bodies than just here in the churchyard.'

Lore stopped and looked at her, he was swaying a bit. 'Really, and where might they be?'

'In my family's private vault, housed within the crypt of the church,' answered Chantry matter of factly.

'Really? Well, in that case, I trust you would have no objection to taking us to have a look around?'

'None at all, Inspector. Follow me,' said Chantry.

'Paget,' called Lore, 'come with us.'

Sergeant Paget actually wanted to sit down and go to sleep, but he pulled himself together sufficiently to follow his superior.

Chantry marched on towards the church. As she did so, Alice made her way around to the back of the churchyard.

'What's she doing?' said Penny, somewhat stunned.

'God alone knows,' answered Neil, 'but she's up to something.'

'I do hope you filled that doorway in properly,' said George. 'If he finds that, we're all sunk.'

Chantry stopped at the large wooden door to the crypt and put the key in the lock. Paget plonked himself into one of the choir stalls. He took a handkerchief out of his pocket and wiped the sweat off his forehead.

'I trust Inspector, that you understand that these are my ancestors, and that you treat their remains with the utmost respect.'

'Would I do anything else, madam?' said Lore fighting the urge to belch.

'If your behaviour over the last day or so is anything to go by, the odds are heavily stacked against it.' She pushed the door open and put her hand around the corner to turn on the lights. Nothing. She clicked the switch several times. 'Oh. I'm afraid that the bulbs seem to have blown. Do you have a torch?' Chantry looked around to the two detectives.

'Torch, Paget,' snapped Lore.

'I'm afraid I don't have one, sir,' said Paget, attempting to get up.

'Bugger,' exclaimed the Inspector.

'Oh, wait a minute, sir. There's a small light thing on my mobile phone,' Paget said taking his phone from his pocket and trying to focus on the keyboard to get the correct app. A small tight white beam pierced the darkness.

'That will have to do,' said Chantry, as she started, gingerly, down the stone steps to the vault. 'Come Inspector, the steps are quite steep so be careful, I should hate anything to happen to you both,' she said, looking up at them.

The two policemen both took deep breaths and descended into the gloom.

Alice Elms entered the church via the vestry door holding something weighty tucked up under her cardigan. Quietly, she opened the door into the main body of the church and crept along to the open crypt door. She could hear Chantry talking to the detectives and heard the clank as the key was put into the lock of the Bowman-Leggett family vault. At the same time, a figure appeared from behind the pulpit. Alice jumped back.

'It's only me,' whispered Ryan.

Alice let out a sigh. She then noticed that had something growing out of his cheek.

'Microphone,' mouthed Ryan as he saw Alice peering at it.

'Oh, yes, I see,' said Alice, not seeing at all.

Ryan turned back a few steps and whispered over his shoulder, 'Stand by, Kylie.'

'Standing by,' called Kylie a little too loudly out of sight.

'Alice, is that you, dear?' called Chantry from below earlier than she had planned but trying to drown out the noise of the teenagers above.

It was her cue.

'Yes, Chantry, I just thought I'd make sure that everything was all right,' answered Alice in the most convincing way she could, which wasn't that convincing at all and then starting to make her way down the steps.

'Be careful, dear, the lights appear to have blown but the Sergeant has a little torch on his telephone.' At which, Sergeant Paget shone the light over towards the steps and straight into Alice's eyes, blinding her long enough for her to drop something from under her cardigan. The sound of a large solid object hitting the ancient stone floor echoed around the room.

'What was that?' said the Inspector, suspicious. The noise thundered through his head and he leant against one of the coffins for support.

'It's all right, Inspector, I just kicked something,' lied Alice as Chantry got herself between the beam of light to shield her friend, who was now scrambling around the floor looking for the object.

'Are you all right, Alice?' called Chantry.

'Yes. I have...I'm all right,' said Alice, retrieving the offending article and shoving it back up her cardigan front.

'Hold that bloody light still, Paget,' snarled Inspector Lore as he groped his way around the dusty decaying coffins. Paget swayed and slumped against one of Chantry's forebears trying to hold the light as steadily as he could.

'Please be careful,' called Chantry as she strained to locate Alice's whereabouts, 'most of these coffins are hundreds of years old. I don't want my ancestors' remains all over the floor.' Chantry then reached out and grabbed hold of Alice's arm as she spotted her in the spilt light coming from the torch. She could see that the two detectives were over in one of the corners, surrounded by a pile of coffins. It was now or never.

'Oh!' she said as loudly as she could. 'Oh, what was that noise?'

Above Ryan, who was peering around the crypt door, waved his hand towards Kylie whose head was popping out around the choir stalls. Kylie ran the few steps to behind the screen, which hid the sound equipment and pushed up the fader on the desk.

'Who are you looking for?' came a voice out of the darkness.

Inspector Lore and Sergeant Paget stopped.

'What the bloody hell's that?' exclaimed Lore, his eyes darting about the darkness.

'You'll never find them,' said the voice, 'you'll never find them without my help.'

'Shine the torch, Paget,' said Lore crossly. 'What's going on here?' Suddenly the gate to the vault slammed shut. The sound of the iron bars meeting echoed around the room. At the same time, the light was knocked from the Sergeants hand. The phone crashed to the floor and the place was left in darkness.

'Miss Bowman-Leggett? Come on now, enough of this nonsense,' said Lore, the noise exploding into his brain. 'You can't scare me that easily.'

'Oh, I've not come to scare you, Inspector,' answered the voice, 'I've come to help you.'

'Oh, aye,' said Lore, 'who are you then?'

'Haven't you guessed?' Ryan was getting into his role as he peered down the stairs, 'it's me, Philip Bennett.'

'That's the Rectory's owner,' said Sergeant Paget as he crawled about the floor feeling for his phone.

'I know that, Paget,' said Inspector Lore gruffly, 'but who is it really? Come on, who are you?

'You don't believe me?' the voice started to chuckle menacingly. 'You don't believe me.'

'All right, enough now. Stop this silly game. Miss Bowman-Leggett, Miss Elms come out from where you're hiding.' The Inspector cleared his throat trying his best to sound confident and assured. He was now finding it impossible to focus, but was determined not to give in to whatever it was that was happening to him.

'We must call in back up, sir,' said Paget, 'we need help, sir. I feel sick, sir. I think I've been poisoned.'

'Get a hold of yourself, Sergeant,' said the Inspector doing everything in his power not to let on that he, too, was on the verge of being violently sick. 'We can do this. We don't need anybody else. It's just you and me, Paget. He summoned up all his reserves. 'Come on, you bastard. Come out from wherever you're hiding. You're dealing with Alistair Lore!'

Chantry held onto Alice to steady her nerves as they crouched behind a pile of coffins very close to where the Inspector was standing.

'Calm yourself, Inspector. Only I can tell you where the bodies are. You do want to know where the bodies are, don't you?' Ryan now felt himself in the zone.

'All right, all right,' said the Inspector slowly, desperately trying to get his eyes to adjust. 'Okay I'll play along. Come on then, you tell me.' Lore's heart was beating so fast now he thought it would explode. His entire body was soaked in sweat.

'The far corner, the far corner on the left, there is a row coffins. Can you guess who you'll find there?'

Inspector Lore turned, and his head spun as he attempted to peer into the corner of the vault. He could make out some shapes of coffins and started to clamber towards them. A piercing scream came from below him as he felt something soft under one of his feet. Sergeant Paget writhed in agony as the Inspector put his full weight on his hand, crushing it.

'Get up, Paget,' yelled the Inspector, his temper and nerves getting the better of him.

'Christ, you've broken my hand, you crazy bastard, you stupid crazy bastard,' Paget snapped. The adrenaline rushing through his body made his head spin. He no longer thought it was attached to the rest of his body. Tears filled his eyes and he wanted to be violently sick.

'Temper, temper, gentlemen,' said the voice mockingly. 'Behind that pile of coffins, Inspector.' Ryan couldn't see where the Inspector was but he was enjoying himself too much to care.

Lore put his hands in front of him and felt his way amongst the coffins. Ryan made a calculated guess that Lore was sufficiently hemmed in by the two piles of coffins he had seen on his recce of the vault earlier.

'Just there, Inspector. You're right on top of them.'

Inspector Lore bent down to look. The last thing he heard was the sound of something hard crashing into the back of his head. The Detective Inspector fell to the floor.

'Inspector? Sir?' Sergeant Paget scrambled over the floor toward where he had heard the noise. His hand was killing him. Suddenly he felt something soft ahead of him. He groped at it; it felt like the material of a trouser leg. 'Oh, Christ!' exclaimed Sergeant Paget.

Chantry brought the large stone down onto the side of the Sergeant's head. He tried to look up but a second blow to his temple finished him off.

She groped her way up both the bodies and felt for a pulse in their necks. Neither had any signs of life.

'It's all right, Alice,' she said, trying to hide the quiver in her voice, 'All done. Nothing more to worry about.'

Alice gave a whimper and emerged from behind one of the piles of Chantry's ancestors.

'Thank you, Ryan,' continued Chantry, 'You and Kylie pack up your things and run along home. We don't want your parents worrying about you. Oh, but before you go, dear, would you be kind enough to put the light bulbs back in?'

Outside the remaining villagers waited. They had no idea what was going on. Had the Inspector found the walled-up doorway into the Monks' Cell? Had Chantry had a change of heart and told him everything? Were they all about to be carted off to prison and spend the rest of their days incarcerated? Chantry came out of the church closely followed by Alice.

'Neil, dear,' she started, 'I'm so sorry but I'm afraid that I must ask you to open up the Monks' Cell. There are two bodies in the vault that need to be deposited there. When you've done, wall it up again, if you'd be so kind.'

The others stood open-mouthed. 'Chantry, you can't mean...?' exclaimed George.

Chantry looked up at him and gave a little smile. 'Oh yes. There was only one thing I could do wasn't there. Otherwise, well the consequences hardly bear thinking about,' she answered.

'Oh my God,' said Penny, weakly.

'George, here are the keys to their car. I wonder if you could pop it up to Borley and ask him to put it with the others.' Her eyes met George's. 'Not long, now, George,' she said quietly.

'Oh, Chantry,' exclaimed George through his breath. He squeezed her hand as she handed him the key fob.

'Now if you'll excuse me,' continued Chantry, 'I feel in need of a little walk.' And saying this she tottered past them looking very frail.

She felt totally exhausted as she turned into Church Lane and started to walk away from the village but she had an unstoppable urge to walk around her domain before going home. Pausing for a brief moment, she turned back towards the church and looked at the others as they watched her in stunned silence.

'It was for the good of the village,' she said, 'the good name of the village comes above all else, you see. My family built it from scratch. I had to save it. What choice did I have? I had no choice.' She gave a weak smile, turned and walked on.

Her head was hurting badly now. Her pills were no longer working for even a moment. Tears filled her eyes as she made her way past the Old Rectory and up Church Lane to Broome Farm. She looked across the field and saw the steaming dung heap, sending its stench towards her. *Eau de Cologne*, she thought and smiled. Opposite the field stood the once beautiful house which was now just a crumbling mass. She tottered around the corner and back onto the street passing the Leggett Arms. The sign, containing the Bowman-Leggett coat of arms, squeaked above in the wind. She smiled up at it and then moved on.

Chantry Bowman-Leggett, the last in the line of the true Bowman-Leggetts, was tired now; more tired than she had ever been. She made her way home, slowly, her head pounding.

Although it was still quite early, she went about her ritual, laying the tray with tea things for the morning. She took down two cups and saucers from the dresser for her and Alice, as she always did, then, having paused for a moment and closed her eyes, she took one of the cups and a saucer back to the dresser.

Having glanced around her charming little kitchen, she made her way to the kitchen door to lock it, but then she stopped short of turning the key. Again she hesitated for a moment and then turned away and started to climb the narrow stairs to her bedroom.

Chantry Bowman-Leggett undressed herself slowly, folding her clothes, neatly, as her mother had taught her and she had done throughout her life. Sitting on the end of her bed a moment to catch her breath she proceeded to pull her nightdress over her head. Taking a few more breaths she stood up and made her way over to the window and looked out across the village below. Her eyes filled with tears once more as she stood, her own reflection in the window glass peering back at her. She stood, motionless for a while, and then with a brief smile, she wiped away her tears with the sleeve of her nightdress and shuffled over to the side of the bed and got between the sheets.

Sitting bolt upright she leaned over to the bedside cabinet and brought out an envelope. It was the one which she had picked up from under the rug. Chantry looked at the words *"To whom it may concern"*. Before taking a pen from the cabinet and a book to lean the envelope on, she wrote something on it and then put it back in the bedside cabinet. Wincing with the pain in her head, she slipped down the bed and placed her head gently on the pillow. She lay staring up at the ceiling and then very slowly her eyes began to close.

The next morning at the usual hour, Alice Elms cycled around the village and leant her bicycle against the wall of Chantry Bowman-Leggett's cottage. She made her way to the back to the kitchen door. For the first time, Chantry was not to be seen. She was not doing her usual duties of putting the kettle on the Aga. Alice looked through the glass door and called out. Then she tried the door; it was unlocked. Alice smiled to herself. *That's all right then,* she thought as she let herself in.

'Cooee, Chantry. Cooee.' Nothing came back. She looked down at the scrubbed pine table and saw the tray laid out as usual. No, wait a minute, it was not as usual; there was only one cup and saucer and not the usual two. Alice felt a little flutter around her heart. She went over to the door which led to the narrow winding staircase; she opened it and popping her head around called up the stairs. Nothing. She let out a sigh and started climbing the stairs one by one. At the top there were two doors. She had no idea which was Chantry's bedroom so she lifted the latch on one and opened the door. The room was filled with boxes and old suitcases along with a large wooden trunk with the Bowman-Leggett coat of arms carved into it. Alice closed the door gently and then put her hand on the latch of the door opposite.

She did not want to open it. She closed her eyes for a moment and took a deep breath; she lifted the latch and pushed the door a little. She called out in a whisper, 'Chantry, Chantry dear, are you all right?' There was no answer; there was no sound. Alice pushed the door until it was fully open and looked in. She could see the shape of Chantry's body lying very still in the bed.

Alice entered slowly and walked over to her.

'Chantry dear? Oh, Chantry.' Alice touched her friend's face. It was quite cold. She knew then that the final true Bowman-Leggett had breathed her last.

Alice was quite calm. She was rather surprised really how calm she actually was. She made her way downstairs to the kitchen and then outside and tottered off around the corner to George Alexander's cottage and knocked on the door. George answered.

'What is it now, Alice?' he asked quite grumpily.

'It's Chantry, George. I think she's dead.'

At that moment, George felt quite cold and lost. 'Where is she, Alice?'

'In her bed, George; I believe she must have died in her sleep.'

'Well, let us go and see, shall we,' said George gently, and so saying, took Alice's hand in his and walked her back to the cottage.

Once Chantry's body had been removed to the undertakers, Alice decided to give the place a good clean. Not that it was dirty or untidy but she wanted to make sure that everything was in its place for her friend. She persuaded the undertaker that when the formalities had been taken care of and Chantry was safely laid out, her body should be returned to the cottage in her coffin and put in the little cosy sitting room prior to being interned in the Bowman-Leggett family vault.

Alice opened and closed cupboards, dusting and sweeping. She vacuumed the stairs and the bedroom. Opening the bedside cabinet, she came across the envelope. On it was a scrawled a message to her, it said:

"Dear Alice,

Do what you think best with this. I found it on that fateful day in the Old Rectory. I know you will do the right thing.

Your friend,
Chantry."

Below were the words:

"To Whom It May Concern."

She turned the envelope over and discovered that it had not been opened. Should she open it and discover its secret? She stared down at it for a moment and then made her way downstairs. In the lounge, she walked over to the fireplace and took up the gas firelighter in her hand. She looked at the envelope and re-read Chantry's last words to her. Igniting the gas flame, Alice moved the corner of the envelope towards it and held it there until the paper was alight. She held the flaming envelope in her hand.

'Well, it doesn't concern me,' she said watching the flames lick out the words on the front. She dropped it in the grate and watched as it disintegrated into blackened dust.

As there was no family, Alice and George took charge of the funeral. As the church filled with villagers, the coffin, borne on the shoulders of the pallbearers, was taken from Chantry's cottage along the street, past the villagers who lined it and who then followed the coffin into the church with Reverend Jonathan Martin at its head.

After the main service, the coffin was borne down the stone steps of the crypt and through the iron gates into the vault of the Bowman-Leggetts. It was placed on two trestles which Neil had made especially. A few words were said over the body in front of all those who could squeeze into the space and then they all dispersed leaving Alice and George alone with Chantry's remains. Alice shed another tear and then nodding that she was ready, they walked out of the vault. Alice locked the iron gates with the key and put it in her pocket.

Stones had been brought in from the wall of the graveyard by Neil and were in a pile by the crypt door covered with a dust sheet. As soon as the church had emptied, he put on his overalls and mixed some mortar. He then proceeded to wall in the doorway to the vault as laid out in Chantry's will and agreed many years before. No one now would be allowed to enter the vault of the Bowman-Leggetts again.

END
